What Readers Are Saying About "The 5th C"

"This is a page turner. Thrilling adventure through Miami, Paris, Moscow and the Siberian diamond mines. Watch out for graphic violence though, not for the faint of heart." Anonymous, Amazon Reviewer

"Suspense, intrigue and romance! Elaine Gallant caught my attention as soon as I started reading 'The 5th C'. Wonderfully written. Hoping to read more from this talented author!" Kahuna, Amazon Reviewer

"It's intriguing...a page turner...compared to David Baldacci, which I love. I don't want Elaine Gallant near me after I die! This one is hard to put down." Deborah L. Woehler, Houston, TX

"Couldn't put it down. Telling all my friends and family about Elaine Gallant's first novel (hopefully more to come) and definitely recommend reading it." Jeanne Friedman, Maui, HI

"How exciting this is. It's intriguing and a page turner...very happy to pass this on... Great job!" Oliver Gold, author, Maui, HI

"Fun to read, lots of twists and turns, and I learned something too... It reminded me of James Bond...I was left in suspense." Diane Pure, Maui, HI

"As superb as any of my favorite authors!!" Kathy Jones, Seattle, WA

"We both enjoyed Elaine Gallant's story. Trust no one for sure!!" Cindy and Stan Catugal, Maui, HI

"The first line, paragraph, chapter takes the reader hostage..." Wm. Sayles, Maui, HI

The 5th C

The CIA, an Unknown Force, And Russia's Secret Cache of Diamonds

Elaine Gallant

ISBN-13: 978-1541039483
ISBN-10: 1541039483

Published by Elaine Gallant in Lahaina, HI
Poem by Elaine Gallant
Cover Photograph by Kristin Hettermann, Grace Delivers

1. Action 2. Adventure 3. Crime 4.Thriller 5. CIA 6. Murder 7. Espionage

To my brothers,
Ed and Donnie,
One man living, the other passed
Both men of action

Acknowledgements

Every story needs an audience, so my overall gratitude goes to you, the reader. Every story also needs inspiration, so I give nod to what most ignited mine--an *Associated Press* article of Sept. 17, 2012 that introduced me to the Popigai Crater and its secret cache of "trillions of carats." Another was *The New York Times* International section article of Dec. 29, 2012 titled, "If Assad Is Exiled Here, He'll Find Plenty of Company" regarding Barvikha's sanatorium that morphed into my hermit kingdom.

The novel, "Tommy's Wars: From Paradise to Hell and Back" written by Howard Fields with and about Takuji Sarashina (the kindest, most gentlest man to ever meet) gave me insight into the saga experienced by thousands of post WWII Japanese prisoners of war.

To write a story additionally takes a team, so my thanks begins and ends with my husband, Gary Weiss, a talented medical professional, voracious reader, armchair editor, advisor, and personal sounding board. His talents are many and forever appreciated.

Enormous gratitude goes to those relied upon professionals who shared their expertise over similar situations to my characters. The first is M.T.S., a retired CIA officer, who asked to remain anonymous but pointed my toes in the right direction at the start. The second is Gene Yu, author of "Yellow Green Beret" Volumes I, II, and III, and a former US Army Special Forces officer who offered valuable technical and personal insight whenever asked and without reserve. Cheers back to you, Gene, and to your mother, Lee-Chun Yu, for introducing us. The privilege was indeed all mine.

To the many editors and authors, both professional and volunteer, who poked holes and severed prose in the mutual effort to make this story better, I can't thank you enough. They are: Jennifer Pooley, William Bernhardt, James Vance, Tamara Hanks Grantham, and Rick Ludwig.

I give special thanks to Rick and Shirley Lantz for technical support and to Kristin Hettermann, who honored me with the cover photo. To her I say that, indeed, earth holds no bounds when Grace Delivers.

Without question I hold immense appreciation to all the writers in my writer's groups and workshops who are too numerous to mention but might chuckle over seeing some portion of their name in "The 5th C." If not, they're free to cast mine about in turn because really, where would we be without each other in the trenches? It's where the magic happens, friendships are formed, and sweat equity is traded. Thank you, especially, to all those involved with Maui Writers, Ink.

To my multi-revision readers who never gave up: Faith Batchelor, Rolin Holsteen, Barbara Brown, Helen Weiss, Elaine Wingfield, Kathryn McCullough, Mihaela Stoops, Terrence Gross, and Suzanne Webster. Your support and encouragement means the world to me.

Merci and spasibo to my French and Russian linguists, Susan Bradley and "Katya", who asked to remain anonymous with a mischievous smile I still can't decipher. And to those who didn't know they contributed except by their own experiences that I hope they recognize and feel pleased to have been included, Lili Neale and Jeffery Kelly.

I'm honored by and grateful to all.

I took liberties with some people, places, and settings in order to enhance the story. I would also like to note that any existing errors are mine.

Even though men look,
they don't always see
because life often counters
what they plan for it to be.
There are times when it falters
and others when it slides
and then there are times
when it fails critically to abide.

It's only at the end of life
when he takes a look around
to count his friends and enemies
or to whom he is bound
that finally he understands
it is the man who can bend
who frees himself from the twists of life
as it is coming to an end.

1
Eric Dane
Dead or Alive

Eric opened his eyes wide to the singe of chlorine. It hurt and burned them around the edges. He blinked, then closed them tight.

What the hell?

Relax, don't panic.

But I'm face down, floating in my pool.

Assess the damage.

Wine? No, blood all around me. Everywhere. My blood?

Yes, in the water. Streams of it. Diluting. Red and pink like the sunset.

It's recent descent returned with sudden clarity…he'd been standing at the edge of his deck with a glass of chilled merlot in one hand, his cell phone in the other, talking to someone new in his life–Glory Milan, beautiful Glory--as the sun faded below Miami's skyline and painted the heavens a mango-red blush.

Turn, breathe.

I can't.

Paralyzed?

No, but I'm hurt badly.

Eric released a few air bubbles as faces he knew appeared below him.

Mom, Dad.

Long gone.

Fanny, Annette.

Oscher.

He recalled *fzzpt, fzzpt, fzzpt* sounds through the water and twitched.

Bullets?

Yes, bullets.

When?

Seconds ago.

He strained to hear more but there was nothing.

His chest ached, building with pain from a large pocket of air. Compressed and stuck.

Not much left.

Please, not like this, not by drowning.

Lift your head.

Eric tried to tilt his head as Glory engaged him in a kiss. But when her soft lips landed, covering his completely, he panicked.

I need air! he begged while gripping her shoulders to rise up for a replenishing breath but they struggled, entangled. The gulp, when it finally came was too small, having been cut off amidst Glory's screams as she pulled him down. Time ticked louder, harder.

I need more! More!

He was then slammed by something fierce, and slammed again. He spewed blood-tainted water, then drew it back in, choking on the rush of it. So rough, so final. He gave a long, last thrash. The assault was over. And then?

Sorry.

Is this death?

Yes, and isn't it beautiful?

Eric's body fell limp, the conversation in his head stopped, and all the images disappeared, except for Glory's face that stared at him lovingly. Her mouth, turned up from pleasure and gratitude, left him in absolute peace. He smiled back at her from the tranquility it brought.

Their bodies, now pressed together in a powerful vacuum, spiraled down into darkness until a faint light caught his eye. Its intensity grew until it burst, filling him with a warm sense of absolute and complete awareness.

He understood now.

They had found him.

They had shot him.

But he knew *exactly* who they were.

2

Philippe Simone
Les Mines de Paris

Two Weeks Prior

By late afternoon, Philippe Simone had arrived at Place Denfert-Rouchereau in Paris's left bank. At its center square where numerous inroads met, sat an immense, bronzed statue dedicated to the so-named commander of the Franco-Prussian War in honor of his siege of Belfort.

To Philippe, the mighty Lion of Belfort with its head reared and mouth agape, lorded over the convergence of boulevards arriving at its firmly planted feet. But not today. Today it looked trapped in a spider's web. Like him. And why? Because the prime minister of France, Jean-Luc Nanterre, had taken an uncustomary action against him over his now missing friend, Ambassador Jacoub Arnoult.

In the past whenever Nanterre confronted him on any issue, Philippe's thoughts had remained clear. In order. Defined. But now they were kinked because Nanterre blamed Jacoub for a most serious offense against their livelihoods. It had caused an argument that forced the prime minister, a man of usual impeccable groom and manner, to lose all control of his senses. He'd simply come undone. Even his black hair had fallen limp, as if all the oil he used to keep it slicked to his well-shaped skull had been rubbed out. The heated exchange of only an hour ago still rang in his ears.

"Your instincts are piss, Philippe," Nanterre had shouted. "You say you trust Arnoult? Explicitly? Have you not yet learned? Trust is something we cannot count on in this business!"

"But I have known Jacoub all my life. I promise you, it's not possible that he would simply disappear. He's only in hiding until it's safe again to show himself. It's temporary, of this I am most certain."

That is when Nanterre had slapped him across the face, nearly knocking him out of his chair. It had taken all of Philippe's resolve to not strike back. Only in self-defense had he stood with his fists clenched. Meanwhile, the prime minister, now red faced, had gone behind his desk, picked up a lamp and smashed it against the wall, tearing open the drywall.

It had been an immediate, regrettable act because the prime minister had at once turned to him and stammered, "Excuse me, Philippe, I did not mean. I…I am sorry. There is just so much at stake. If he told anyone about the diamonds…"

He'd then covered his mouth with a shaky hand and added, "I…we cannot afford any loose ends, understand? And with Arnoult missing, I am concerned that all will be lost. It could be disastrous, Philippe. Find him because we cannot afford this. It could mean the end to us all."

Philippe had understood well. But in the sizzle of the moment, he could not afford his anger to rise. He needed his keener senses to gather beneath the storm that rioted in his head.

"I will do my best, and when I find him, I will report it to you. Until then, let me do my job."

"Yes, yes, but of course, Philippe. And again, my apologies." Nanterre had extended his right hand but Philippe ignored it and had instead reached toward the door.

"I am afraid of what he might do, Philippe," he'd

5

heard the prime minister whisper.

"As well you should be," was all he could think to say on his way out.

Since leaving Nanterre, Philippe had been in a whirlwind of anger. And now? Now that that anger had marched him to where Jacoub had last mentioned he'd been before everything escalated to the breaking point, what did it all mean? What was the prime minister's rage really about? Their private business? The diamonds? The possible ruination of them all? Not entirely.

It was about Jacoub Arnoult, the loose end, and whether or not he could be trusted. Trusted! For the first time in his life, even Philippe now questioned that bond. But a bigger problem loomed unbeknownst to the prime minister, for what a turn of events Jacoub had truly pulled. Thank God he had not informed Nanterre of *that* conversation, a tête-à-tête of only yesterday when Jacoub had informed him there'd been an unfortunate outcome with an American by the name of Tobin Corbett.

He'd told Philippe that they'd met two days prior and that Corbett had stated he wanted to work with them in moving their "product" into the United States. He'd even reiterated that in spite of the many cautions that Philippe had given him over the years to be wary of anyone who might even so much as hint of their private business, he'd panicked and made a mess of things.

Philippe had shaken his head at the thought and he was shaking it now.

Why hadn't Jacoub done as he'd asked and brought the American to him? After all, wasn't he in the better position to judge the legitimacy of Corbett's demand? And wasn't he more able to take advantage of the opportunity to turn it toward their benefit? Instead what had Jacoub done? He'd taken it upon himself to interrogate the man and then he'd killed him. And now that he had? *Somewhere* Corbett's body was decomposing. On top of that, it needed to be sanitized before someone else found it. So what would the prime minister have done besides slap him in the face and thrown a lamp across the room if he'd known? Philippe took a deep breath and exhaled with a flap of his lips. He already knew the answer. Nanterre would have ordered Jacoub eliminated and he might still, unless he could find his friend to protect him.

"My God, Jacoub," Philippe whispered. "What a liability you've become in your old age."

With nothing left to do but to get down to the business at hand, he looked around the square and loosened the strap of the backpack. Only a few people milled about. He figured they were tourists because no Parisian would tolerate the mid-day heat. Instead, they would prefer to emerge later in the evening for a chilled glass of wine or café noir to begin their nightly rituals. Even the thousands of students in the area were indoors. It was a good time for him to be out on the street.

So he retraced Jacoub's last known footsteps and proceeded on foot to Rue du Faubourg-Saint Jacques, a shady boulevard that passed a mid-seventeenth century hospital that Louis XIII's wife, Queen Anne of Austria, originally built as a church called Le Val-de-Grâce. And where still, an old quarry remained beneath its lavish grounds that served as a cellar and large catacomb for the monks who'd once lived and died there.

This was his intended destination. The unmarked tunnels. The secret catacombs. The City of Lights crisscrossed with hundreds of them, many of which were now sealed. There were exceptions, of course, a few tourist attractions and government-controlled sections, but based on what details Jacoub had volunteered, it was the one at Le Val-de-Grâce that most came to mind. He should know because it was a place he'd often ventured himself many years ago. Although as it happened, when Philippe had pressed Jacoub to verify his suspicions, Jacoub had hung up the phone, too shaky to continue the conversation.

He knew then that his friend would make a move, but disappearing wasn't what he'd expected. No, not after taking a life. He thought Jacoub would take to his bed after killing Corbett, for he wasn't a healthy man. He was a widower, lonely and frail. And to commit murder required much strength, both physically and mentally, something Philippe had mastered and wasn't sure Jacoub possessed. But Jacoub had, and now that he was missing, he was making everyone, especially the prime minister, very, very upset.

Philippe walked east past the Jardin de l'Observatoire and after that, headed north several blocks, keeping his head slightly bowed and the brim of his duckbill cap low over his eyes. Along the way, he slipped into a noticeable stoop, more from occupational habit than age, but age had indeed crept into the deeper features of his face and graying hair. The prime minister once complimented him that the look was distinguished but whenever he compared himself to Nanterre, who was at least a head taller and ten years younger, he didn't agree. Instead, he felt he more resembled the warmed patina of a well-crafted clock. He still ticked, he still tocked, but all the distinction resonated from the refined inner confidence in his craft.

At present, his pace was angry but controlled with his mind focused on the job at hand. He studied buildings and cafes, looking for the few people who might have been watching Jacoub and Corbett closer than expected. It might be that someone had taken notice of them. Perhaps a nurse or doctor from the nearby Hôpital Cochin had made an observation. Or maybe one of the patrons or wait staff at any of the brassieres had either served the two men or watched them stride by. If necessary, he would ask. Eyes were in unexpected places and definitive answers always came to questions correctly posed.

He crossed Boulevard de Port Royal and through a restoration entrance, ventured onto the back property of Le

Val-de-Grâce to walk the length of the car-packed parking lot and point of entrance that Jacoub would have used, if indeed he had. Once there, he knelt and felt around the stones for the metal ring of the manhole cover. Finding it, he pried off the lid. It opened with relative ease, evidence enough that someone had recently entered. He slid inside and perched himself on the iron ladder attached to the wall. He next pulled a mini maglight from his backpack, turned it on, and put it between his teeth before closing the lid that creaked and landed with a soft muffled poof.

Darkness consumed him. The air turned cool. Philippe took a deep breath of it to fill his lungs and thought, *Ah...no wonder the monks of old stored their famed liqueur here.*

No longer true but the sudden vision of his own prized bottle of Chartreuse nestled on a shelf above his desk between his twenty-year-old XO Cognac and introductory bottle of Grey Goose vodka came to mind. Deep amber-green in color, it always reminded Philippe of how perfectly those monks had captured the essence of the many herbs they'd secretly used to make it.

Philippe exhaled away the image and began his decent, only to land in a puddle of chilly water. It seeped through his canvas shoes to wet his toes. He stepped aside and pulled from his pack a pair of small rubber boots. He put them on, accepting that the water level could very well rise from here. As he did, he surveyed the low ceiling, telling himself to watch his head, too.

The tunnel narrowed but was plenty wide enough for one man to march ahead of another at gunpoint. He could see Jacoub doing so in his mind's eye. Darkness did that. It made one's thoughts more clear. It also conjured up fears of robbery, torture, rape...and of course murder. Especially the ones he knew himself to have committed in these pitiless places. He'd found the tunnels ideal. They were soundproof and abandoned for long periods of time. Surely Corbett, like

9

many of his own victims, must have known his fate. At the thought, a pleasurable surge rippled through Philippe's chest. He closed his eyes and pondered what Jacoub might have done to the man, what information he had obtained, and more importantly, what he was doing with it now.

He sloshed forward, touching the wall as he did. After several bends, Philippe climbed a few stone steps that led to a crevice almost too small for him to fit. He squeezed through and once inside, sensed a high but small, dry room. He panned his flashlight. The vaulted area appeared as Jacoub had described it.

Philippe then directed the beam of light at the body he now saw slumped on the floor against the opposite wall. He suppressed a chuckle, thinking not of Corbett, but of Philibert Aspairt, the legendary doorkeeper of Le Val-de-Grâce, who in the 1700s got lost and died in a room similar. What he had been doing in there no one knew, but even today many a French student could recite his tomb's inscription. So, too, could Philippe for he fancied the legendary tale and for all his life had been working hard to create one in his own right.

So in honor of Aspairt, he spouted, "In the memory of Philibert Aspairt lost in this quarry on November 3rd 1793 found eleven years later and buried at the same place on April 30th 1804."

The sound of his voice filled the room but then died a silent death into the thick earth. He walked toward Corbett and added, "Eh? So it took them eleven years to find Aspairt? How many years, Monsieur Corbett, will it take them to find you after I am done?"

Again he panned the room with his light and in doing, looked for any sign of activity. There was none. He next jutted his nose forward and took a deep, long sniff. Absent was the smell of decay, a clear indication of why the rats had yet to start their job. He bent over Corbett and inspected his corpse. The man's hands and feet were bound and a small bullet hole appeared in the crook of his neck under the chin, but no blood spilled. Philippe half smiled in appreciation of the unexpected neatness before him until he recalled Jacoub's objectionable explanation.

"I gave him fifteen milligrams of aconite and then I questioned him. It was over too soon. I am sorry, Philippe. I could not break him."

"Not break him?" Philippe remembered shouting back into the phone. "You killed him by giving him too much. Half a milligram alone would have done the job. But why did you have to shoot him, Jacoub? He was already dead!"

And now here he was, face to face with Corbett's body and having to take care of any identifying properties. He whispered, "Ah, Jacoub, my friend, my dear, dear friend, why did you have to do this?"

After another long, hard look, he shook his head and placed his backpack on the floor. From it he removed a pair of industrial rubber gloves and a military gas mask to lay near the body. He next unrolled a leather mechanic's bundle containing a small ball-peen hammer, pliers, screwdriver, and ratchet pruning sheers and arranged the tools in a neat surgical row next to the gloves and mask. Lastly, he removed strips of cloth and a Ziploc bag of rotted meat scraps from which he tossed pieces around the room after placing a few chunks down Corbett's shirt.

He put on the gas mask, the heavy gloves, and then with great care, removed a small metal box holding a vial of sulfuric acid. This, too, he placed on the floor.

He again inspected Corbett. Rigor mortis was fully set, perhaps at its peak, due to the room's coolness. Under normal conditions, a body's stiffness dissipated and the limbs became more manageable, but not in a cold cellar. No. Instead, Corbett's limbs were firm and the muscles contracted. In the meat industry, the condition is called "cold shortening." It was also a term he'd come by firsthand from certain doctors and surgeons who served the prime minister

11

in his underworld.

Philippe was the undertaker within that world and highly compensated for his efficiency. He was absorbed in all its functions. As a result, the prime minister had come to depend on his unique skills, especially now that their diamond business was fine-tuned and he could be counted on to handle the less savory aspects of the job. In return, Philippe's notoriety rose in magnitude to his station in life.

Much was expected of Philippe, even now, so he said aloud, "You are yet another identity for me to erase, Monsieur Corbett. And since superstitions already float through these tunnels, let's add a bit of flair of our own, eh? After all, it is *my* reputation at stake."

Saying this helped lighten the seriousness of the task at hand, something he always recognized but had not in his earlier years, always appreciated. As a result, his past ignorance nearly got him killed on a number of occasions. But he'd learned well and from it understood much more, including the true value of his instruments. Back then he'd tried everything, running the gamut from low- to high-tech performance tools. But in his later years, he'd settled on the less obvious. Anything manual. They were cheap and more available and as common as any household item. His conclusion was that the simpler the tool, the greater the art.

He came to love the way he held a screwdriver, for instance, or turned it about. He'd see the thumb muscles tighten or soften as he angled it one way or another. There was beauty in his actions. It took time and patience to control every aspect of what he did but it was in the subtle nuances that he knew his legend would come.

So he began by prying Corbett's mouth open with the claw of his hammer and using its head to break the jaw with a single, clean snap. He next picked up his favorite screwdriver, and with the pliers, removed each tooth, digging them out from the root. The work was time-consuming, especially when removing molars where space was limited.

When he finished, he inspected Corbett's mouth and collected what tooth fragments and teeth he could. He placed everything in his pocket to grind later. He then filled Corbett's desecrated maw with strips of torn cloth.

He next untied Corbett's hands, picked up his small pruning sheers, and began to snip off one frigid fingertip at a time. They fell to the ground as he did. When the last phalange dropped, he rounded them up in a small pile. He then cupped the two hands in prayer, forming a well that he filled with the leftover fabric, and rebound the wrists at Corbett's chest. Afterward, he repacked the backpack with all his tools.

He opened the container holding the vial of acid, removed it, and put in its place Corbett's fingertips. He next, and with great care, opened the vial to pour some of the acid over the cloth between Corbett's cupped palms. He then laid Corbett on the floor on his back, noticing for a moment how the man's legs had hardened. Bent and splayed. He poured the remainder of acid into the man's toothless, but now stuffed mouth before wedging the empty vile into the mix. As the sulfur vapor rose, he picked up the metal container, shoved it into his bag, and backed away to the chamber's opening.

In a farewell salute he said, "Alas, monsieur, my job is done and it is time for the rats to make a meal of you."

Philippe slipped out of the crevice and ran to the ladder, storing his gas mask and rubber boots before he grabbed a rung. He looked back once more and climbed.

Lifting the ancient lid, he saw that the night had come. And as he looked beyond the tree line, witnessed many a Parisian making his or her way to dinner and drinks. The parking lot was empty as he slipped out of the tunnel and ran to the bushes. There he turned to the street and made his way north. It would be a long walk…about thirty minutes, giving him plenty of time to decompress. Once he was far enough away from Le Val-de-Grâce, his thoughts returned to Jacoub.

Where are you my friend? He patted a top pocket for his phone and finding it, pulled it out and hit the number. After the fourth ring, the now familiar beep rang in his ear.

"Hello?" he said into dead air space. "Jacoub? Are you there?"

Nothing.

"Let's meet, eh? At the café Notre Dame. Eight thirty. You know the place. I want to see you, okay? It's all good, my friend. I've seen to it. We'll have a glass of wine and a chat, hmmm?" But still there was no answer, so Philippe ended the call and continued on his way.

He followed Saint Jacques to Rue Dante, a street that led him directly to the River Seine. On arrival there, he paused to take a breath before deciding to cross its bridge at leisure. The site of Notre Dame on the opposite bank reminded him that this passageway, the historic Grand Pont, was the city's first known overpass. To cross it without some reflection of its significance seemed disrespectful. Besides, he had at least an hour before Jacoub might possibly show himself. So at its midpoint, he stopped and peered over its low rail into the water. It gave him an idea.

He retrieved the small metal container that held the snippets of Corbett's identification, opened it, and studied them. They resembled boiled peanuts. He glanced around at a couple that were walking arm in arm toward him. He smiled to them as they neared and wondered who would question a man at night simply eating peanuts on a bridge and tossing the hulls into the River Seine?

No one.

The couple smiled back and nodded a good evening, just as another couple stopped to admire the same view. Still, too, groups of Parisians and tourists passed back and forth.

Philippe laughed at the audacity of his lifting a nub in the company of others and pretending to crack it open. Going further, he threw a fake nibble into his mouth. Then one by one, he tossed each tiny crinkled shell into the gently moving current below.

As expected, not a single person on the bridge noticed.

3
Jacoub Arnoult
L'immigrant

After leaving Paris by train on the very day he'd spoken with Philippe, Jacoub Arnoult was now in London and from there would fly directly into the United States. It was late evening and he was on the run.

The trip had commenced earlier than planned but he'd really had no choice any more. He'd killed a man and apparently not just any man. Tobin Corbett was CIA. It was the one vital piece of information he'd been able to extract before the aconite had taken effect. Jacoub had hoped to interrogate Corbett much more before he died, but Corbett had admitted little. Instead, he'd only begged.

"I just want to help," he'd said. "You know, to be a connection for your people in the United States. I have access to their CIA files. They're mine, trust me, and I can take care of everything for you internally. And like I've told you, I have outside connections, too, because a cousin of mine's already helped you. That's why I'm here. He said your diamonds are of a size and quality that no one's ever seen before. So why wouldn't I come to you with what I've got to offer? Mr. Arnoult, please, you've got to believe me."

At the time, Jacoub was dizzied. The diamonds were not his, per se, and he had no involvement with other people outside of Philippe and Nanterre. Yes, surely he knew a great deal of how the diamonds were distributed and how the network operated, but no one outside their powerful triad did, especially in the United States. It was much too intricate. Movement happened in sectors through various means. A receiving end did not know the sending end. A shipper once was not a shipper twice. The venues constantly changed and required close management through a separate and distinct network. It had been Jacoub's good fortune through the years to have been groomed by Philippe and given the positions he'd held with Nanterre to do what was required of him now. So he was not about to lose it because of a liar, especially this liar.

He scolded himself again. "You dope, you idiot. You allowed this breach. How could you not see that Corbett was CIA from the start? How much poison did you think it would take to extract the truth, huh? Too much. And now what? You're running like a dog with its tail between its legs because no matter what you do, or where you go, they'll find you. They will...they will. You're as good as dead."

Jacoub took a deep breath and rubbed his sweaty palms across the tops of his pants' legs. He was jittery and tired with exhaustion from the traumatic experience. He hadn't slept since and still couldn't eat. His mind, filled with fear, circled. All he could think of was of getting to America. Once there, he could at least put some time and distance between himself and those who were surely after him.

Jacoub warmed his hands at his mouth debating if he could do this.

You must go, he told himself. *It's your only salvation.*
And Philippe? What about Philippe?
Philippe will be there for you. Always.
No, not this time. I've gone too far.
There is no too far when it comes to Philippe. You know that.

And Jacoub did know that. Philippe would do whatever it took to protect him. He was the other half of his protective shield, wasn't he? With Philippe in France and diplomatic immunity as one of Nanterre's attaches around the rest of the world, how could he not feel protected? And hadn't Philippe always had his back and given him the courage to do what he needed to do? But had he crossed the line this time? Left too big a problem? Oh, how he wished he'd told Philippe everything, especially where he could find the body.

He also should have told him that Corbett was CIA and that was why he'd had to kill him. Corbett was no ordinary man. He was a threat, a real threat, and if he hadn't done what he did, well…Corbett would still be out there trying to get in. That's right. There was no way around this. Corbett had to die. He did everyone, especially the prime minister, a favor by killing him. He'd saved Philippe and Nanterre the trouble, isn't that right? So wouldn't that make him the hero? Wouldn't that be reason to celebrate?

Jacoub lowered his hands and opened them to study his wet palms. *This palm. And this palm.* Perspiration beaded in their creases as the stubble of Corbett's neck returned to prick them. He squeezed them shut of the memory.

"My god," he whispered. "It's too much, too much."

Agitated, Jacoub ventured into a restroom to face himself in the mirror. All of his seventy-three years looked back. Thinning white hair from the top of his head to his chin framed a bony face. His skin sagged, his brows drooped, and his nose appeared longer, wider, and more pocked. His eyes were red and glassy. He leaned into them, but for a second, and only the briefest really, it was Corbett's eyes that suddenly stared back. They were wide and frightened and at that desperate moment when Corbett knew he was near death. That the poison…the poison he'd been given was lethal and there was nothing more he could do but succumb.

Jacoub willed himself away from the image on shaky legs that couldn't hold him. He stumbled, then banged against a stall door that swung open against his fall, and landed on the rim of the toilet. He allowed himself to sit back for a moment to regain his wits, but there was no escaping this. Never in his life had he eliminated a man. It was Philippe who always did the dirty work. His only responsibility was to point his mottled finger and Philippe would go out and fire the bullet. Very simple. No fuss, no trace, until now. This error was fatal and it had happened in Paris, no less. If caught, he'd be tried as any other criminal. A murderer, plain and simple.

Oh, why couldn't it have happened in America? At least there, he'd have had immunity. But not in France, no, everything would be lost. His career, his savings, his retirement. And his diamonds? Maybe, if they found them too. He took a deep breath that, when exhaled, became a sickly cackle.

"I used to be so important. So above the law," he laughed through tears that formed. "It's over. It's simply, simply over. I'm done. Philippe will never understand."

He leaned back ready to release them until a thought trickled in...Philippe would understand everything except why he'd stolen the amount of diamonds he'd had after being compensated so well. It was obscene. They'd had an agreement–he, Philippe, and Nanterre--and Jacoub had broken it. There was only one way out now and he was taking it. Jacoub had spent years building this very escape and it was time to be implemented.

He'd secretly built and secured a private agreement with the head of US Homeland Security in Paris where he'd gain American citizenship in its witness protection program in exchange for detailed information about a terrorist plot against the US Embassy on Avenue Gabriel. He had plenty of bogus evidence. And Homeland, in return, would secure him and his assets. Everything was in place, although it was tenuous at best. But no matter what, he had acted upon it. All he needed now was to get on US soil and in touch with Homeland headquarters. He also had to do it before Philippe

19

caught up with him. How much time he had depended on how soon Philippe figured out he'd left Paris. Then Philippe would need to figure out where he was and how he did it. And that would prove quite difficult.

He'd covered his tracks, used false identification, paid in cash, traveled with the masses, and there had been no lull. He'd moved with speed. Could he still have a week? Ten days? Yes possibly, because he'd been so careful. He knew how Philippe and Nanterre operated, what they looked for, and how they found it. And he had taken care of all that too. No credit cards. No cell phone. Still on the nightstand, right? And his apartment? Exactly as he'd left it. Not a single suitcase missing. Even his identification papers would be found locked in his safe.

The thought of having laid this prior plan calmed him and allowed a small measure of security to return. He'd soon be out of the diamond business for good. He'd be free of the prime minister's hold on him and able to live out his remaining years in peace. No more smuggling and no more arrangements and contracts and under-the-table deals. No more spotlights and public appearances. He could step off the stage. Fall behind the curtain. He could grow a garden and think only of Eleanor, his beloved wife. God rest her soul. It was all waiting. Waiting for him in America. He just had to get there. And…he had to tell Philippe about Corbett. He owed him at least that much, an explanation. But there were gaps in his timeline that he needed to fill.

In particular, he'd have to explain to Philippe that it was several hours after killing Corbett that he'd taken the man's own gun and shot him. That he'd simply been too unnerved to leave the cave after watching him contort into such grotesque postures. That's why there was no blood splatter. It had already drained and settled. But Philippe, the consummate professional, would see that. Yes, he would. He might even laugh about it. But no matter, whatever he'd done, Philippe still deserved to hear the details from him.

Yes, this circle of doubt was almost over. He would live. It would all work out.

With that he went back to the mirror, washed his face and hands, and dried them. He pulled a clean shirt from his newly purchased valise and ironed out the few creases with the wall-mounted hand dryer. He put it on and found another tie to wear. It was the best he could do. At least he looked more presentable, and once he purchased a hat from one of the gift shops, he'd appear more like the Londoner in the picture on his second-hand passport.

He was walking a thin line and he knew it, but all he wanted was to board his plane and get to New York. There, its population of over one and a half million people, would swallow him in anonymity. He'd reserved a private suite for two-nights at a swanky hotel on Central Park West that afforded him ease of movement to a more obscure location if necessary. Within a week or two he'd tell Philippe everything, be given his new identity, and come under the complete protection of Homeland Security.

He again looked at himself closely in the mirror and checked his teeth. Then nodded at his own image saying, "Two weeks at best, my friend, but you have only this night to figure out what you will eventually tell him."

He next headed to the gift shop where he bought a gray tweed cap embroidered on its back with the seal of England.

Finally his flight was called and he joined the other passengers. After taking his seat, he felt better. Yes, much, much better. He ordered a cognac, drank it down in one swift gulp, and soon fell into a heavy sleep.

*

Jacoub arrived in New York under a cover of darkness.

All the better, he thought as he strutted into the hotel.

He paid in cash without question, and after receiving his key, took the elevator to his suite on the thirty-first floor. It was spaciously appointed and faced the famed and brightly lit Broadway, a thoroughfare in the heart of New York City's theatre district. At the door, he stood for a moment to survey his room and then as if pulled by the city lights, walked over to the bank of floor-to-ceiling windows. A wave of vertigo rolled over him until he placed his hands firmly on the glass.

The mass of streets below blinked with headlights and taillights, neon signs, and sparkling marquees. Yellow and green cabs jerked and stopped. On the sidewalks, a hell-of-a-lot of people walked this way and that or waited on street corners to cross. Others darted between trapped automobiles. Jacoub, though, saw none of the details. Instead he envisioned an assembly line of activity, something he found amusing to watch from so high. To him the tiny lives moving about were like small gems cascading down this shoot and out that one, being sorted and weighed and scrutinized for their street value.

Even as hectic as New York City was known to be, Jacoub knew better that it was the hodgepodge of immigrants that created its buzz. There was Little Italy, Little Manila, Russia's Brighton Beach, and Chinatown. There was also the Latin Quarter, Queens and the Bronx where the majority of African-Americans, Haitians, and Jamaicans carved out their lives. As a result New York City, to him, was the epitome of a melting pot and not at all like his refined city of Paris. Sure New York could be sophisticated, but it was nothing like Paris, no.

The French were more systematic; their streets easily navigable. It was a circular city that from its historically geographic core at arrondissement one–home of the Louvre, Royal Palace, and hundreds of other significant sites— spiraled clockwise outwardly with hundreds more thoroughfares throughout the remaining nineteen boroughs. The French had always been proud of their city for having maintained their cultural heritage. That is until recently, he sighed, what with the thousands of immigrants escaping intolerable regimes. Was there no end?

He shrugged and turned back into the room, eyeing the bed with its luxurious, pure Egyptian cotton sheets and thinking of the comfort of a hot bath. But oh how jangled he still felt.

"A nightcap," he chose instead.

After deciding the hotel's bistro was too bright and brusque for him, he ventured out toward Central Park to locate something quiet and less high end. He found it a few blocks away and there ducked into the dark tavern. He claimed a table near the wall with a small window that looked out onto an alley, ordered a cognac, and drained it hungrily on its arrival. Afterward, he brooded. It had been a long seventy-two hours, but here he was on American soil at last.

He eyed the bowl of salted nuts on the table and ordered another drink. He knew explaining to Homeland why he was in the United States so soon would be his first hurdle, so it was imperative that he nailed down the details. The most difficult part would be whether or not to tell them about Corbett. Homeland and the CIA were linked in spite of their separate functions, and if the CIA had known of the diamonds, wouldn't Homeland know as well? If so, how would they receive the information of Corbett's death if he told them? Would it cost him his new identity? His new protection? Should he risk jeopardizing his future, or would telling them about Corbett, Nanterre, and the diamonds enhance his credentials? If he informed them, would they have another reason to protect him besides the terrorist information he claimed? He understood that mentioning the diamonds would be a gamble, because he couldn't be certain that Homeland knew about them. The CIA, on the other hand, was a different matter.

He had to admit that his involvement in the diamond

23

trade contained great value—even more so for the right party. The question was, was Homeland the right party to trust with this information?

Jacoub accepted the second drink, thinking he should acknowledge the death of Corbett as some sort of accident by someone else. Surely this was the better and more probable answer. But how would he have come to know this information? How could he, as only an attaché for the French government, know the name of any covert person killed in Paris, unless of course, it was connected to a terrorist group? Yes, yes, a terrorist killed Corbett and because he has the information to trade with Homeland on that very subject, it would be a suitable link. Who wasn't connected to terrorism these days?

"Bien," Jacoub whispered before swallowing a last long sip that brought with it some former confidence.

As he stepped outside, he took a look around. There were a great many people about and yet none made eye contact. He was invisible to them and still under the protective cloak of night. How little they knew of whom walked amongst them. Him, a killer. The power of it all sharpened his focus and made him feel as if he was canvassing the streets with the eyes of a predator.

Jacoub wondered if this was how it felt for Philippe to shoulder such clarity of mind and single purpose. It was an intoxicating drug that he could very well get used to.

4
Eric Dane
Miami, Florida

South Beach hummed with a mixture of music, people, and late afternoon heat as bikini-clad women lounged in the sun and graced tables at outdoor cafes along its shore. The sounds of heavy metal, rap, and rock vibrated from convertibles and t-tops, SUV's and giant Escalades that paraded slowly down Ocean Drive. Mopeds darted around. Bicycles glided by.

From beneath a large umbrella on the outdoor terrace of Miami's Ariel Hotel, Eric Dane raised a mug to his three companions and said, "To our future, mis amigos, and may it be everything we hope."

"Here, here!" they cheered.

Eric took a long, celebratory swig as a passing breeze ruffled a few blond curls against his forehead. He reached up to calm them only to hear David Holdberg exclaim, "You already asking for another round, Dane?"

So without hesitation, he raised his hand further and signaled to the female server. She nodded before turning away and heading back into the much cooler building.

"Awwwwrighty," David said. "Now you're talking, because this is the only way I'm gonna survive this heat, fellas."

"You and me both," came the smooth baritone of

Francis "Fanny" Bergan, who whenever he spoke always delighted the ladies, especially those in college who had said he sounded silky and sexy.

Eric had bore witness to the effects. Fanny would simply whisper into some luscious co-ed's ear and she'd come up giggling from the timbre of it. Neither of the two had heard so much nervous laughter since their choirboy trebles started to crack in puberty. Eric's own voice was only slightly higher but, according to similar conquests, it was velvet lined, giving him equal leverage. The two men were amused by it until their perplexity became the bluster they needed going forward.

Today, Eric considered Fanny manly and lethal, well defined and compact. He was built like a truck. Powerful. He trusted him to have his back, as did Fanny of Eric. Always. Not only during college at the University of Florida in Gainesville, but also during CIA training and most assuredly now.

"C'mon, Fan, what are you talking about? We grew up here," Eric chided. "Are you saying you're still not used to this heat? It's not like these guys who came all the way from D.C. just to join us." Eric nodded to David Holdberg and Tripp Marsh.

"Yeah," David agreed, "but whose idea was it to sit outside?"

"Dane's," Fanny answered, pointing a finger at him while he checked his cell phone for messages.

Eric laughed, shaking his head, knowing he had his reasons. "Put that thing away," he told his friend, "or you're paying the bill and c'mon, guys look around. You think you can see any of this action sitting inside?"

Just then he saw David's eyes fall on a particularly tall woman sauntering by in a cover-up that moved in sheer, gentle waves over a deep-cut bathing suit. She smiled as David peered back at Eric with a sleepy crooked grin.

"Now that is the very definition of hot," David said as

they all watched her go by.

"Case in point," Eric added with a wink to Fanny who flipped him off with his wrist.

Eric chuckled out loud at the long familiar motion and wondered if he'd be flipped off after he told him what he most wanted to share.

"What're you laughin' at?" Fanny asked, putting his phone into his pocket.

"You," he answered.

"Why?"

"I don't know, man, memories, I guess. You remember Charlene?"

"Rennett?"

"Yep. Remember you and her at her locker?"

"You're asking for trouble, Dane, so stop right there."

"Yeah, you remember. You'd have one eye on her and one looking up the hall. And when I'd come knocking, you'd at least think to come up for air. But no, what did I get? That...that wrist flick."

"Worked didn't it?" Fanny asked, grinning and reaching out to wrap a muscular arm around Eric's shoulder.

David leaned over to separate them. "Hey, come on, now. What's this? We're here to celebrate our graduation and if so, I for one am ready to par-tay."

"Amen," Tripp said, who up until now had been relatively quiet, then added, "And where the hell is that second round?"

The mugs arrived, as did a third and who knew how many more that poured from the tap. By evening's end the men were rowdy and well into tales from the academy.

"Man, oh man," David joked with Tripp as he talked about their superiors. "That Brockman was something, wasn't he?"

"Yeah," Tripp answered. "Especially during black out training. Remember that?"

"Sure do," Fanny whispered. "That black out room

was a challenge. I mean, c'mon, furniture, traps, hidden assailants? But tagging the instructor took talent, Tripp."

"I stumbled over a rolled up piece of carpet."

They all laughed as Tripp continued, "He shouldn't have been there! I mean, if he'd have been an actual target, I'd been a star."

"Too bad the C.E.O. didn't quite see it that way," Fanny added.

"Oscher?"

"Yeah, now that one's got some smarts. Kind of reminds me of you, Dane," Fanny said, turning the conversation his way.

"Me? Fanny, you are way past sober."

"I don't know," David chimed in. "He was pretty keen on you and that'll put you on the fast track."

"Oscher knew his folks," Fanny offered. "So get used to it 'cause this guy's whole life's been CIA bound. Shoot, it wouldn't surprise me in the least if he isn't head cheese some day."

Eric coughed. "Now that's stretching it some, don't you think, Fan?"

"No I do not," Fanny answered. "I know who you are and where you came from, remember? And so does the director. Your folks? They were something else."

Eric lowered his blue eyes and pushed away his silverware with long, fine fingers.

Fanny cleared his throat and added, "Sorry, man, I loved them too, you know that. But they gave the ultimate sacrifice and Oscher will never forget it. Now you're willin' to do the same. You swore to it. Hell, we all did, but your mom and dad? They opened doors for you. Now granted it's not the way any of us wants them to open, but I gotta say I agree with David on this one. Oscher has a special place in his heart just for you, so sit back and let it shine, bro."

Eric shook his head at the thought of his parents. Their duties as investigators of international property under

President Ryan Newcomb had helped the CIA in many ways and their constant travels had taken them to countries and places he could only dream about. But their successes were theirs, not his. He'd have to earn his in his own time. About the only thing he agreed with was that growing up under their auspices had shown him a much bigger and more dangerous world than any of these guys knew. And it came after waiting nights, sometimes weeks to hear from them what had unfolded on their latest journey, even up to their last, which had been Kazakhstan.

There, rebels deep in combat against their Soviet leader, Sabir Niyazbekov, had destroyed their small plane. Their bodies were never recovered but posthumous awards piled, including two Exceptional Service medallions, an Intelligence Medal of Merit, a Career Commendation, and the rare Intelligence Star. Whatever they'd been doing for the CIA had been epic. At fourteen years of age, Eric was lost, knowing he'd never hear of another adventure from them again.

He was placed immediately under the guardianship of his beloved uncle, a physician and brother to his mother by the name of Doc Munroe, who kept him enrolled at Ransom Everglades School, a private facility located in the quiet grandeur of Miami's Coconut Grove. It was during this time that he received the dedicated direction he needed to become the man he was today. Fanny, too, who never left his side.

The two teenagers had flourished at Ransom and embraced its objective to "believe that they are in the world not so much for what they can get out of it as for what they can put into it." In turn, they focused on foreign languages, physics, politics, and in particular, world history, affairs, and economics. They studied together, worked together, and more often than not, played together.

Between their two homes--with Eric on Key Biscayne and Fanny at Coconut Grove--stretched the watery continent of Biscayne Bay. Here's where they'd sharpened the skills needed to conquer their greater world. They studied and charted deep-sea maps and night skies, became practiced sailors, fishermen, and divers. And along the way, they mastered all types of watercraft and gear that later led to more complicated forms of transportation, guns, and weaponry. Eventually, through an infinite number of staged acts of heroism and survival, they became adventurers who overpowered whatever imaginary or real foe stood in their way. These early days groomed them and later proved to be their first training grounds for the CIA before being tapped in college and invited in. Admiration between the men never waivered, and now here they were, a pair of Central Intelligence Officers sitting at a table getting wasted on chilled mugs of Heineken.

Eric took a minute to study his best friend, whose precision showed in his very dress from the short spike of his chestnut hair on the top of his head all the way down to the details of his intended relaxed look. He raised a glass to Fanny, who raised his back. They took a drink and set the mugs back down on the table.

Eric took it as an opportunity to pull Fanny away and asked, "Had enough?"

"Yeah, I'm full, I'm drunk, and to tell you the truth, I'm tired. I need some sleep."

David laughed. "Sleep? The night's still young."

Tripp agreed.

"Well, you two go right on ahead." Fanny told them. "Miami's waitin'."

"Don't mind if we do," David accepted. "And what about you, Dane? You coming?"

"Afraid not. Me and old man Bergan are going to hit the road. So be careful out there, okay? South Beach can be a wild ride."

David and Tripp threw an arm around one another and staggered out onto the sidewalk.

Fanny trailed them with his head until they were out

of sight, then asked, "Think they'll be alright?"

Eric sighed. "Well I sure feel sorry for the guy who tries to mess with them."

"You got a point. They're officially dangerous."

"And armed," Eric added.

"No shit. So how's about we get outta here too?"

"Sure, Fan, but hang on because now that they're gone, I want to talk to you."

"Okay," Fanny drew out the word, resting his elbows on the table. "What's up?"

"I got asked to do a job."

Fanny's eyebrows rose.

"Nothing too exciting," Eric said, holding his hand up to his friend's enthusiasm.

"So you say, but what is it?"

"You know I can't answer that, Fan, although I did at least want you to know."

"And now that I do, can you tell me how you snagged it?"

"No, except that he wanted someone outside of Washington."

"That right?"

"Yeah."

"Well I'm outside of Washington and I didn't get asked, so how'd he come to you? Was it your good looks or your connections?"

"You mean my parents? Don't even go there."

"You're right, that was a bad joke. I'm just jealous, I guess, because really I don't have a problem with it."

"Good, because it's nothing you'd want anyway. It's grunt work."

"What kinda grunt work?"

Eric stared at his friend without answering, except to say, "I leave on Thursday."

Fanny shifted in his seat. "Shiiiit, Dane. I knew you'd get the first tour."

"It's not a tour, Fan, that's the military. Besides, if he'd of thought of you first, you'd be the one downplaying it to me."

"Why?"

"Because it's beneath your station."

"But not yours," he said, poking Eric in the chest. "And you leave on Thursday."

"That's right."

"And it's nothin' but low-grade grunt work."

"Like I said."

"Well then, I trust you'll tell me all about it when you get back?"

"Will do. Wish me luck?"

"Always, brother, and thanks for telling me, really. Now let's move."

Fanny started to stand until a pressing thought crossed his mind. He looked at Eric and signaled for him to wait. After sitting again, he said, "I've got a piece of advice for you about grunt work. Be careful, you hear? Because *in* the military, it's the rifleman who bears that burden and it's that *same* rifleman who's on the front line. He's the one getting shot at."

"I got you, Fanny, but I doubt this job will have me getting shot at. Besides, something like that could play heck with my future. So, yeah, I'll be careful. I'll also promise to tell you about it when I get back, although I suspect by then you'll be on an assignment of your own. So buckle up, big guy, the train is leaving the station."

5
Jacoub Arnoult
New York City

Jacoub huffed his way across the room with the heel of his hand pressed to his heart. The sudden sharpness in his chest peaked, then receded slightly as he rested against a nearby wall.

"My god," he gasped. Was it a heart attack? Was the stress too much? Had the last few days been too costly?

All night his mind had spun, producing torturous dreams. First it was Nanterre shouting at him and Philippe walking away. Then it was himself being thrown into a long, black tunnel where his panicked screams whooshed out into the darkness until they turned into Corbett's haggard wails as Philippe turned to shoot the man dead. He'd heard his own laugh full of pride and reassurance at the thrill it gave him. He then saw Corbett's wide, fearful eyes as poison spewed toward him from the man's mouth. Then, at last, he felt his own hands around Corbett's neck. Squeezing, snuffing the life from him, all the while asking *why, why, why* to either the man or himself, he knew not which. And he was asking himself that now.

But he knew the reason. Because there was nothing else he could have done. He had to kill Corbett and he had to report it to Philippe, who in turn would destroy the evidence as expected. And then he had to…simply had to…leave the country, which he'd accomplished with much success and suddenness. Yes, everything thus far had been the right thing to do. It was empowering and in knowing this, his heart regained its rhythm. He took a deep breath and leaned against the closet's doorjamb as a chuckle escaped from his lips.

So you are so sure of yourself? So omnipotent, eh? No, no you are not. You're a fool to have done such a thing. Yes, it was smart to have killed him, to leave, even, but now what? What exactly have you walked away with, huh? What more had Corbett withheld?

These were questions he'd asked himself a hundred times. How unfortunate he'd been to not extract it all, other than who Corbett was and why he'd connected with him. Also that Corbett had known of the existence of their diamonds on the market and that they were being moved between France and the United States under the prime minister's directive. But what else was there? What else had the man known? And lastly, what could either country benefit from with what little he'd learned in the last few days?

Jacoub closed his eyes and continued to breathe with measured effort so that he calmed himself further still, an old technique his wife had taught him through the use of yoga. She had always cooed, "Jacoub, mon amour, breathe slowly and you will find peace."

"And what of happiness?" he would ask to which she would respond, "Only in my arms."

The thought of her brought his own arms up around his shoulders to caress himself as if it was her. The comfort allowed him to wonder further still at the many retirement plans they'd made. They'd had no children. It was she who was damaged much to her own regret, so desperately they had tried until testing proved positive and more than one fetus had aborted before term. After the fifth one, she'd said, "Enough, Jacoub. With that one goes my desire. I want no more. I want only you and the life you have chosen."

34

The life he'd chosen…the one that had forced every child out of her. Yes, she'd worry to the point of exhaustion while he was away. And yes, she'd accepted the same risk as he in sheltering the diamonds he'd stolen, for even she knew what gain they were to their future. She'd even died protecting them, just as he would if it was ever discovered. But what good were they to her now?

Had she not passed so prematurely, they would have retired early and been living in the south of France on the diamonds and pension they'd so carefully invested. They would have lived as they intended. But life for them was not to be like that. Instead here he was weary and working still, only now on the run while conspiring with a foreign country to save his very life.

"I am so sorry to have let you down again, Eleonore," he said to the fading feel of her as an unexpected tear trickled down his dry, rough cheek. "How ever did it come to this?"

He turned back toward the window where the sun streaked between the gaps of the closed shades and pulled them open, knowing that it was six hours later in Paris and that Philippe would already be working hard to locate him. He could phone to fill him in on the final details now, but that would cost valuable time and pending protection. No, the prudent thing to do would be to call Homeland first. Get them onboard so to speak and to let their actions dictate his. So he went to the closet, selected the tie he'd come for, and dialed the private number given him.

"It's me, Jacoub. I am now in New York City," he greeted Homeland Security's director, Mark Feldon.

"On official business?"

"No, no, it is only me. I have come under a new passport, you understand?" he said with a small laugh.

Feldon replied kindly. "You mean you slipped through? Come now, don't tell me TSA missed someone as important as you. But why are you here? We weren't expecting you."

35

"My apologies, but maybe Homeland should do a better job of keeping track of me, no?" he teased and then added, "So why am I here now? Well, you see there were complications in Paris and I had to go."

"What kind of complications?"

"I, I had to eliminate an obstacle. Of course it was totally unintended but he was asking a lot of questions about your Embassy."

"Like what?"

"He wanted scheduling details of meetings and staff functions so that he could work out an exact timetable."

"And?"

"And naturally, I said I would assist but then he asked about security, particularly on the second floor where your ambassador maintains a private studio, which as you know, I have no clue. He said I must seduce Madame Osbourne there and gain her confidence, but I thought that is ridiculous. Me? A seducer? I laughed, he hit me, and things turned rather disagreeable as I have said," Jacoub rattled on with his lies.

"Do you have a name?"

"Certainly….a Nicholas Bouchard," Jacoub lied again. "But of course it is not his real name because I checked as soon as I could."

"Nicholas Bouchard, you say?"

Jacoub hesitated before answering, "Yes, and well, I thought that maybe it was some kind of trick at first. You know, like you or the CIA sent him to test my sincerity."

"Me or CIA?"

"Yes, but I see now that was not the case."

Feldon fell silent for a long moment before saying softly, "But you eliminated him anyway before you were certain."

"Yes, it was regrettable, I assure you."

"As you say."

"I do."

"We do need to meet then, the sooner the better, but

please don't speak of this to anyone else because if he is indeed a person of consequence, you have as we say here, stirred the pot. But I'll give you my word, Mr. Ambassador, to look into to the matter immediately. Where are you staying?"

"The Grosvenor on Broadway."

"I'll send a car. Ten a.m.? Can you be ready?"

"Yes, ten o'clock. I will be prepared. And ah, today, I am Mr. Caldwell," Jacoub confirmed before hanging up the phone.

It was hard for Jacoub to judge how Feldon truly felt about what he'd just confided. His instincts leaned toward Feldon not being so duped, although he had seemed nonplussed. And yes, Feldon had stopped the conversation when he told him he thought Corbett as Bouchard was an officer, but Feldon had expressed no alarm. Could it be that it was indeed a trick? And wasn't Feldon sending a car so they could speak privately about it? Once there, would he be taken hostage, or was it that Feldon would only once again press him for the information he wanted? After all, Feldon's first priority was to secure everyone's safety within the US Embassy against whatever threats there were in Paris. Even though, in this case, none actually existed.

Counting in his favor would be that Feldon would find no "Bouchard" in his system. But if he knew of Corbett, if he and the CIA were working in conjunction, how would that play out? Jacoub didn't know. So he rose and repacked his valise. Chances were good that his two-night stay would be short lived.

After coffee and just before ten o'clock, he went down to the lobby and watched as a black Buick arrived at the entrance. An impeccably dressed man got out of the car and stood beside the right rear passenger door in typical military stance with his hands clasped below the waist. Jacob stepped toward the exit and nodded to the doorman who waved him through with white-gloved service.

"Your car, sir?" he asked.

Or my coffin.

"I believe it is, I'm Caldwell," Jacoub answered with a British accent as he placed the tweed cap on his head.

"Caldwell, yes sir," the doorman directed the name toward the driver who acknowledged.

Jacoub tipped his hand at the doorman and slipped into the Buick's comfortable leather interior as the driver closed the door.

Within the hour, he was sitting fitfully across the room from Feldon, who at that moment was reviewing a dossier that Jacoub could only assume was his. Their greeting had been warm, which comforted him, but now Jacoub felt a slight change in temperature, perhaps in part due to the lies he'd told and would have to tell again only this time in more detail.

Jacoub watched the director lay down the file and walk toward him, then stop to lean against a chair before sitting down. It was a walk of deep concentration, as if he was weighing the most effective tactic to use against him. Even seating took Feldon some time what with the jostling of his suit jacket, the straightening of his tie, and the pulling at the knee crease of his left pants leg as he swung it over his right. Several times he even stretched his shirt's front collar to clear his throat.

Jacoub, meanwhile, continued to watch Feldon, allowing his concentration to sharpen. He liked nothing more during negotiations than to observe people, to analyze their unconscious tics, to see if they were nervous, or about to assert themselves. He could always predict the results of his negotiations before things ever concluded simply through the body language of the person or people in front of him. And right now, Feldon was feeling a high level of discomfort.

Finally Feldon folded his hands on his lap as if closing a book, which meant a decision had been made, and said, "As you say, Jacoub, there is no Bouchard. Perhaps you can describe him to our sketch artist later and from there we can determine who he really is. But for now, I think, we need to get you secured, especially since you have learned that other people are contacting you directly. This is very unfortunate."

"I agree," Jacoub said with relief.

"And now, tell me more about the US Embassy."

"You mean besides what I have already expressed?"

"Correct."

"Well, I would say things continue to escalate and if my sources are to be believed, which I am certain they are, the Embassy is clearly the target. I would expect, if I were you, an attack of great magnitude," Jacoub warned now that he realized he was back on top.

"And you have proof?"

"Proof?" Jacoub asked. "Have you not been listening? What about Bouchard? Is his life or mine not proof enough? And have I not already provided you with certain specifics over the last couple of weeks to know that it exists? I will provide no more *proof* until I am certain I cannot be found by any of them. I am a high profile person and this is a high profile situation. If I die, the information goes with me and the hundreds of lives lost will rest on your shoulders. "

Jacoub paused and leveled his eyes with Feldon's, which studied him in return.

After a steely moment, Feldon spoke. "Yes, yes that's true, Mr. Arnoult. It is a most serious situation and we are taking it as such. No one wants another Embassy attack."

"Especially in Paris."

"*Anywhere,*" Feldon emphasized. "That much is clear. So while there's still time, let us move up your schedule. I'll make the arrangements myself for your citizenship and once you're processed, we'll take you into Federal protection, after which you'll be required to reveal everything as agreed."

"I shall."

Feldon stood and presented his hand. "Have you any qualms with Buffalo?"

"Buffalo? The meat or the city?" Jacoub asked with some confusion, clasping his palm to Feldon's in a firm handshake.

"The city, of course, for your ceremony."

"Oh, yes, I understand, but no, of course I have no problem with it. It's fine. And until then?" Jacoub inquired.

"Enjoy."

6
Eric Dane
D.C. Bound

That same morning, Eric had risen before dawn to complete his morning routine of squats, dead lifts, and pull-ups. And after breakfast, he'd shaken off the buzz through meditation. His re-entry thoughts had centered on his return to Washington and speculation over his first assignment. It was a simple job, he'd been told. A pick up. Someone the agency wanted to question, that's all. Nothing dramatic, sorry, pure routine. But if he did this one well, who knew? Yes, who knew where it would lead? So was he ready? Yes, he was ready. He was definitely ready.

Now dressed, Eric inspected himself in the floor-length mirror to linger over the look of his inherited blond curls. They were his father's and something his dad had always kept docile on the job with a crew cut. During down times though, he'd let them grow into tiny wild cues all over his head so that his mother had something twirl around her baby finger when they sat together on the couch to watch television.

"To straighten him out," she'd teased only to have his father wink at him and say, "She twists my heart in the same manner."

"Mine too," young Eric would add, smiling broadly.

"Yep, she's got us both, son. Lock, stock, and barrel

and there's nothing we can do about it."

"Nothing," Eric would echo.

And she did and they couldn't and neither wanted to anyway. Their family life seemed perfect then, except for his parents' long journeys away. But they'd always come back to share amazing tales of faraway places. It's where Eric's dreams thrived and his imagination took rise. It was the reason that he and Fanny had had such spectacular boyhoods. Because once filled with whatever new world his parents brought back, he'd grab Fanny and off they'd venture into their private wonderland of intrigue and espionage.

He looked again into the mirror as the shape of his mother's oval face looked back. He had her smooth Eastern European skin and clear, blue eyes. But his upturned mouth, strong Scandinavian nose, and overall proportions were purely his dad's. They were within him all right and there they would always be, this much was true.

Eric smiled and touched the mirror. "Who'd of thought, hmmm? Thanks to you two, I'm finally in. I know, I know, it's a small job, but I'm going to do it well, you'll see. I've wanted this as much as you have and it's finally happening, so watch out for me, would you?"

He dropped his hand as another thought grabbed him. *C'mon, Dane, you're twenty-six years old and there are more people to thank than yourself or your parents. Doc deserves some credit.*

Doc, the uncle who'd raised him in the Dane estate, had instilled a lot of sense into his loss. He'd told him that they'd died doing what they loved for the people they loved most. Above all that meant they did it for Eric. But they were of the greater world, weren't they? So then, they were doing it for all of America, too. There was no higher calling than to serve one's country and to do so by putting your life on the line for it. They'd given the ultimate sacrifice and because of that, they would be remembered forever. They were national heroes.

Eric, of course, had mourned them only as his parents, but had finally wrapped his head around their deaths and his arms around Doc. His uncle had kept him whole, both physically and mentally straight into adulthood. It was then that Doc had retired from being a surgeon and purchased a home down the street, confirming in his no-nonsense sort of way, that they both needed to be on their own. It was this straight and narrow of Doc that saw Eric through the roughest part. He was the steel to lean against and the advisor to seek. Why if it hadn't been for Doc, he might have missed his calling all together. There were many avenues he could have traveled, but Doc had kept him pointed toward the CIA.

"This *is* your life's work, son. It's what you've always wanted, so go after it. Let's make it happen not *for* your folks, but for you. It's your future, and by god, you can count on me to see you through to the finish line."

And he had. And he was still there only a stone's throw away. Eric had every reason to feel secure in all he'd done: college, the academy, this chance. And it was Doc who was behind it all. He'd helped him climb the rungs in the ladder of the life that he wanted to live and it was happening, starting today.

*

After boarding at Miami's International Airport, Eric settled into his business class seat just as a hurried female flight attendant dropped a few magazines onto the aisle floor next to him. He reached down to help her. Unfortunately she stooped too, butting her head into his right ear.

"Oh my goodness," she stood and exclaimed. "Are you all right?"

Eric bolted upright with his eyes closed and laughed. "Are you?"

He heard an anxious "yes" as she placed the remaining magazines on the seat opposite. The sound of her made him smile. He was surprised, however, when she next massaged his temples. He opened one eye and then the other to find a bronzed nametag pinned to a silk blouse that read "Glory Milan."

Eric looked up to her face, taking in the sight of her. She was biting her plump lip. Once they made eye contact, she stood upright and smoothed her skirt. Perhaps she realized how inappropriate it was to touch a passenger, but whatever had stopped her, she bent again and asked softly, "I'm so, so sorry, sir, but are you in any pain?"

"No."

"My fault entirely," she admitted.

"Or mine, but it was worth it."

She smiled at the remark. "Would you like a drink? A pillow? Maybe a deeper rub?"

Eric's surprise registered in a widening of his eyes.

"I could ask if there's a licensed masseuse onboard," she continued and then said something about the competitiveness of other airlines before picking up the remainder of the magazines so that the other passengers could board.

"You headed home?" she inquired with the stack pressed to her chest so that a large man could squeeze past.

"No, my home's here in Miami…Key Biscayne to be exact," he answered as she handed him the latest edition of *Cigar Aficionado*. "And where's yours, D.C.?"

"Yes, but this is my regular route. Every week. Back and forth. D.C. to Miami, Miami to D.C. Gets a little boring except when the politicos are on board, if you know what I mean."

"No, I'm sorry, I don't."

"Well we, all the regular flight attendants that is, call it the 'Playpen Express' because most of the guys travel without their wives and they like to have a little fun. Understand now?"

"Sort of."

Glory made full eye contact. "Not with us, I mean!"

"I didn't think so," Eric said, watching her shoulders relax as even more passengers squeezed by.

"Goodness, I hope not. I mean they have some amazing stories to tell but others get a little wild with their intentions. But we would never partake, no, too creepy," she said while shaking an open palm in front of her face at him. "On the other hand, if you'd ever like to hear what they tell us. Well, I'd be happy to share it with you sometime because some of the stories are just so, so…"

"Over the top?"

"Exactly."

"I'd love to sometime, really."

"Me too," she said with tenderness just as the loudspeaker squawked and a woman asked for a glass of champagne.

"Gotta go," she said. "But, um… I'll come by later and see how that head of yours is doing, if that's okay."

"That's very okay, Miss Milan. My name's Eric, by the way."

"Oh, I'm sorry, we never did introduce ourselves, did we? But it's Glory, please."

"Yes, it's on your nametag. Very nice to meet you."

Eric watched her walk away in her snug uniform, the magazines now cradled in her right arm. She was lovely, he told himself. Fit and toned and beautifully made up with a head full of deep, auburn hair. He was certain that once it sprang loose from that carefully pinned-up bundle, it would tumble down the back of her neck like a silky mane. He'd love to touch it, run his fingers through it, and maybe even rub her head as she'd done his. He hoped he'd have the chance.

Midflight, Glory came down the aisle and placed a piece of paper on the keyboard of his open laptop. He hadn't seen her coming, so he was startled at first but didn't show it as he closed the lid on top of it.

45

"Is that what I think it is?" he asked.

"Yes, and I hope I'm not being too forward, but you did say you'd like me to tell you more about your representatives."

"Yes I did," he replied with a big smile. "And it would be a real treat, but it might be a few days before I'm free. I have some business to take care of first. That said, I hope you don't think I'm putting you off. But if you're free when I'm done, well, I'd like very much to give you a call."

She smiled and wiggled her shoulders.

"Using this phone number right here," he said, breaking eye contact to look at the top of his closed case and then back at her.

She nodded her head yes, then tilted it. "What kind of business are you in?"

Eric cautioned himself at the question. *It starts the minute you say yes to the profession.....*

"Nothing political I assure you. My work's much more boring. If I tell you now, though, you might think less of me and not answer my call. But I promise when we do meet, I'll fill you in."

"It's a deal," she said with added tenderness. "Although I can't imagine what a man such as yourself would be doing that is so incredibly boring, especially since you're not one of *them*." Her laugh was light, elegant.

As she turned to continue her duties, he found her reaching out with equal delicacy to touch the top of his head. Again he watched her go and again he saw himself being with her but wondered, how soon would that be?

He felt his star was on the rise. First with this upcoming assignment and now with meeting a gorgeous flight attendant named Glory, of all things. Seeing her on a regular basis would be out of the question, certainly, but if she was willing to be flexible, and indeed she did look flexible, well, she might just fit into his schedule rather nicely.

"Yep," he chuckled to himself. "Things are definitely looking up and it feels pretty Glory-i-ous indeed."

7
Conrad E. Oscher
Operation Pop Up

Central Intelligence Director, Conrad Ezrah Oscher, stood on the opposite side of the conference table thumbing through some paperwork as Eric walked into the room. He stopped to study Eric for a moment and size him up, comparing him to his parents who seemed to descend upon him in a flash of immense fondness. He was, as promised, about to do what they'd asked.

Oscher remembered the day well when they'd stood in this same room just as Eric stood now. He was the director's assistant then and it was just prior to their leaving for Kazakhstan. The moment had felt odd, as if their confidences had slipped or they'd had some sort of premonition. It happens to the best of officers, especially when the stakes are high. But, they'd been on dozens of prior missions with similar stakes without ever making such a personal request.

"If anything happens to us," Mike had said but Marian picked up, "promise to take care of Eric when he appears at your door." And without missing a beat Mike had added, "he's being groomed and will serve the organization just as fiercely as we have."

Oscher invited Eric to take a seat as the images of Mike and Marian faded.

Once settled, he informed Eric of Tobin Corbett's demise in an underground catacomb in Paris at the hands of Jacoub Arnoult, who CIA once considered an unlikely candidate given his age and political position. And then he reminded Eric that while Arnoult was the target of Eric's mission, he could very well kill again. So Eric had best keep that in mind if he planned to succeed in bringing him in, which was all he was really assigned to do. Bring him in.

"So you understand the situation?" he asked Eric as a second round of doubt punched his gut. *Careful now, go slow. This kid might be agency blood but he's still a rookie.*

Eric nodded with the affirmative and thanked him for the opportunity.

"Good," Oscher said. *But what else would the kid say?*

Oscher turned his back to ward off his collusion with Eric's dead parents. Behind him, on the table, several photographs, maps, and flight schedules lay scattered over a short list of names and a printed copy of the oath for US Citizenship.

"I meant," Oscher added, turning again to face him, "do you think you can pull this off with as little difficulty as possible?"

Eric, who was now leaning against the table's edge, pursed his lips.

Oscher took note. *Just like his dad. Doesn't go for the knee-jerk response, but how's he going to pull this off in such a public place and under such scrutiny? Simple enough for his parents but does he have their street smarts? Will he deliver?*

Eric's answer was, "Anything's possible so long as the plan is followed to the exact detail."

Okay...

"And you have that plan?"

"Not entirely but it tends to present itself along the way."

Oscher smiled over Eric's assuredness.

"So this is the man who serves directly under the prime minister of France?" Eric asked as he lifted a photograph of Ambassador Jacoub Arnoult to study it.

"Yes."

"And he's the person we're certain killed Officer Corbett in Paris's underground?"

"Yes," Oscher said before offering some background. "He currently has diplomatic immunity in the United States but is on the run for his part in what we're calling Operation Pop Up."

"Operation Pop Up?"

"Code name for a newly recognized diamond smuggling ring that we here at CIA want to kick in the ass before it becomes a fully blown international affair. Seems Arnoult is privy to how some rather impressive diamonds are being moved out of Russia's Popigai Crater into the United States…all without alerting Homeland Security. And, he's diverted Homeland's attention to that by convincing Director Feldon that a terrorist attack against our embassy in Paris is imminent. In order to stop *that* from happening, he first wants US citizenship and full witness protection. Feldon, of course, has agreed to provide it in exchange for whatever terrorist information he provides."

"I see," Eric said.

"No, I'm afraid you don't," Oscher said, stopping him. "Because Feldon is being lied to, or at least that's what our intelligence indicates. There is no terrorist threat to our embassy in Paris, although the Popigai hole in US security through an undisclosed route could certainly be considered one. The biggest problem we've had thus far is in identifying Arnoult and his part in all of this. And now that we have, we need to obtain whatever knowledge he holds regarding those diamonds before Homeland provides him the protective custody he's demanding."

"So why not work directly through Homeland?"

"Because we choose not to and because we're deeply offended by what this man is doing to our country and our fellow agency. It's a smack across all our faces. And because it's our job at CIA to look at the bigger picture, something this man can draw for us as to who's pumping those diamonds out of that crater and how. And lastly because Operation Pop Up is ours, all ours, and we intend to see it through to fruition. After which we will have done our country and Homeland Security an immense favor."

"And who do we think is pumping out the diamonds?"

"We don't know for certain, although we can plainly see that Arnoult is a pawn in it. We believe ultimately that it's a rather elusive Russian major general by the name of Gregor Niembriev and it's our goal to find him and shut him down. We also believe Arnoult is the only person who can tell us where he is and how he's exporting. We get Niembriev's location from him, diffuse the major general and his diamond mine, and it all closes down before anyone's the wiser. In the process, we brick up that hole in our border as well."

"Okay," Eric said. "So, tell me about Popigai."

"Well, first, Popigai isn't part of your mission, but you'll find the background helpful. Popigai itself is manned by a Colonel Rabokov and is located in a remote section of Siberia at Krasnoyarsk Krai but it's more than a mine. It's part of an entire collection of mine-filled craters. We think Niembriev and company traffics for the entire network but commands only one location…Popigai, and that's why we're so focused on him.

"Now ever since the Kremlin's early years, especially under Stalin's reign, they've been mining those craters with the help of World Ward II German and Japanese prisoners as part of the reparation agreement signed at the end of the war. Since then, the mines and the goings on in those mines have been very top secret.

51

"Over the past few months, we've learned that they contain 'trillions of carats.' Mind you, that translates into a colossal mass of gemstones and industrial-grade diamonds. They say it's enough to supply the world market for the next three thousand years, although Russia has yet to begin doing that for reasons they've so far and again kept to themselves."

Oscher stopped and walked to the window. "Imagine what that could do to the balance of things. The diamond and stock market trades, banking, etcetera. But before all of that, consider the manufactured diamond industry, for instance. A flood of this nature could outsource its function. The Popigai diamonds would replace them and we'll end up using them for practically everything, including cavity fillings, for Christ's sake."

Eric interrupted. "And is there anything special about these industrial diamonds? I mean, are they better or worse than what's being manufactured now?"

Oscher walked back to the table to answer. "Well, they're better on many levels because you simply can't beat Mother Nature, that's first and foremost. They're not synthetic, which is what a majority of the world's industrial diamonds are now. Plus they're harder. They're tubular like most gems, but their size is quite extraordinary. Many measure a foot long. They also have a very large grain making them useful for scientific purposes on a major scale. Think semiconductors, high performance bearings, heat shields and the like.

"Some people call the stones extraterrestrial diamonds or celestial diamonds but the industry recognizes them as impact diamonds because they're the result of meteorites that fell to the earth some twenty million years ago. Popigai's alone is sixty-two miles wide. Naturally, the pressure at impact turned its graphite into diamonds."

Eric whistled softly. "And the gemstones?"

Oscher hesitated a long while before answering. "They deny it, but they're better and more colorful than any we've ever seen, plus they've begun showing up in very limited numbers in the US. More importantly, we understand that Russia still has a lot more to discover inside that crater. Niembriev, in particular, has created a handsome side market and must be making quite the profit too. But how he's doing all of this, we don't know. It's ours to figure out through Operation Pop Up before it becomes a global situation."

"You mean before Russia goes full production?"

"Yes, and because the other diamond-producing countries like Africa, Canada and Australia, won't take it lying down. Another world war could be right around the corner. For now, however, the Popigai diamonds aren't being marketed through regular channels, making us believe it's being privately managed which brings us back to the snake that's raised its head here and the reason we need to talk with Arnoult.

"What we know is that he's involved somehow and he's the one who can connect everything for us. Your job is to simply bring him in, nothing else. He holds the key to the vault and we want it."

"Where is he?"

Oscher rested his hands on a black-padded computer bag then rapped it with his knuckles.

"New York. I've put all the data I think you'll need in here but you'll have to commit everything to memory. Sorry for that but nothing leaves this room for long. Don't even think about making copies or taking written notes. You'll have twenty-four hours to review, memorize, and then return the bag. I'll tell you how later. In the meantime, try to impress us by bringing Arnoult in before he becomes a US citizen. Should be simple enough with your training. Once you do, we'll get out of him what we need to know about Niembriev."

"And when is Arnoult supposed to claim his allegiance?"

"According to our sources in six days. It's all in

there," Oscher said as he slid the computer bag to Eric. "Take it and put it over your shoulder like any other D.C. professional walking safely down the street, and get out of here."

"Are they?" he asked. "Safe, I mean…these D.C. professionals? I hear this city can be quite the place."

"No fear, Eric," Oscher assured. "We've got your back."

Eric looked at him from the corner of his eyes as if he didn't believe what he'd just heard and said, "Yeah, well, truth is I'm counting on that, sir. I kind of like the life I hope is ahead of me."

"Right, but don't get carried away. It's just a pick up, Dane." And then on second thought Oscher added, "Sorry, you're right. We've already lost one man in Paris although there's no indication of anything like that happening here. But still, yes, of course, whatever you need."

Oscher watched Eric pick up the computer bag and place it over his shoulder then hesitate.

"Sir?" he asked.

"Yes."

"I appreciate this opportunity, I do, but why me?"

Oscher looked down, splaying his fingers out on the table.

"I won't lie to you, Eric. I made a promise to your parents and I'm going to keep it. This assignment, on a project under my own supervision, is the first step in keeping that promise. That said, whatever happens next is entirely up to you. You fail and there won't be another one in Operation Pop Up. You'll go into the rank and file with the rest of them, so do your best. Everyone's watching, mostly to witness my own embarrassment. But I'm a betting man and if you're anything like your folks, if you've learned anything from them or from us, you'll save me from that."

"But didn't you tell me my getting this assignment had nothing to do with my folks? That it was because no one

54

in D.C. would know me on the street?"

"I did and you can be certain that no one will know who you are, that's for sure. It's a big plus, trust me. However, I told you it wasn't because of your parents because I wanted you to believe that. It was unfair, I'm sorry, but there you go. I'm indebted to them and want to repay them in the way they asked. That said, don't think less of the assignment or of me, because if you weren't up to the challenge, I wouldn't put you on the project. Operation Pop Up needs to stop Niembriev before he establishes more routes and bringing in Arnoult will do that. So just go do your job, Dane.

After Eric left the room, Oscher closed his eyes and thought of Mike and Marian. "Okay, the ball's in motion, now you've got to help him meet the expectations."

8
Eric Dane
The Laissez Passer

Eric exited the building through a side entrance and hailed a cab. His resentment at being lied to about why he first got the assignment was palpable. Oscher *had* given it to him because of his parents. What a burn. He had half a mind to turn around and tell the director to go screw himself. But what good would that do? His parents weren't so immortalized that insubordination on his part would be pardoned. So what was going on here? Was it loyalty or guilt on Oscher's part? Whichever it was, it was best he put his anger to work at figuring out how the situation might later benefit him because it proved one thing--Oscher could be swayed by his emotions.

A cab zipped into the curb and turned its service light off.

"Take me to Vineyard's on Twelfth," Eric told the driver.

Without a reply, the driver whipped out into traffic as fast as he'd come to the curb.

"Whoa, partner! What's the hurry?"

"Sorry, sir, I thought I seen somebody approachin' when you jumped in. Probably a tourist thinkin' it's a share fare." The man stole a glance at Eric in the backseat.

Eric twisted around only to see a man's suited leg

disappear into the cab behind them. "Keep an eye out, would you? If that cab follows us, take me to Fifteenth and let me out."

"You got it boss," the driver said.

After making a few false turns, Eric figured the second cab was still in sight. So he looked out the back window again as the driver quipped, "Hope you don't mind the extra expense, sir, but I'm guessin' you don't wanna play tag."

Eric pulled his computer bag onto his lap and threw a twenty-dollar bill over the front seat, saying, "Okay, next block take a right and stop fast."

The minute the car lagged, he scrambled out to hide in the shadow of a tall building. The driver sped off and veered left. Within seconds, the second car appeared. In the back, a man dressed in standard government garb sat forward jabbing his finger in the direction of where his driver had turned. Eric neither recognized him nor believed he was friendly. His mission must have been compromised. If that was the case, he'd have to leave his hotel immediately.

Eric closed his eyes to make a mental imprint of the operative he'd witnessed and took a deep breath. *What was he wearing? Gray...a gray suit, pale blue shirt, dark tie. Hair? Brown, cut short. Glasses? Aviators, silver metal frame, something Fanny would wear. Anything remarkable? No, nondescript, middle aged, could be anybody.*

Stepping from the shadows with the computer bag clutched to his body, Eric sprinted to his hotel still several blocks away. His real fear now was time. How long would it take him to pack up? Where would he turn? To what other hotel or establishment should he go? Where would he be safe? A bar? A library? Yes, a library. Preferably a large one, something the size of an institution, and then he'd call Oscher.

It took him twenty-seven minutes to reach the lobby and another three to reach his ninth-floor room and throw his bag onto the cream colored linens of his king-sized bed. In that thirty minutes time, he'd already processed a lot of additional information.

Someone other than Oscher and Fanny had known he was going to be in Washington. And after his supposedly private meeting, they'd followed him with the intent of forcing contact. It could also be that some other agency had known about Operation Pop Up and put a tail on him. In all cases, whoever this person was or other agency might be, they either knew or wanted to know what he had in that bag.

As Eric grabbed his belongings, he wondered if the pursuer knew where he was staying, but as soon as he looked at the coffee table, he knew that he did. His switchblade, folded earlier inside a napkin by a bowl of Fuji apples, was missing. He'd meant to slice into one but decided instead to wait until after his meeting with Oscher. Now only the folded napkin remained. *Was it the maid? No, that's too obvious. Not here, they wouldn't dare. Plus, they would've set out a fresh napkin and placed the blade, folded, conspicuously on top.*

He moved about the room with extra caution. He peeled away the curtains and opened the closet doors. Returning to the bed, he noticed the bathroom door partially ajar. He kicked it back, hoping to startle anyone there, but there was no one anywhere. He returned to the sitting area and took another look around. There were no other disturbances. Suddenly, the connecting-room door flew open and the man with the silver aviators stepped through with Eric's switchblade extended.

"Where is it?" he asked.

Eric raised his hands. A subconscious whisper floated up, *fight or flight*, but he knew the answer.

"What?" Eric asked, pointing to the computer case. "That?"

The man nodded and stepped forward.

Eric ventured toward the bed, and in doing, stopped at

the chair rolled neatly under the desk. The man tracked him with the knife raised.

"Now," he said.

"Okay," Eric replied as he wheeled the chair around and rammed it into the guy's knees.

Grimacing in pain, the man bent to shove the chair away, a move that gave Eric the opportunity to blindside him with a downward punch from the heel of his hand. The man stumbled. Eric kicked the chair aside to grab and twist the guy's wrist so that the blade was at the man's chest. They scuffled. Eric wrapped a leg behind his attacker. The squeeze brought them hip-to-hip; then torso-to-torso. The momentum slapped Eric's body hard against the man's arm. The blade entered silently through the ribcage.

Eric clung to him for a few seconds and then released his embrace to watch the man fall to the floor. Placing his foot on top of the man's chest, Eric then bent down and felt around his pockets for identification. Finding a green passport, he checked inside.

The name printed was Victor Chagell from Seine-Saint-Denis, a prefecture northeast of Paris. But French passports were burgundy, Eric knew, so why did this man have a green one? Green was for people who needed a replacement passport or were traveling emergently for humanitarian reasons for organizations like the United Nations. Green passports served as a temporary "laissez-passer" or "let pass."

Eric looked down at the man and asked, "So this was to be a short trip, huh?"

The man made no reply, so Eric answered for him. "I guess it was. But who do you work for?"

Again he got no answer, except for the implied statement that came from the soft roll of the man's eyes. Eric checked for a pulse, felt it fade, and stepped away. That's when a tremble, from deep inside rose up as the magnitude of what had happened hit him. This was his first kill. He drew a deep breath and tried to calm his tingling nerves. He rubbed his hands, arms, and fingers, hoping to return them to normal. He felt sick and gagged but held it back. And then, as the shock ebbed and burst forward again, the presence of this now dead man took on a whole new meaning. Someone *outside* the United States, presumably connected to France, knew about the mission.

Eric stepped back to gather himself again. He wondered what he carried in the computer bag and whether or not this intruder was in D.C. on Arnoult's command. If so, who then was the leak inside the CIA? And if not them, which agency and why? The alternate answer was that some other international authority was in the mix. In addition, Chagell, or whoever he was, would only be the first of many operatives to follow, of that he was certain. Eric added the latest information to his mounting arsenal of knowledge. Grabbing his phone, he dialed Oscher's office. When he was passed through, he blurted, "I had a visitor. French."

"Had?"

"Yes, sorry, but I needed to, ah, dispose of him."

Oscher quieted. "You okay?"

"I think so, sir, yes."

"You sound shaky."

"I am but I'll be fine."

"Of course you are. That's what you're trained to say at times like this. It comes with the territory. But, Dane? Take my advice, do as you were taught and find a reason to make it acceptable."

Eric searched his mind and thought of his parents. How had they handled it? They never said, did they? Was it because he'd been too young or did they just never talk about it, ever? And then they were gone....

Oscher cut in. "Mine is God and country."

"God and country," Eric repeated automatically, allowing it to settle. "Yes, sir, but what now? How do I...?"

"Leave it to me, son, but listen, you've got to watch

out for yourself. You said French?"

"Yes, sir, as per his passport. A laissez passér, I might add."

"Really," Oscher stated more than asked. "That's unexpected. Best to keep your eyes open from here on out and report *everything* directly to me. And I mean everything."

"Yes sir, everything. My eyes…they're open fully and I will report directly to you, sir."

"Now get out of there and take the bag with you. Protect it with your life, Dane."

"Yes, I will, I mean I have, sir. I've got it."

Eric ended the call and returned to the bed where he sat very still. After a minute or so of more garbled thoughts, he shouldered his bags. He then stood and went again to the dead man. He needed to justify the killing on his own terms.

His thoughts spiraled wildly around Fanny's warning of the frontline rifleman. Then they tightened when he connected this killing with the untimely death of his parents and to the people they must have killed. Eventually they landed on his training and the years he'd spent preparing for a moment like this. It all meant something. It was the cement in the wall he was building as a CIA officer. He was truly one of them now. Pure and simple. What becomes of his career moving forward was entirely up to him. *Fight or flight.* And again he knew the answer.

He moved his eyes up from the bloody chest to the man's face. The look upon it was calm--peaceful in repose--although only moments ago it had been contorted in rage. It was kill or be killed Eric told himself, and at that, Eric stepped away. He didn't look back or waste any time leaving the hotel. All that consumed him now was to find a safe haven to review what was in his computer bag and to quiet the hammer pounding inside his head.

9
Eric Dane
Buffalo Bound

Eric half sprinted through the main reading room of the Library of Congress toward its north corridor. There, a small gold-paneled nave beckoned him with an inscription, "Ignorance is the curse of God, Knowledge the wing where with we fly to Heaven." He understood the message well.

Knowledge, and the gaining of it, had saved him, especially after his parents had died. His voracious studies at Ransom, the University of Florida, and Langley had kept his heart and mind busy. As a result, knowledge cleared his ambiguity, settled his nerves, and solidified his future. And given this current situation, additional knowledge was exactly what he needed. The unexpected developments over his self-acclaimed grunt work had him feeling ill informed. Even Oscher had called his assignment a "simple pick up", but was it? No, it was clearly more complicated. Something sinister lingered underfoot that calculated into multiple outcomes. Of course the central character in all this was Arnoult, so bringing him in for questioning was vital. But in order to solve the number of rising unknowns, he first had to educate himself about the Frenchman and then he could better face the task at hand.

He found a table and chair that kept the north corridor in view and threw down the computer bag. He removed its contents and spread them hurriedly out in front of him. There were some government stickers, red zip ties, a blue file, a packet of photographs, and a small velvet bag from which he removed a five-inch rectangular gray rock. It held an equal length of what appeared to be a long, octahedral-shaped diamond. He studied the mineral closely.

In the pale yellow light of the library, hints of blue, green, gold, and bronze glimmered below a slightly opaque surface. He imagined it polished and full of luster. What prism of colors would it show? What spectrum would it hold? He traced it with his finger and then rubbed it with his thumb. Nothing changed. It was still cold, hard, and earthly, just what you'd expect from a rock.

So this is an impact diamond? Eric asked himself before deciding that it was. *Man, it looks so...so what? Deadly? No, it's just a rock although I could kill someone with it; bash them over the head with it, really. But first it's a just mineral...created by a big meteorite. Don't kid yourself...it's also twenty million years old and just so happens to contain a natural buried treasure. This is a very expensive stone that will one day either become a million specks inside a precision saw or have color, cut, clarity, and carat weight. And what makes it so special? Because it's celestial...making this baby right here, what? The fifth "c"? But who's behind the killing for it? Who took the stab at me? Who knows I'm involved and how deep does it go?*

Eric glanced up to survey the corridor. There were a few people walking about or reading at their tables but no one looked suspicious enough to cause concern, so he returned to his thoughts.

Okay, then, what now? Can I trust Oscher to have my back, especially when I know he's capable of lying to me? What choice do I have? He did confess, though, didn't he? Besides, it's his operation, so how can I stop being knocked out at the starting gate? Somebody's already tried...and there might be more. Yeah, but isn't this what it's all about?

Putting my life on the line for good versus evil? Chasing bad money and corrupt power? Yes, that's the ultimate and it starts here, right now with this...this diamond in the rough. What's the lot worth? Can it even be calculated? Whatever it is, it's definitely more than the price of life...Corbett's, mine, and hundreds of others, maybe, but only if I'm foolish enough to let them.

He felt the rock's heft and again rubbed his thumb over its embedded crystal with interest. This was what Chagell had been after. What he'd died over. Eric laid it on the table and spun it around. He nervously massaged his eyes then wondered what stories the stone could tell and how many people were after it. Oscher hadn't gone down that road, had he? All he'd told him was where it came from and where it was going, about Russia's decades of silence and the prisoners who mined them. There was much more to the story of that he was certain. He cupped the rock and slipped it back into its protective bag, then opened the blue file and began to read in earnest. Inside there was nothing new about impact diamonds but there was plenty on Arnoult.

He was a seventy-three-year-old widower and his wife, Eleonore, had died five years prior at age sixty-nine. She, a housewife, had dabbled in local politics, yoga, and other personal interests while Arnoult, a lawyer and diplomat, had negotiated major airway contracts for France. The expertise awarded him a multi-state ambassadorship where he now reported directly to Prime Minister Jean-Luc Nanterre.

Arnoult's current whereabouts: Buffalo, NY.

Previous: Paris, France, two days prior.

Note: Assumed assassin of Officer Tobin Corbett.

Eric flipped forward to a page marked "Corbett".

Corbett when found, had been severely disfigured and burned by acid. He could not, at first, be identified. Confirmation by CIA came from the recognition and documentation of a triangulated scar on the inside of his left thigh, an old wound resulting from a knife fight in Japan involving the Boryokudan or Yakuza, also known for its extreme violence. The Yakuza were a highly organized crime syndicate spanning all of Asia. Its signature form of penance was to cut off a fingertip.

Since Corbett had been missing all ten of his, at first glance, it appeared that the Yakuza might have been involved and had extracted a harsh revenge. But surveillance and further evidence proved otherwise. In the end, all ten missing tips pointed directly to Arnoult and/or his conspirators. Other individuals had yet to be determined. An ongoing investigation by CIA was currently in place.

Eric cringed at the grotesqueness of Corbett's death, then flipped the pages closed. He would not allow himself to dwell on what happened or what could happen to him if his involvement in Operation Pop Up deepened. Crazy, certainly. Life threatening, for sure, but right now, he needed to focus on Arnoult if he hoped to survive the assignment at all. So he reopened the file to the list of national and local contracts that Arnoult had won and lost for Nanterre and studied them.

Clearly the wins outweighed the losses. Eric could see that Arnoult had indeed been a valuable asset to France. He memorized several highlighted agreements that had become familiar headlines due to alleged corporate issues either in the news or from conversations with colleagues. He then scanned the remaining articles, all of which expounded on Arnoult's significant contributions. In the back of the file, he found a printed version of the oath for US Citizenship that the Frenchman was expected to take within the next few days. Eric examined it line for line. At its conclusion, there was a renunciation of title that simply stated: *I further renounce the title of (blank) for the country of (blank) which I have heretofore held.* In reading it, Eric mentally filled in the blanks with "ambassador" and "France".

Attached, he found a schedule of where and when Arnoult would be sworn in the following Tuesday: City Hall,

65 Niagara Square, Buffalo, NY at 10:15 a.m., the Honorable Judge Elizabeth Vickers presiding.

Eric next turned to the packet of photographs and saw pretty much what he expected. Arnoult speaking at a podium. Arnoult at his desk. Arnoult with Nanterre delivering a public speech. Arnoult waving from the tarmac at a small airfield. Arnoult in the cockpit of a Cessna. Arnoult with his wife. And on and on. Many of these photographs he'd already seen during his meeting with Oscher but hadn't had time to study them. Now he did.

Several nervous hours passed after which Eric collected his things. He left the building with a half-baked plan rising in his head. He now had to get somewhere secure so that he could work out the details of how he would find Arnoult before his swearing in next Tuesday. He also needed a place for the night, so he headed to the Capitol Hill Hotel. Once there, he rented a suite and ordered room service. He then studied again every detail of the contents given him. He had this one night only and needed to understand as much as he could in order to see his job through.

He pulled out his laptop and commenced researching well into the early hours following leads and painstakingly putting together what he felt was the most effective and least disruptive method of abducting Arnoult. The knowledge piled on.

In the morning, still groggy from his lack of sleep, Eric showered and packed his things. He put everything back into the computer bag Oscher had given him and placed the call.

"I'm ready, sir," he told Oscher.

Oscher responded with "good" and then instructed, "Secure the main compartment of the bag with the red zip ties in the front pocket and place the 'Confidential US Government' stickers over them. Then leave it with the front desk to be put in their safe. Tell them a courier will be there shortly."

"Yes, sir."

"And Dane? Good luck. I'm certain this'll be over in no time."

"Yes, sir, it will."

"I'll see you and Arnoult soon then," Oscher said before hanging up the phone.

"Yes, sir," Eric replied as the full weight of his mission landed squarely on his shoulders. He took a deep breath.

With all the unknowns of this simple "pick up", he believed in the end it would, in fact, be the beginning of a long career, especially if he pulled it off with the finesse he had in mind. More importantly for anyone watching, he also hoped they'd see that he was capable of not only doing an outstanding job but also of doing it in a way no one expected. He wanted their eyes opened as far as his had been pried in the last twenty-four hours.

He lifted the computer bag from the desk where he'd zip-tied and sealed it shut. Then, after dropping it off at the front desk as instructed, he left the Capital Hill Hotel. Next stop Buffalo, New York.

10
Eric Dane
Niagara Square

On his second loop around the block of the Federal Building, Eric considered switching tack over to City Hall. He'd been in Buffalo all weekend, spending most of that time scouting areas Arnoult might visit or happen to pass, but so far leads to his actual whereabouts had been few. Moving to a new location felt prudent. However, just as he was turning his chin over his shoulder, there, in his direct line of sight near a window inside a coffee shop across the street, sat Arnoult. Eric stopped.

At first, Eric couldn't believe the twist of fate. It was, of course, a given that Arnoult would be at the swearing in and that he would carry out his assignment at that event, but still, finding him beforehand established his presence and provided Eric options. Now here he was.

As alternative actions entered his mind, Eric leaned back against the building's brick façade to watch a waitress fill Arnoult's coffee cup while he read *The Buffalo News*. She interrupted him with some friendly banter and in return he nodded and smiled until she left. He then laid down his newspaper and lifted his mug up, stopping midway to stare out the window in Eric's direction.

Is he looking at me or someone else? Eric wondered, as he instinctively pressed harder against the wall.

Arnoult held the mug steady in front of his face for a few seconds more before placing it back down on the table without taking a sip and again lifted the newspaper. Eric checked his watch. It was quarter to nine. He figured Arnoult must have simply been musing, perhaps over something he'd read or something to do with his upcoming transition. He might even have been thinking how his life will change once everything was behind him, which mattered little, since Arnoult's fate depended entirely on the information Oscher dragged out of him as it pertained to Operation Pop Up. Whatever it was, he wasn't looking now, so Eric relaxed and assumed that he either didn't see him or if he did, considered him an office worker.

Eric stepped away from the building and walked toward the nearby obelisk at Niagara Square to reassess his objective. There he'd be able to keep an eye on the coffee shop and have the opportunity to put a respectable distance between them. He busied himself with the plaque memorializing President William McKinley's death from a gunshot wound while attending the Pan-American Exposition held in the city of Buffalo in 1901. Then he looked around before deciding to sit on one of the many benches to gather his thoughts.

Should he take Arnoult prematurely or wait until the celebration as planned? What were the risks? His original idea was well constructed and he'd rehearsed it a hundred times in his head and on paper. It was familiar. Also if he waited and didn't capitalize on this present opportunity, his target might be less attuned to him when it came time for the ceremony. Not like he could be at this moment, if in fact, he'd been compromised by Arnoult's observation.

A woman's loud laugh interrupted his thoughts. He ignored her until her male companion said, "Oh c'mon, Shirl, Vickers at least has some flash."

"Sure she does," she chuckled.

Vickers? As in Judge Vickers?

69

"Yeah," the fellow argued. "All that sweat makes it stuffy in there sometimes. The fresh air will do us good."

The woman laughed again and raised a clipboard from the man's lap.

"I don't know," she said to him. "Let me see what you've got."

The man leaned into her.

Eric sensed an opportunity and walked over to them. "Excuse me," he said.

The two looked up.

"I was wondering if you could tell me of any tourist activities around here? Maybe for tomorrow? You know, like sailing or going to a farmer's market? Something local. Something interesting."

The woman eyed him up and down. Smiled at his good looks. The fellow suggested he take in the Buffalo Museum of Science. "They have a wonderful Seymour and Stanley exhibit."

"Were they early explorers?"

"No, they're a mastodon and an albertosaurus. Kin of the elephant and Tyrannosaurus Rex."

"Sounds fascinating."

"Or you could come to the swearing in," the woman suggested.

"Swearing in?"

"Yes, of new citizens. The public's invited and it'll be right here. Tomorrow. Around ten."

The man nudged the woman. "Haven't you got anything better?"

She laughed. He hit her shoulder.

"Just ignore her," the fellow said. "She doesn't get out much."

"Maybe not," she retorted, "but at least I will tomorrow."

The man grimaced at her obvious flirtation. "Look, we've got a lot to do today, Shirl, so why don't we go get that cup of coffee we talked about, hmmm?"

Shirley pursed her lips and stood. "I don't even know why people come to Buffalo for this kind of thing anyway," she teased Eric. "There's a million better places. I'd pick Hawaii if it were up to me. No brainer, right?"

Eric chuckled, because according to the dossier he'd read, the Federal Government used Buffalo for high profile immigrants simply because it *was* Buffalo and not a more luxurious location. Plus, Judge Vickers made it an easy in, easy out, no fuss process for CIA, FBI, and Special Ops when it came to moving keepers. She was, if anything besides "flashy" as these two people thought, quick and efficient.

The man stood up and put his hands in his pockets. "Let's go, Shirl, we've bored this gentleman enough."

The woman eyed Eric one more time before walking away.

Eric sat in their places and began to reconstruct images in his mind of the changed venue. Gone was the thought of taking Arnoult any earlier because having the service outdoors in the square was an absolute bonus. He'd have to come back later in the afternoon to see what those two had put together, but for now, all he needed was to peruse the area. He studied every bench, tree, bush, and waste can with renewed energy. There wasn't much, so open was the park's layout, but he was happy with what he saw and with how much easier his work would be. All he needed now were his supplies.

*

Meanwhile, Arnoult was paying his bill as the same couple from the park walked into the coffee shop. He studied them with heightened suspicion. His goal was close and he needed to be vigilant of everyone and everything. He simply couldn't afford any mishaps so near the finish line. Already

71

he'd watched a man walk around the Federal Building several times before stopping to rest against the building and looking, it seemed, right at him.

Had it been this man? No, this one's too young. Maybe I'm dreaming or maybe that first guy was just stretching his legs before going to work. What do I know about the habits of these people?

He went back to counting his money.

When finished, he angled his cap into his left brow to better block what he could of his face and hurried out the door. He walked down Genesee Street and headed for his temporary safe house, something Homeland provided on occasion to visiting dignitaries such as himself. Its closeness to City Hall and the Federal Courthouse was beneficial to conducting business, both legal and otherwise. And while he'd never personally been to Buffalo, Homeland had assured him that the city was "tight as a bank" and that he shouldn't worry about a thing "aside from following the script", which was pretty straightforward: remain in the apartment as much as possible, stray no further than Niagara Square if one had to venture outdoors, and speak to no one.

So far, that's exactly what he'd done.

Tomorrow's ceremony, however, had been moved from the courthouse to the square. A special federal clerk had notified Feldon, who in turn had notified him. It would begin at ten and last forty-five minutes, depending on how quickly everyone could be processed during the nine-thirty check-in. All told, he understood that about twenty-seven people of varying nationalities would be in attendance. He, however, was the only one that Feldon had sent. This meant he alone was going directly into protective custody once he crossed the threshold of the Federal Building with his naturalization papers in hand. In spite of Homeland's well-oiled routine, Arnoult still felt vulnerable. He couldn't say exactly why, but given his private business with Nanterre and Philippe and all that had transpired up until now, he felt he had good reason.

72

"What does Homeland know?" he asked himself repeatedly. "Things go wrong all the time and if they go wrong now, it will be unforgivable."

He deemed himself fully exposed for the first time in his life. He had no wife to console him, no immediate protection from the United States, and no reliable assistance from his own country that he could or would contact. So why had Homeland left him to his own devices without a bodyguard or companion? Was it really part of its *purview* as he had been told when they'd transported him here? *Purview?* Did they not have the manpower? The funds? The interest? No, none of that. They would leave him, they said, to his own devices because they trusted their system. His requests were inappropriate. After all he still had a country he belonged to that brought with it diplomatic immunity, didn't he? Besides, his business with the United States was still pending. What more could he expect? A private swearing in? No, because he had refused until then to exchange real information, so good faith had to be part of the equation and the risk for both parties. He would just have to go through the process.

Arnoult thought of all he'd left behind, entered the apartment, and double locked the door.

*

Eric, on the other hand, believed the start of the event would happen closer to ten-fifteen, with the actual swearing in somewhere between ten-forty five and eleven o'clock. He'd based his timetable on the confusion often brought on by multiple nationalities to any given affair and on the number of chairs he'd seen set up at the square. It was in this extra fifteen minutes that he would execute his plan. All he had to do now was analyze the periphery once more in order to install the props he'd purchased.

At sunset, Eric returned to the park for a second time,

stopping only to pick up a canned soda. He was standing across the street with it in his hand when the last worker left in a van painted on the side with "All the World's a Stage."

"Good name," he said to no one in particular.

He stayed at his post for several minutes to study the people who were admiring the work already done or reading the "Public Invited" announcement board. He watched a few of them lean over the metal barricades surrounding the ceremonial area as couples strolled by holding hands or found benches on which to sit and cuddle close. He also saw a security guard sitting in his SUV on the other side, something he expected but wondered if more would arrive during the night.

He figured it was possible because enough equipment laid about, although it didn't really matter. Right now, however, was a different story. A single male dressed in dark clothing, walking around the entire park alone with a soda can in his hand was anything but a coincidence to someone trained in surveillance. The question was, just how good was this guy?

Eric refused to take any chances. He needed a ruse in the shape of a vulnerable female to act as his girlfriend. So he went to the coffee shop where he'd first spotted Arnoult and sat at the counter next to a young woman who looked as if she was grabbing a bite after work.

"I'll have what she's having," Eric told the waitress with a smile at his intended shill.

"Chicken Caesar salad?" the waitress intoned dryly.

"Yes, please," he answered cheerfully and then whispered to the woman, "It is good, isn't it?"

She giggled. "Very."

Eric extended his hand. "Hi, I'm Sam."

She shook it. "Mandy."

They ate and talked with Eric making up stories in order to cast his hook. Finally he told her that he was a Konica copier salesman. And, after a brief pause added,

"From Jersey."

She smiled, so Eric continued to let out some line.

"I'm in Buffalo to claim a government contract that could be the biggest thing I've ever put together, so I'm kind of nervous. Well, excited, I guess. What do you do?"

"I'm a stenographer."

"For anyone in particular?"

"Bindenal," she answered.

"Judge Bindenal?"

"Yes, but everyone calls him 'blind-and-all' behind his back."

"Like Lady Justice."

"You could say that."

Mandy moved in her seat. Settled in. "He's mostly called blind-and-all because he's extremely fair except when it comes to wife beaters and pedophiles who crawl out from under the snow come March. They get housebound, you know? Must be the cold winters. If they're guilty, he really takes a hard swing at them," she explained with a smirk.

"Hang 'em high, does he?" Eric asked, pushing them deeper into conversation.

"Hang? I guess that's what you'd call it because he really has no problem subjecting them to any kind of public humiliation. Once? Before he sent a guy to prison for beating his wife? He put him under guard and had him hold up a sign in the Square all day that read, 'I beat my wife because she bought a poodle.' Well, guess what happened?"

"I can't imagine."

"People pelted him with doggie doo," she laughed. "They were merciless! The guy had to be hosed down before going into his cell because Bindenal wasn't about to let him in covered in all that! And the people loved it, I mean, it was street justice and kind of old-fashioned, you know? To let them punish him?"

"And you love Bindenal for that, don't you?"

"Yes," she admitted. "It somehow seems fair."

"Hey," Eric said, leaning into her. "How about you show me where it all happened? I mean, isn't the park right down the block? What's say we take a stroll?"

She looked at him.

"It's a lovely night," Eric offered with arms spread.

"Okay," she said, sliding off her stool and swallowing his bait.

Eric paid both tabs and left a tip on the counter. It was now seven-fifteen. The park, well lit on both sides of the wide concourse, was bathed in a double halo of soft light. This would be romantic under any circumstance, and for Eric's purposes, it served as a perfect backdrop.

Mandy, unaware, was excited by Eric's attention and pulled him by the hand across the street. She pointed to the sky with her other and shouted, "This way! This way!" Something Eric remembered as a quote from a poem etched into the monument. Once there, they slowed. Eric surprised her with a passing kiss that swept lightly across her lips. She looked into his eyes.

"That was nice," she whispered.

"And so are you," he whispered back before kissing her again a little firmer this time with the hope that the security guard caught a good peek.

They walked around the park like ordinary lovers. Eric scanned the grounds as she told and retold, at his insistence, where and how the wife beater was so mercilessly pelted. They laughed, leaning in close to one another. They claimed an empty bench behind the stage. Here they sat talking for about fifteen minutes more. When Mandy looked away to dig around in her purse, Eric reached beneath the seat to install a few of his props and when she was finished, pulled her into his chest.

"You're lovely," he said.

They nuzzled with Eric making sure security noticed by wrapping his arms tightly around her as if he'd just proposed and she'd accepted. Then he suggested they again walk back to the coffee shop where he said his goodbyes. Only this time, it was she who reached up and kissed him on the lips.

"You're a good man, Sam, I can tell. Will I see you sometime again in Buffalo?"

"It's doubtful unless I get a lot of referrals from this contract, but thank you for tonight," Eric answered, reaching out and sweeping stray hairs to behind her ear. "The offer is very tempting but after tomorrow I'm off to Philadelphia. But, hey, if I was staying longer, I'd certainly treat you to a dinner with complete linen service."

Eric reached into his shirt pocket and pulled out a pen. "Got a piece of paper?"

Mandy smiled and again dug around in her purse. She found an old receipt and handed it to Eric. He wrote on its back. "Here's my e-mail address and phone number. Contact me anytime."

Mandy's eyes danced as she fanned herself with the piece of paper. "I just might. And that linen service you've suggested sounds like fun."

Eric laughed at the innuendo and kissed her again before parting.

Back in his hotel room, he reviewed the schedule one more time and prepared his clothing before deciding a good night's sleep was his best weapon. He next slipped between the sheets and put his mind to rest. In the morning, he dressed in a suit and tie. He wanted to blend in as a government employee, which, technically, he was, only from a different branch. He made coffee in his room and sat on the windowsill overlooking the city as it came to life.

Despite all its industry, he admired how efficient Buffalo appeared with its crisscrossing of bridges over wide, meandering waterways that connected people and places and made everything accessible. Even the college and all its young lovers lent a warm presence to the city. He determined that aside from the fact that Buffalo was covered in ice and snow for long periods, it currently appeared quite tranquil. But it wouldn't be for long. At seven forty-five, it was time to roll.

Eric strolled toward the square to check on the activities. He spotted a new security guard sitting on one of the risers, drinking from a thermos jug, and watching joggers run by. And already, two people were draping tables and moving boxes of paperwork and flags around. He decided to go in the opposite direction until more people arrived.

Within the hour, more were lined up in separate queues. One was for the general public; the other for attendees. There was no sign of Arnoult still, so Eric walked away, preferring to join the festivities when the swearing in actually began. He strolled around the block and down a side street that eventually brought him back to the park behind the spectator's area. Perfect.

He spotted Arnoult filling out forms and talking with a person from Immigration. As she smiled at the Frenchman, she held out her hand to the rows of folding chairs. Arnoult stepped in that direction and chose a back row seat on the left aisle where he sat and removed his hat, a gray tweed cap. Eric concentrated on him. Arnoult looked calm, something Eric attributed to him believing that he'd soon be an American citizen. But how would he look after his existence was erased, Eric wondered? Because if Eric's plan succeeded, France was about to loose a valuable diplomat and America would gain a very surprised informant.

11
The Swearing In
Buffalo, NY

Eric slid in behind the growing number of bystanders to get closer to Arnoult, who had yet to lift his head from reading the paperwork he'd picked up at check-in for the ceremony. He then moved into a better position and palmed the contents in his pants pocket…a small push-button remote that when pressed would discharge the bells and whistles the organizers had staged. There would be plenty of smoke too, from the devices he planted beneath the bench where he and Mandy had enjoyed the park the night before. Tucked in his waistband was a Glock 21 Gen 4, a .45 caliber, semi-automatic pistol and newer generation of the gun his parents had used in the field years ago. The weapon gave him a sentimental measure of confidence.

He watched Arnoult scan the crowd as Judge Vickers took her place at the dais and a local brass band played "God Bless America." On either side of her stood several employees from USCIS, the United States Citizenship and Immigrations Services.

When the band's music faded, Vickers addressed the audience.

"Welcome," she enthused with a calculated pace so that her words didn't reverberate. "Welcome each and every one of you. Today it brings me great pleasure to see you here.

And, as you are about to become citizens of these great United States, it is an honor to know that while you have lived in foreign lands, your view of America and the treatment of its people, has shown you that in the land of free, you can have the same right. May our country welcome you and your allegiance with open arms."

The crowd applauded wildly, the band played a long riff, and everyone waved their American flags. Only Arnoult remained still. Judge Vickers continued with her opening monologue and when finished, the head of Immigration took the dais. As he addressed the crowd, for what seemed about twenty minutes, Eric focused on Arnoult from behind. And, as the Frenchman wiped his brow with a handkerchief and bounced his knee, Eric surmised that Arnoult was indeed anxious. But then so was he. His timing had to be impeccable.

Next to the dais stood a large monitor draped in red, white, and blue bunting on which at the conclusion of the ceremony, a previously recorded video of the president would appear to welcome them as US citizens. It was just too bad, Eric thought, that Arnoult wouldn't have the pleasure to see or hear it.

Taking the mic for a second time, Judge Vickers asked everyone to rise, place their right hand over their hearts, raise their left, and repeat after her:

I hereby declare, on oath,

Eric leaned forward and held the remote more firmly in his left hand…

that I absolutely and entirely renounce and abjure

Arnoult repeated the lines and continued to stare straight ahead…

all allegiance and fidelity to any prince, potentate, state or sovereignty,

Eric placed his right hand on his gun…

of whom or which I have hererforto been a subject or citizen;

And with his left hand, he pressed a finger on the button.

From behind the stage came the popping sounds of high-powered firecrackers. Smoke billowed up over the band. People screamed and scattered in various directions. Arnoult grabbed at his chest, at which time Eric pressed the hard nose of his Glock into his side. Arnoult turned wide-eyed to look at the gunman behind him.

"This way, Mr. Arnoult," Eric said into his ear after placing a strong arm over his shoulders.

Arnoult twisted back toward Eric and smiled with recognition. "Up close you are but a boy."

"A boy with a gun," Eric replied, digging the Glock deeper into Arnoult's ribcage. "This way. Now."

Someone from the stage was shouting, "Calm down! Calm down! It's only the fireworks! You're not in any danger," as security moved in to help handle the crisis. But no one paid attention, so frightened they'd become.

Together Eric and Arnoult moved against the excited mob down Court Street. Arnoult resisted, so Eric mostly carried him across the street to the Veterans Affairs Building and pushed him toward the subway station.

Arnoult's breath came out in grunts. He stumbled. Eric pressed him harder. He then forced him into a building's indention and allowed him a moment's rest. Here Eric holstered his gun while securing his wrist to Arnoult's with a zip cuff and then shoved him back out onto the street where he stumbled again. This time against an SUV.

Eric reached for his Glock a second time. This time, however, he leveled it at Arnoult's chest, put his face only inches from the Frenchman's, and threatened, "One wrong move like that, one more stumble, you die. Now let's get going."

Sirens sounded from every direction as police and fire departments barreled through intersections. Car horns honked, trucks braked hard, and buses hissed to a stop. Chaos mounted. When they started walking again, Eric turned them back toward the square and pushed Arnoult forward.

"What are you doing?" Arnoult asked with much surprise, his head turning swiftly to Eric who told him, "Calm down, remember? It's only fireworks. So why don't we just go see what's happened like every other curious person?"

"Are you crazy? Do you not think people will notice these?" he shouted, raising their entwined wrists.

Eric slipped his opposite arm out of his suit jacket to let it rest in sloppy folds across the cuffs that bound them. "Move," he said.

He kept Arnoult close to the buildings opposite the square and away from the growing scene. Then forced their way into his hotel by dodging the nervous staff that hustled past. He grabbed the first elevator, all the while holding hard to Arnoult's hand. Once in the room, he cut himself from the tethered cuff and rebound Arnoult to his own wrists with a new one. He picked up the phone and dialed Oscher's office where he was immediately connected to the director.

"I have Arnoult," Eric told Oscher.

"Good, well done, but hold the details."

"Yes, sir."

"Give me five to reposition a car at the lobby's side entrance. Then bring him down."

"Yes, sir, and thank you, sir."

He hung up the phone, as Arnoult asked, "And now what? I am supposed to sit here in handcuffs until when, monsieur?"

"Until I take them off."

Arnoult's laughter was laced with anger. "Who are you and why am I here?"

Eric turned to the window and looked out. "I'm nobody but you're a man without a country, Mr. Ambassador, that's who you are and why you're here will soon be revealed. My job's to make that happen."

"What do you mean I am a man without a country? I am a Frenchman. I have a passport and diplomatic immunity. You do not know what you are talking about."

"Are you sure?" Eric asked, turning to face Arnoult again. "After all, you said it yourself, sir, under oath to Judge Vickers when you denounced 'all allegiance and fidelity' to France, remember? That makes you a man without a home. Without an identity. Without protection. Your passport is no good. You are, as they say quite frankly, de facto and de jure stateless. France can no longer protect you and, well, the United States has yet to bring you in. So you're nowhere, Mr. Arnoult. You're a citizen of nothing. How does that make you feel?"

Arnoult's stare told Eric that he was processing the validity of what he'd just been told. His face registered neither here nor there and looked locked in space both politically and physically. That meant he could tell him anything right now and the man might just believe him. He saw Arnoult's eyes darken, the tip of his tongue dart out like the head of a serpent, and pull back. His head started shaking slowly before his mouth opened to say, "This is preposterous. You're preposterous. Who exactly are you anyway and who is it that you work for?"

"My name's Eric Dane. I work for CIA, not Homeland as you're probably expecting. My job was to pick you up and bring you in and that's exactly what I'm going to do."

"But why? Why would the CIA want an old diplomat like me? I've done nothing," Arnoult protested.

Eric paused, locking his eyes into Arnoult's and wondering how long the stare down would last.

Finally Eric asked, "Nothing? Are you sure? Because one of our men went missing. Presumed dead in Paris, no less. You might have something to do with that."

Arnoult bit his lip.

"Tobin Corbett was his name in case you didn't

bother getting to know him before you killed him and tried to erase his identity. But you missed something. A very unusual scar on his thigh. Had you bothered to fully examine him, you might have seen it, but you didn't, did you? You were in a hurry to go where, Mr. Arnoult? Here? To beautiful downtown Buffalo to become a US citizen? For what reason? Who exactly are you running from, huh? And who was it that you sent after me in Washington?"

At this Arnoult closed his eyes as if offended or afraid, Eric couldn't tell. What he could determine, however, was that based on his initial response when taken from the ceremony, was that the man had expected someone older than Eric.

Arnoult shifted in his chair. "If you think, monsieur, that someone is after you, you may very well be correct. But it was not me, I assure you."

"He was French."

"Ah, so I am guilty by association? I see, but have you considered they were not after you but me?"

"What? By coming after me?"

"Yes. Why not if they know in the end it is me you have come for?"

Eric laughed at the man's train of thought for it was the bag Chagell was after, not Arnoult. That said, however, Eric made note that Arnoult's involvement must be immense to think that way. But then…what if there was an element of truth in what he was saying? That there was more reason than the bag to send an assailant? What if the entire pursuit was related to Arnoult? Had the prime minister sent an operative to America? Would he send more? And if so, how much did the prime minister already know? Was he behind all this? Was the CIA aware? Was he walking into a trap?

Arnoult opened his mouth again to speak when the phone rang. Eric answered it and told valet that he'd be right down and, no, he would not be in need of any other services.

Arnoult asked for the bathroom, so Eric lifted him

from the chair and walked him to it but stood in the doorway.

"Not even any privacy?" he asked.

Eric turned and gave him a cold look.

When finished, Arnoult washed his hands and said casually, "I would never betray my country by killing one of your men."

Eric's anger escalated at the obvious lie. So he grabbed Arnoult's jacket from between the shoulder blades and pulled him backwards out of the bathroom. He then took him roughly down the hotel's emergency staircase to get to the lobby's side entrance where the driver waited.

"After you," Eric told Arnoult who hissed over his shoulder and slipped into the car.

12
Not Nyet
Leaving Buffalo

Meanwhile back at Niagara Square, a gray tweed cap lay on the ground amongst the scattered aluminum chairs until an unfamiliar man lifted it to dust some dirt off the embroidered seal of England and scanned the now smaller crowd. Seeing nothing more of significance, he tucked it under his arm and walked away. A hidden rage, however, had him gnawing at the inside of his mouth, enough to make it bleed in an attempt to hold tight his emotions.

He climbed into a dark blue sedan parked across from Niagara Square and when seated, addressed his partner with Russian sternness, "How the hell did we lose him, Iosif?"

Iosif, with his hands clutched to the wheel, shrugged and waited further instruction. The man hit the dashboard with his fist. "The airport!"

Iosif pulled the car away from the curb but at the on-ramp of I-90, he pointed to another vehicle sitting in traffic just two ahead of them and said, "Alexei."

Alexei took from his breast pocket a small set of binoculars and aimed them at the backseat passengers. His face turned rigid. His jaw clenched. He took out his pistol and checked its full magazine. He gestured to Iosif to lay his identical pistol on the console between them. Alexei lifted it and checked its magazine as well. Traffic moved slowly but he was ready, and when it was their turn to merge into traffic, he signaled Iosif to move into the passing lane. Iosif progressed seamlessly between cars, keeping Arnoult's and Eric's vehicle in view at all times.

As they approached the next exit to the Buffalo Airport, they fell in behind them. Alexei considered the three men ahead. Arnoult, he saw, was in the back seat on the driver's side with another younger man to his right. They were not talking. The driver, nondescript, seemed focused only on driving. He signaled for Iosif to bring their car up to Arnoult's. As Iosif brought them parallel, Alexei lifted both pistols and started shooting.

The driver of the other car swerved, hitting the guardrail. He then over-corrected and rammed his car into their sedan. Alexei opened fire again. This time blowing out the rear window of Arnoult's as his sedan crashed into a semi truck that had been coming up too fast behind them. The driver of the semi lost control before engaging the air brake, forcing his rig to jackknife and flip. It flattened the sedan beyond recognition.

Traffic knotted to a standstill, as Eric's driver pulled onto the far shoulder. Eric raised his head over Arnoult, who lay cowering across his lap. He pushed Arnoult off and then crawled through the now missing rear window.

"Keep your eyes on him," Eric told the driver on his way out.

With his weapon raised, he ran over to the toppled semi and circled around it to inspect the car. And while he was unable to detect any movement inside the flattened sedan, he did spot a gun that had been thrown from it. He removed a handkerchief from his jacket and picked it up by its barrel, wrapped it, and ran back to the car. Once there, Eric pushed Arnoult across the glass-speckled seat and yelled to the driver, "Let's get the hell out of here."

"Yes, sir," the driver responded as he threw the car in gear.

Eric craned his neck to survey the accident scene for witnesses to their departure, but everyone was busy either checking their own vehicles or running to the toppled semi truck with cell phones to their ears or to take photos. Meanwhile, with a dazed Arnoult sitting upright next to him, Eric lifted the wrapped gun from his lap and carefully examined it. What he found surprised him. First was the ancient look of the engraving imbedded in its grip–a flaming meteor tipped with what looked like a bursting diamond. And second was the gun itself. It was a modified Russian Baikal IZH-79-8 with a barrel that had been rebored from a 8mm to a 9mm. Its modification to Eric seemed strange, considering better technology existed. He'd studied similar pistols at the Academy and recognized it as the next generation of 9mm Makarovs popular before the collapse of the USSR in 1991. He also recalled that the United States had since restricted its use.

So he wondered, what was a gun like this doing in Buffalo and why was it being used to shoot at him? Who with any ties to Russia even knew he was here? Did this have any connection to the situation in D.C.? If so, how? Had they followed him too? Or was Arnoult, the target? Was it both of them? The only answer lay in that whoever they were, or had been, they'd almost succeeded.

Placing the marked gun back onto his lap, Eric felt bruised but not bloodied. Arnoult, however, seemed slow to move, making him wonder if he'd suffered a wound or concussion.

"Exit here and find some isolated parking lot," Eric told the driver.

After he located one, Eric asked the driver to get out of the car and walk away. When he was a safe distance, Eric turned to Arnoult and pointed the Glock at him. Arnoult didn't immediately move. Instead, he stared only at the pistol on Eric's lap.

"Are you hurt?" Eric asked him. "Were you hit?

Answer me."

Arnoult pointed a weak finger at the Baikal. "What you have there is a very big problem and it will, mon ami, be our death."

"What do you mean?"

Arnoult opened his mouth and exhaled. "That symbol. On the grip."

"Go on," Eric insisted.

Arnoult winced. "Well, that particular weapon with that particular symbol could only have come from one place in the world, and trust me, it means we are doomed."

"Doomed? That's a pretty dire thing to say, isn't it, Arnoult?"

"No, monsieur," Arnoult answered, closing his eyes. "Doomed would be my word of choice."

Eric held his gun to Arnoult's temple.

Arnoult remained motionless, saying only, "Go ahead, please, do me this small favor."

"Why?"

"Because I am as good as dead already. They know where I am and that means they have been watching my every move. "

"Who's they?"

"They? They are gods. Angry gods. People of such distinction that they are their own kingdom. No one rules them but themselves."

"That's impossible," Eric said as he lowered his gun to Arnoult's shoulder.

Arnoult opened his eyes unwillingly and pointed again to the Baikal, adding with a measured breath, "That symbol there? I will tell you. It is representative of a hermit kingdom so deep inside Russia that it has been kept secret for more than five thousand years. Its source of income is diamonds. Celestial diamonds. Diamonds that I have effectively stolen in great quantity to fund my retirement and something I might now never see. I should have known that I

89

could not cheat them."

"You're talking about Popigai," Eric said as he watched the driver take a position beneath a tree with his eyes on the passing traffic.

"Ahhh, yes, so you do know of Popigai and its diamonds," Arnoult replied with a weak smile. "But do you know that the keepers of the kingdom are somewhere else entirely? In effect, those who operate the mines do not control the distribution and it is quite possible that even they do not know who pulls the strings."

"But you do. And are you in contact with these keepers?"

"I was," he answered with a twinge. "But I had the vain idea to get lost in your witness protection program that Homeland so eagerly wanted to provide me in exchange for some information."

"What information? Something about the diamonds?" Eric prodded already knowing of the arrangement.

"No," Arnoult answered, his voice pained. "They know nothing of the diamonds as you and yours might already suspect. It is another matter and I'm afraid the wild goose chase I have them on will be revealed for the fraud that it is before much longer. My window of opportunity, as you Americans call it, was rapidly closing anyway. And now you have gone and how do you say, slammed it shut?"

Eric thought for a moment before again pushing Arnoult. "Tell me who's after you because if they're after you, they're after me."

"Oh, of that you can be sure and they will not stop until they do because they are most determined. You should be very careful to trust no one, not even the people who command you because they are everywhere, no?"

Arnoult coughed hard and closed his eyes again. He then whispered, "Excusez moi, how little you know for you are so naive."

Eric planted his pistol firmly against Arnoult's temple

yet again.

Arnoult groaned this time and reached for his heart.

"And why should I trust you? You're a traitor," Eric whispered into his ear.

As if to agree, Arnoult smiled and pointed at the gun. "And I shall die because of it, but so will you, guaranteed."

He then slumped against the door, a move that allowed his hand to fall from his chest onto his lap. Eric put two fingers against his exposed wrist and found a faint pulse. He then opened Arnoult's suit jacket and saw he was wounded just above his heart where a spread of blood was soaking the man's shirt.

"No, no, no, no, no," Eric vented as he reached across the front seat and blew the sedan's horn. "We need to go!" he shouted and waved to the driver who sprung into action.

Eric laid Arnoult across the back seat and used his own jacket to compress the wound. The driver threw open the door and climbed in, placing his cell phone to his ear to call Oscher.

"He dies, we die," Eric yelled as they peeled out of the parking lot and he worked as hard as he could to keep Arnoult alive.

13
Double Talk
Washington, DC

Eric's debriefing started with Oscher shouting at him as soon as he walked into his office. "What the hell, Dane? How did you let this happen? Arnoult wasn't supposed to get shot at, for Christ's sake, much less be fighting for his life right now!"

Eric put his right hand to his chest and asked, "May I sit down, sir?"

Oscher relented with a wave.

Once seated, Eric began a counterattack of his own. "No offense sir, but I was shot at too. So was the driver you sent. And again, with all due respect, you said that you'd have my back so I can't tell you how I let this happen."

Oscher leaned in as his face darkened. "What are you implying, Dane?"

"I don't mean to, sir, but trust me, the whole situation from I-90 on was a surprising affair to us all."

"Expect the unexpected," the director spat. "Don't let this be the first litmus test of how green you really are. No one, and I mean no one, forgets such a simple rule so soon after graduation. Have you wasted all our time and money? I hope not because you had no business being in any crossfire! And what happens when you do? You damned near get our guy killed! It's unconscionable!"

Eric let Oscher's words settle as his own thoughts somersaulted. He felt vulnerable and betrayed but accepted, at the very least, that a tongue-lashing was warranted. After all, he did almost lose a valuable asset not to mention the intelligence that Arnoult would have brought to the table. On the flipside, did Oscher think that he *and* the driver were any less affected? Had he again been lied to? And, truthfully, did he really deserve this? No one on their side had died...not yet anyway. And if Arnoult's warning about his commander was to be believed, what was Oscher's responsibility in all of this? How much had he kept from him about this mission that would have made the difference?

As Oscher ran his fingers through his dark hair in a moment of deep thought, Eric wondered what more was to spill from his mouth. He hadn't a clue, so he concentrated on the reflexive drawing of Oscher's lips into a tight line. About the only thing he could decipher was that he was trying like hell to keep whatever it was inside. So with caution, he took a another stab.

"Can you tell me who came after us? I mean, do you know if they were with the French government or from Popigai?"

Oscher turned to him and barked. "Me? I can't tell you a damned thing because no one even knew you were in Buffalo!"

Again, Eric waited for Oscher to settle down. He seemed too enflamed. But what did all his anger mean? That the bodies piling up proved his own game was off and maybe, just maybe, Oscher wanted an outcome so different that he couldn't contain his dissatisfaction? Was that it?

The director came from behind his desk with arms crossed and planted himself on the edge of it in front of Dane. He stared at Eric. "Okay, for the record. What happened? And start at the beginning. You skip one detail and it'll cost you. I'm all ears, capische?"

Eric repositioned himself and decided to tell Oscher

what he felt was essential. Nothing else. In particular that Arnoult had mentioned the hermit kingdom and that he should be suspicious of his superiors. He wasn't ready to surrender all that just yet. Besides, if it really existed and Oscher really could be trusted, shouldn't he be the one telling him?

So over the next hour and a half, Eric described the weekend's events. As he did, Oscher interrupted on occasion with questions of his own. Why did you involve that Mandy woman? Did you get any intel on the Judge or any of the other immigrants? Were any of the security personnel suspicious? Did you notice anyone who might have been there for any other reason? Did you look along the building tops? Did you talk with anyone or see anything else at the site?

Eric answered every question with ease. He felt he might have missed some opportunities by not paying more attention to the other immigrants. But, no, he had not noticed anyone on the rooftops or witnessed any other suspicious personnel either. And, yes, he had perused the square in great detail.

He felt complimented when Oscher said, "good that you reverted fault onto the organizers, Dane," referring to the simple incendiary device he'd used to prematurely set off their scheduled fireworks. He also felt patted on the back after he explained why he had timed the abduction the way he did.

"Let him think he was left without a country. Very clever and very useful to us all right now because if he thinks his diplomatic immunity is gone, he might even believe the UN can't help him now. In his mind, he's positively stateless. Brilliant. Good job."

Eric again felt encouraged and more importantly, felt he had turned the director's temperament around. So he continued with the details. However, when he started on the particulars of the accident, he pulled back, knowing this was a moment of truth.

Consequently, when Oscher asked what happened after he approached the shooter's car, Eric said nothing at all. Instead, he reached into his pocket and pulled out the now bagged Baikal pistol to present it to the director.

Oscher took it and turned it over in his hand. What escaped from his mouth was a deep, unintended growl. Eric settled back into his chair as Oscher leaned forward and pressed his index finger against the symbol to trace the deeply engraved meteor.

"What's this?" he asked, his voice strained.

"I don't know, sir, because I've never seen this symbol before. But, again, I'm thinking it has to do with the creation of celestial diamonds. As for the gun, I picked it up off the highway. I'm hoping ballistics can tell us something."

"Has this gun been looked at for prints?" Oscher inquired without commenting on Eric's reference to the diamonds.

"No, sir. I'm leaving that to you."

Oscher sucked air in through clenched teeth. His eyes narrowed. Eric made note of everything before adding, "The gun is a Baikal IZH-79-8. Russian made and a marked improvement over the Makarov previously used by the Russian military. But after the country's collapse, the market became flooded with Baikals. *This* Baikal, though, is rather special, not only for its unique engraving, but also for its modification to an 8mm. What that means, sir, is that this particular weapon is capable of shooting gas cartridges. Something street thugs in Moscow favor."

Eric waited to allow what he said be heard but Oscher was lost in his own thoughts, so he continued. "Now one can assume that the two men shooting at our car were visiting hoodlums or we can simply accept the fact that they were hired killers...sir?"

"What? Yes," Oscher said looking up at Eric quizzically for the first time since he'd handed him the gun.

"Yes, of course. A Baikal. Russian certainly. To tell you the truth, I didn't know they were still in use. I've heard stories, but you can't trust stories. This one's old and this symbol." He traced it again.

A ripple of laughter came from Oscher, who then said, "Thugs. Funny, Dane, but you're right, hired killers, definitely. And we'll have to assume first they were after Arnoult unless, of course, it had something to do with your attacker in D.C. If it did, well then, it opens up a lot more questions, doesn't it? But that's not your job to figure it out. It's mine. You did yours. You brought Arnoult in and now he's safely in our hands. Near death, but still, God willing he'll come out of this whole. He's in critical condition, you understand?"

"Yes, sir, I do."

"Yeah, well, we're doing what we can for him. When he's out of recovery, we'll get to the root of all this. I trust his story will back yours?" Oscher asked as if that might even be in question. "But I have to say, for your first mission, it sounds like you handled yourself fairly well. You made some good decisions under extreme circumstances. Mind you, this was supposed to be a very simple assignment, so in spite of my initial reactions, we're all very happy that you returned to us unscathed. The information you provided me today is extremely useful. And bringing in Arnoult? Well, for that you're due some real compensation."

"Thank you, sir, but all I hope for is another assignment with Operation Pop Up."

Oscher laid the Baikal on his desk. "It's under consideration, but for now, why don't you take some time off? A couple of days should do it and you can use the rest. As you've discovered, being shot at is serious business. When you get back we'll all have a better understanding."

"If you insist, sir."

"I do, but you won't be going home because when I say rest, I mean rest. We've got a designated safe house in

96

the Caribbean for our recovering officers."

Eric's brows pinched.

"You should see your face, Dane," Oscher commented. "You're wondering why I'd send you off. But the truth is that I can't afford to have you floundering around Key Biscayne for three full days, although I will let you stop briefly on your way back. So take the authorized break I'm offering while we check out the gun and figure out why it showed up on our turf."

He paused.

"Anything we assign you to next could very well require everything you have mentally and nothing assures a more stable mind than a quick trip on company money. I'll have Sally get you out of here by morning."

Eric managed to say, "Yes, sir, thank you, sir" as the promise of another assignment lifted his spirits.

"Don't mention it," Oscher responded with a laugh.

With that, Eric stood and shook Oscher's hand. He took a final look at the bagged gun on the director's desk and noted that Oscher hadn't fully responded to it. So on his way out, he asked, "Is it possible, sir, to let me know what ballistics says about that gun and its symbol?"

"When it's pertinent, Dane."

Eric left the office with Oscher trailing him, who went to his assistant to make arrangements for his departure. As he exited the building, he decided he needed a drink and he needed to have it with someone who would take his mind off business. So he dialed up Glory Milan, the lovely flight attendant he'd met on the plane.

"Still in Washington?" he asked.

"Yes, what's on your mind?"

"You, and maybe a drink? When do you leave?"

"Tomorrow morning."

"Me, too, how odd."

"Very."

"How about we meet on the roof of The W around

seven thirty?"

"The W? Oh, yes, the hotel near the White House."

"The one and only."

"Sounds politically motivated. I'll be the woman in red. See you then," she concluded and hung up the phone.

Eric smiled. It was the first real sense of relief he'd felt. It was also a hint of the fringe benefits his profession might provide from traveling around the country for the CIA. Because if meeting women like Glory Milan was a distinct possibility, it could be well worth it. He'd have to make sure, though, that he took it slow with Glory, for he had intentions of seeing her again in Miami—days, even months from now, should she be so willing.

Yes, Glory was significantly better than a designated safe house for the type of recovery he wanted.

*

They met on The W's rooftop at the open-aired POV lounge. She arrived in red as promised, only it was limited to the thin belt she wore at the waist of her short, black lace dress. They walked to the edge of the covered lounge and looked toward the White House, the Washington Monument, and other landmarks. The air was cool but neither really noticed.

"It's beautiful," she said. "I can see why they call it the Point of View."

He raised his glass to her. "It hardly compares."

"You're charming."

"I hope so."

"What was it you said you do?"

"I didn't because I didn't want to bore you. Besides, I'd like to get to know you first."

"Oh?"

"Yes, and I'm talking from experience because whenever I divulge that I'm a copier salesman, it seems that, well, women just disappear."

"Copier salesman?"

"Uh-huh."

"Really? You don't look like a copier salesman, so fess up and tell me the truth."

Eric held his ground by holding his tongue.

"Well I'm not into games," she said, eyeing the expensive cut of his Brooks Brothers suit before letting out a sigh.

"No game," he said. "Now if I recall, you were going to tell me about the playpen express and some of our more distinguished leaders' good intentions."

"Yes, and when I get to know you better, perhaps I will."

"Ah, now who's playing games?"

She lowered her chin and took a sip of her martini.

"You're right," he conceded after realizing how offensive he must be sounding. "Neither of us has time for this stuff, so let's not play any games at all. Just know that I'd really like to get to know you better. I have to tell you though…like you, I travel a great deal."

"To where?"

"Washington, New York, Florida."

"My route, pretty much."

"As we've established, remember?"

"When we first met?"

"Yes."

"Well then, it's very likely we'll meet again and again and again."

"I hope so, but I do have a trip coming up. A reward, of sorts, for a job well done. After that, I could be free for a few days."

"You must be pretty good at whatever you do to get a travel reward."

He smiled at her and she laughed, saying, "Call me when you get back. I'm curious."

"Good, the more curious the better."

Later that night he was rewarded with several lingering kisses.

"I haven't felt anything like that in a long time," he whispered.

"Me neither," she replied. "And if you're a good boy, chances are there will be more in your future."

"I'd like that, I'd like that a lot."

Yes, he would. He'd be seeing Miss Milan again, of that he was certain. She was captivating and not at all invasive. She'd be off the books. A woman he wouldn't have to vet personally or professionally. They were just two wandering souls looking for companionship. The only question was when and where?

He hoped he had things figured right, but for now, he'd have to wait. He had an unexpected trip to take...one that further tipped the scale of suspicion and opened up a new line of questioning, most importantly, why was he being sent *away* from Washington when he could have as easily stayed there to do research for Oscher? It just didn't make good operational sense.

14

Chambois des Caribees
Nevis, B.V.I.

The soft, yellow pull of the Caribbean's morning sun enticed Eric out of bed. He stretched with satisfaction, poured orange juice from a bottle in the mini bar into a glass, and stepped out of his room. He felt revived and even more so after he alighted upon something quite remarkable.

It started with a well-manicured foot and stretched the length of two ebony-colored but well-toned calves. Then thighs. And then a stark, white string bikini bottom that laid like a tiny patch of gauze at the base of a dark, flat pelvis. Her stomach, almost concave, bore an impressive diamond embedded in the navel that glistened against well-oiled skin whenever she took a breath. It was all he could see of her because of a large, potted palm strategically placed between their two patios. He announced his presence by rattling the ice inside his glass.

She greeted him with a hint of Creole. "Morning, I hope you don't mind, but the sun is closah to your place then mine."

He smiled. "Not at all, but why bring only the half of you?"

She giggled and rolled over, giving him the completed view of her lower body. "How's that for the other half?" she asked.

The revelation of a thong was also an invitation, in Eric's opinion, to take a closer look at her sculpted buttocks. So he answered her siren's call by stepping forward to lean against the tree. He rattled his ice once more.

"Given time, I'll reveal the rest of me," she teased.

Eric caved at the thought and jutted his head around to find hers hidden beneath a large straw hat. Its brim rested where the ties of her bikini top should have been knotted but dangled instead untied on either side of the chaise.

"You're quite the vision."

"Why thank you," she said without moving.

As Eric searched for what to say next, his breath caught. Finally, he asked, "Would you like a drink?"

"Too early unless it's champagne."

"Champagne?"

"Yes, champagne."

"I was referring to orange juice."

She laughed. "Then only if it's mixed with champagne and includes breakfast, I'm starving."

With that she peeked at him from under her raised hat so that he could see that the upper half of her complimented the all of her. "Let me get my wrap," she said while attempting to tie her top behind her back. "But help me with this, would you?"

Eric sat his drink inside the palm's container to free up his hands and rushed to her side. He bent over her luscious body and secured the ties loosely.

She sat up. Then stood. As she did, Eric found himself staring at one of the tallest women he'd ever seen. She was stunning in every detail although older than him by about twenty years. Her eyes had that foreign depth of only the most exotic places that, as they focused on him, sent out an intoxicating message. The vision of her took the last of his constraint away.

He watched her tiptoe into her room and reappear wearing a lavender-colored sarong tied low at the hips that revealed the braided threads of the thong beneath it. He extended his hand. She took it and walked with him to the hotel's seaside restaurant. Eric wasted no time in questioning her and allowing her to question him, or rather the other him. The copier salesman. Their friendliness grew and over the course of the next two days, he found himself sleeping peacefully to the rise and fall of her hypnotic breath.

In her presence, he felt like a ripened fruit on an unending buffet laid out for her insatiable appetite. She awoke in him an equal hunger intended for Glory, but here he was on a tropical island with a tropical beauty. So when on her last night she arranged a few sweet mango slices in a zigzag pattern up her stunningly brown stomach from her diamond-studded navel to the base of her cleavage, it was all he could do to not ravish her on the spot. Instead he toyed with each slice and as he did, she repeated some of her questions.

"Where were you born again?"

"Kansas," he lied, sucking up a thin comma of fruit.

"You got a girl in Kansas?"

Glory's face flashed through his mind as he answered, "Not yet but I'm working on it."

"I'm not available," she teased.

"Too bad."

"What do you do?"

"I sell copiers," he lied again, licking juice off her belly.

"I don't believe you. You can't sell copiers in Kansas and afford all this comfort."

"And I don't believe you," he said, nodding to the diamond. "That's a rather sizeable inheritance, wouldn't you say?"

She lifted his head and slipped into her deepest accent to poke fun at him. "Aweee, did I be sayin' inheritance? Mo' like benefactor. Me not mention? Truth ta tell, I be born and raised in da Big Easy, mon cher. N'awlins?"

Eric laughed as she switched into proper English. "My family, middle class at best, couldn't afford to send me off to college but it didn't matter because Ralph Lauren found me."

"*The* Ralph Lauren?" he asked, resting his head on a bended arm.

"Yes," she paused. "I was eating a beignet at Café Du Monde one morning when a man walked up to me and said I had a marketable face. From the minute I dropped that pastry and took his card, my life changed. Later on I became an airline stewardess with National Airlines. Remember them? 'Hi, I'm Annette. Fly me'? Well, some men took it seriously and before I knew it, I was under the spell of a darling pilot who kept me landlocked for longer than I cared. I lost my job because of him, and later of course, the airline went belly up. After he left me, I met a wealthy businessman who wooed me with this stone."

"What happened to him or is he still around?"

"Well, let's just say that even he wanted to possess me a little more than I cared. So here I am."

"Yes, here you are."

"On a little island in the Caribbean with yet another lovely man by my side."

Eric traced a circle around the diamond as she caressed the back of his hand. Thoughts of Popigai and Operation Pop Up surfaced only to be speared by her asking, "You won't be a tryin' ta tie me down too, will you, cher?"

"I'm not the warden type, Annette. Besides, unless you want to be a slave to a lowly copier salesman, I hardly think life with me would be interesting enough for you."

She laughed, "Come now, that's just a line and we both know it. But that's okay. I don't want to be tied down again anyway. What we've got here is just perfect. A tryst. And a tryst is plenty fine with me."

"Me too, but really, a diamond that size must have cost a fortune," he said fishing for its true origin.

"Oh, it did, but I'm certainly worth it. Would you like to see why?"

She laughed heartily with the intent of coupling with him well into the night. The next day, she and the vision of her were gone.

Eric wondered if anything she'd told him was true. Had it all been a game? If so, this gal had the sport down to perfection. And what about that diamond stud? Which story resonated most? It being an inheritance or a gift? And what about her being in hiding from possessive men? His senses told him that the truth lay somewhere far away. But no matter how much he'd sleuthed around, she'd deftly sidestepped the issue. Perhaps he wasn't as clever as he thought, or worse, he was starting to believe that every diamond he saw came out of Popigai.

But what about the coincidence of her presence? Had she been sent by Oscher to quiz him? Was she involved in Operation Pop Up? If so, could he handle it? Did he handle it? Or worse, what if she was a honey pot with some other organization charged with coaxing out of him whatever he knew? *His first.* He smiled at the thought, but truthfully, Annette's presence had only confused him.

Eric couldn't trust anyone anymore, he knew, especially now that he was CIA and had already been targeted. He'd only had one minor mission but from it he'd produced three dead bodies--one in Washington and two in Buffalo. So what could he garner from all this?

He mulled over the list: he'd been assigned a minor detail by Oscher in Washington to abduct Jacoub Arnoult before he became a US citizen and accomplished that. Immediately after receiving that assignment, he was followed by Victor Chagell, a temporary passport-carrying Frenchman whom he'd killed and whose body he'd left behind for Oscher to bag and remove. He'd successfully detained Arnoult in Buffalo until such time as Oscher sent a driver and everyone was chased, shot at, and run off the road by two goons with special weapons from—according to the near-dying Arnoult—a supposed hermit kingdom. And now he'd just spent two incredible days courtesy of Oscher on an exclusive dot in the Caribbean with an extremely intoxicating woman who sported *in her navel* a diamond the size of a dime.

The common denominator in every situation was Oscher, not Arnoult. But of course it was, he told himself. Oscher was his boss and commander. So naturally everything tracked back to him.

But what about Arnoult and the hermit kingdom he mentioned? Could he trust that last conversation? If it truly existed, surely Oscher knew about it but didn't tell him. He'd certainly appeared startled at the sight of the Baikal with its strange emblem. So why didn't he include that in his briefing on Operation Pop Up? Would he reveal who these people were on his return to duty? Could he trust Oscher or not? And how were all these people connected, because hadn't his parents always told him they were?

"If one person or thing points to another, then focus in that direction because only the smallest of degrees separate them," they'd advised. "Fill in the minute details and you'll have the whole picture."

With that in mind, Eric spent his last day searching for the missing threads…that smallest degree separating Arnoult, the hermit kingdom, Oscher, Annette, and of course, the three dead men.

He researched online and in the resort's small library. He worked for hours checking sources and resources. He scoured newspaper articles and reference books. He also checked airline routes and airport services. Upon his return to Washington, he wanted to be as up to date as possible on all things French and Russian: travel, politics, history, current events and most importantly, the Popigai Crater and its diamonds. He wanted to know more than what Oscher had provided him in the original dossier, and he wanted to know with whom he was really working for and against. Lastly he phoned Fanny to review as much as he felt he could, omitting what Arnoult had told him before his collapse about the hermit kingdom. He asked his friend for help. Fanny agreed but warned Eric that his life could still be very much in danger.

Eric only said, "Fan, you were always the dramatic one, but listen, I'll find my way through all of this, trust me, and with your help, I might even survive. Right now, we're a team, you and me, but I've got to make a pit stop at the house before going back to D.C, so can you meet me at the airport?"

"You got it, bro," Fanny said. "I'll be there. Meantime, I'll get to work and will have something for you when you land."

"Thanks, man, I'm sure you will."

15
Fanny Bergan
Caelestis Lapis

A worried Fanny stalked the baggage area at Miami International Airport. He had some urgent news that needed sharing with his best friend. As Eric turned the corner, they made eye contact.

Fanny strode in long, firm strides toward him, all the while watching Eric adjust the only piece of luggage he had with him, a black duffle that had seen better days. The carryall was a gift he'd given Eric during their college years and the only piece of luggage Eric had used to tromp around Europe. It now showed its wear, although Eric didn't, in spite of what he'd told Fanny he'd encountered since first arriving in D.C.. As they neared, Fanny gripped Eric's hand and pulled him into a bear hug.

"Good to see you, Dane."

"Yeah, Fanny, good to be back."

Still holding him, Fanny whispered, "Be careful, bro, because chances are I'm not the only one here to greet you."

"What do you mean?" Eric asked, his voice panicked as he reached up and patted Fanny's chest to feel the bulletproof vest under his shirt.

"Just listening to my gut," Fanny answered with a welcoming smile. "And after all you told me regarding your mission? Besides, wasn't I right about the rifleman on the front line? You did get shot at a number of times, as I recall. So lean in, buddy, and let's just get you outta here, okay?"

Eric nodded.

Fanny kept Eric close, using his Kevlar-covered body as a human shield, and together they stepped out to the curb where Fanny's Land Rover waited. Here, he opened the passenger door and gently helped Eric inside, then ran around the front of the SUV and jumped into the driver's seat.

"Buckle up," Fanny told him. "And boy have I got a whopper for you." He said nothing more until they were safely headed east toward I-95 and the city of Miami that loomed in the southeast.

"What gives?" Eric asked as he checked his side mirror, then whipped his head around to look out the back window that filled with the sprawl of warehouses, shopping districts, and commercial properties.

"Everything," Fanny said before pausing to explain. "First off, that little bit of research you asked me to do on the symbol etched into the grip of that Baikal? Well, I've come up with something very interesting. It took some digging but it seems that symbol's been around for hundreds...no, strike that...thousands of years. And according to the history I found, it's got to do with heavenly stones. Now obviously I was thinking meteorites because of the shape of that symbol, so that led me to celestial diamonds and that, my friend, was the key to the kingdom."

He noticed that Eric was deep in thought. So he asked, "Hey, you with me, bro, or are you still having fun in the sun with a certain Miss Chambois inside that brain of yours?"

Eric bobbed his head as if physically hit by the remark.

Fanny stole another glance in the review mirror then turned his eyes back to the road as he continued. "Eric, man," he said unable to resist craning his neck toward the passenger's side mirror this time, "This is big shit I'm talking about with global implications. It's pre-World War, man. I think it might even predate the Freemasons or maybe the Bible, but hey, things are a bit sketchy on the documented side, so how far back it really goes nobody knows. That symbol's ancient. Now what I did find out is that it's somehow connected to the Russian Bratva, a.k.a. today's Russian Mafia. Heard of them? Lethal buggers. Real butchers. That means we could be talking about a faction or secret sect that's been around since time began."

Fanny paused to check Eric for a reaction. "What? Still nothin' to say, partner?"

He watched as Eric rubbed his own chin, making him think that his best friend was wondering where to take the conversation next.

Then Eric asked, "What makes you think it's so secret?"

"Because the trail's as thin as air," Fanny answered. "Furthest I could take it was to a religious sect called the Christ Believers. They maintained that some heavenly powers along with a certain Lord Sabaoth, who was God himself, descended upon the earth in chariots of fire. Sabaoth supposedly assumed the earthly body of a peasant man in western Russia and stayed, thus becoming a living God. The heavenly powers, however, returned to the skies but not before directing a splinter group to travel over two thousand miles into northern Serbia. Now here's where it gets hazy because it seems, and I'm guessing here, that the splinter group wanted to break it off to commandeer their new domain on their own terms. As a result, the heavenly bodies got really, really mad and delivered tons of fiery meteorites to punish them. In the wake of those meteorites, they unintentionally created diamonds. Huge diamonds. Billions of diamonds. Making this sect one of the most powerful and richest in the world. Get the picture?"

Eric nodded with his lips stretched into a closed, tight smile.

"What's so funny?" he asked.

"I'm not sure, Fan," Eric answered, causing Fanny to wonder if his pal was withholding truths he wouldn't confess. And as if to confirm it, the limited response he got was, "That's way, way out there if you know what I mean. But we are talking about diamonds no doubt and celestial diamonds for sure, so it all fits. But a secret sect since time began? Hell, man, even you've got to admit that a story like that is stuff right out of the science-fiction pages."

"I said it was a whopper, didn't I?" Fanny blew air through his lips to release some frustration, then added, "But there's something solid about what I just told you. That symbol you asked me to investigate was sewn into their cassocks. Same flame shooting down toward earth. For Christ's sake, Dane, it's pretty obvious to me."

"Maybe," Eric said, nodding his head in agreement. "But the rest of the story? Now that borders on pure fantasy."

"It gets better," Fanny said ready to go full tilt. "Know what they used those diamonds for?"

"No, but you're going to tell me anyway, right?"

"Castration," Fanny blurted without pause.

"What?"

"Castration, as in cut the nuts off. Seems this new sect believed that the only way to appease the angry Gods was to be like them, meaning no sign of sexuality whatsoever. Not only that, but some followers went a little further voluntarily. Seems they, the extremely devout, cut their penises off too. Can you believe it? How they survived surgically back then is beyond me. Shoot, I can't even imagine how they urinated, I mean, we're talking about a society of eunuchs here. Almost every single one of them. Not all, though. They did leave some for mating. You know, to ensure posterity?"

"That's sick."

"No doubt, brother, but they survived *and* reproduced. But lest you think the women fared any better, get this. Everyone knows that Eve doomed the entire world when she seduced Adam with that apple, right?"

"Right."

"Well think in ancient terms. Think symbolically, man, 'cause it's all symbolic. These people believed that apple was really her clitoris and who's to say it wasn't since it was the enticement to sin. So now can you guess what they did to the seed of that forbidden fruit?"

"Cut it out."

"Bingo. They sharpened those diamonds and removed every single one in town. Some volunteered their breasts too, all in an attempt to appease the powers."

Eric held his head in his right hand, rubbing his forehead. "So how does this connect to the Russian Mafia?"

"Well, like I said, the sect wanted to answer to no one, not the heavenly powers they feared and later, not any church, government, or ruling party. They lived by their own doctrines. They thrived underground by selling diamonds and anything they could make from them, like jewelry, ornaments, you name it. More importantly, they crafted the sharpest damned tools and weaponry in history. All made out of celestial diamonds, precious stones, and meteor rock. They became legendary and extremely wealthy, of course. But get this, wealth wasn't their ultimate goal. Their goal was absolute power, which made them enemies of the state. Needless to say, over the centuries, the state must have won because the Christ Believers trail disappears. Dries up, man. Making any sense here?"

"Maybe, got anything else?"

"Sure, that said, the state might have won the battle but they obviously did not win the war." Fanny exited I-95 for the tollbooth at the Rickenbacker Causeway that crossed onto Virginia Key and then onto Key Biscayne. "That gun you picked up? The Baikal with that symbol? It means they're still out there, bro."

Eric whistled a slow note, making Fanny wonder just how off the money he was, but surely his friend grasped what he was telling him…that what had seemed farfetched, no longer did. That the Bratva and the Russian Mafia *were* together and have been forever. And the hermit kingdom? Still out there. Still selling their diamonds and living by their own rules.

"Now is it adding up for you?" Fanny asked.

"Absolutely."

"But you still can't tell me everything."

"No, not yet."

"Okay then just tell me this, this mission you just did…besides the gun, what did it have to do with diamonds?"

"A lot, except that particular job's done. Over. Mission accomplished, excluding a couple of hitches."

"Hitches? You mean the two hired guns and your target nearly dead as a result?"

Eric nodded and said, "Yeah, but as you and I are now aware there's more to the story, because if those two shooters in Washington were Russian Bratva, which is what your evidence indicates and I tend to agree with, then what are your thoughts as far as the bigger picture?"

"I think that the Bratva are with Popigai and the Christ Believers run the hermit kingdom. They're still out there, brother, both of them."

Eric neither acknowledged nor denied, preferring instead to keep Arnoult's confirmation of that very situation to himself for the time being.

They drove over the causeway in silence and for the next fifteen minutes allowed their brains to absorb what was discussed. As they came to the main intersection on Key Biscayne, Fanny turned west and looked over at the Key Biscayne Yacht Club, recalling their youth. He then turned right at Harbor Point where Eric lived. It was a long familiar sight.

Fanny spoke first after driving up to Eric's ornate gate, behind which stood his stately house. "Whatever happed to those days?"

"The ones when you used to chase me around the bay in that little Sunfish?" Eric asked as he pulled a remote from his pack and pushed the button.

"Naw, I'm talking about your folks and how I used to come over here and get into all kinds of interesting shit with you. I mean your parents were so cool about everything. Us, life, whatever. To this day I feel like they were every bit my parents as yours, you know? They set one fine example. I think that's why I'm in this business with you and I sure as hell know that's why you're in it."

"They were cool all right and I miss them. They lived and died for the agency. That last mission into Kazakhstan..."

Fanny heard Eric's breath catch in his throat, so he reached out and patted his shoulder, allowing the silent grief to fill the cab until Eric broke it with, "I just hope to do them proud. That's all."

"You will," Fanny said as he slid the car under the elegant porte-cochere and came to a stop. "What do you think your folks would have said about all this diamond and secret cult shit?"

"They would have said to connect the dots, Fanny. That everything's connected. They saw a lot in their day, but no matter what, they covered their bases from every angle, before, during, and after their missions. I had a few screw-ups with this first one. Some minor, some large but it ended okay, or at least I think it did. Anyway, with what you've uncovered and I've already been briefed on, this bigger picture isn't done for a Miami minute. Far from it. I'm going back in according to Oscher. So hey, thanks for covering me at the airport."

"No prob," Fanny said as he watched Eric take another look around before he added, "Looks like we've made it without a tail. You'll be fine now, my friend."

"Thanks, and Fan?"

"Yeah?"

"Safe travels. It's…"

"I know, I know….a wild world out there."

"You got it, man. Take care."

"You too," Fanny said in return, "And keep me posted on what else I can do for you. No use wasting all this brain power waiting for the C.E.O. to ring."

"You mean Conrad Ezrah Oscher?"

"The one and only."

"You got it," Eric said as he grabbed his duffle and entered his home.

Fanny idled in the driveway until Eric walked in and closed the door before slipping his Land Rover into gear and leaving the property. He felt satisfied at having delivered his friend home safely. What he didn't know, however, was that less than a quarter of a mile away on Bay Lane, an older, white, four-door Crown Victoria sat facing south toward Harbor Point. Behind the steering wheel, a man dressed in a long-sleeved black t-shirt and black slacks waited. His eyes were locked to the rear view mirror that took in the road behind his car until he saw Fanny's Land Rover head north on Harbor Drive. He then waited another minute before starting the engine and cautiously heading toward Dane's domain.

The man parked near the house after pointing the car in the opposite direction. He then stepped from it with quiet practice. Fortunately for him and less so for Eric, the gate remained open. So he slid past it and got as close to the building as he could to crouch beneath the blooming yellow hibiscus and bushes of blue-flowering plumbago.

His eyes roamed over the lavish landscaping. Mature date, coconut, and cabbage palms framed the house. A jasmine hedge, thick and fragrant, lined the walls, and a brightly colored bougainvillea of pinks and reds covered a painted white arbor that led to the pool. Flowers bloomed in a variety of colors but none of this–not one bud-appealed to him. His focus instead was on finding Eric, who by now had dumped his duffle on the kitchen counter, grabbed a glass of red wine, and walked to the edge of his pool to watch the setting sun.

The man moved closer to settle in behind a thick raffia palm and to watch Eric make a call on his cell phone. He was close now. One more step and he might alert him. So, as Eric continued to talk and sip his wine, the man quietly pulled his gun loaded with silenced bullets from a holster that hung neatly against his chest. He stilled when Eric ended the call and then tracked him again as Eric stepped left of the pool to walk slowly toward his home.

He watched Eric's every move. Marveled at him too, because Eric was young, blond and handsome. Boyish, almost, and stylish. Lean. Not yet fattened by the wealth of age or excess. He guessed Eric to be five foot, ten. Eleven, even. Only slightly taller than himself. But nothing to worry about. Size wasn't important. He had the element of surprise on his side, after all.

The man slipped in closer to Eric and a bit more parallel, then shifted to the right as Eric reached the floor-to-ceiling windows of his sliding glass door and, using them as a mirror, tucked in his shirt and then centered his belt buckle.

He leveled his aim when Eric hesitated over the door's handle. Had he been spotted, he wondered? Not wanting to take any more chances, he rose and fired. The only sound heard was that of shattering glass that clattered loudly to the ground.

He held Eric in his sight until Eric ducked behind some lawn chairs. His first thought was to fire right through them. As he aimed, Eric leapt up from behind the chairs but took a misstep and tumbled toward the now open entryway. The man took a second shot. Then a third. Eric fell to the pool's deck and with a concentrated look for the shooter, tried to roll out of sight, but he slipped into the swimming pool instead.

The man popped off a succession of shots into the water. Heard only the *fzzpt, fzzpt, fzzpt* sounds of piercing hot lead. He then stopped when he noticed a good amount of blood spreading out around Eric and that he was no longer moving. A barking dog alerted its owner who repeatedly yelled "Quiet!" Time was of the essence, so he left the property from the direction he'd come, reached the Crown Victoria, jumped in, and drove away.

At that same moment and several miles away, Fanny kept having little flickers in his head of a white, four-door sedan he'd glimpsed around the corner from Eric's house. Something about it wasn't right at all. Should he keep going or turn back?

"Dam it," he grunted with a hard wrench on the steering wheel of his Land Rover.

16
Eric is Reborn
Key Biscayne, FL

A rush of panic gripped Eric as Glory Milan's soft mouth covered his completely and she began to suck the air out of his lungs. Her embrace was urgent. Tight. Her weight, an anchor. He tried to push her away but she held firm, clinging to him in desperation. He couldn't breathe, although he knew he must. They were entangled. Under water.

His inner voice screamed, *I need air,* as he scratched at her shoulders to rise for a replenishing gulp. He managed a small inhale but it wasn't enough. He needed more. Glory wouldn't allow it, though, and pulled him down again as the loud sound of a clock ticked to the rhythm of his racing heart. He felt something big and forceful slam into him. He couldn't bear it. Blood-tainted water spewed from his mouth then drew back in, choking him. The effect was rough and final. It stilled him.

Sorry, he heard from either himself or from someone else above the congested waters in which he now grew limp. Seconds passed. Perhaps moments, he wasn't sure. Glory was now smiling at him, entwining herself around him, as they spiraled into the blackness where a faint light flickered. As it neared, his surrender to death felt complete.

Then from far away, another voice called, faintly at first, but it grew. "Yeah, baby. You got it, big guy." He was being coached.

His mind latched onto it. He measured its distance to the surface. Objects pressed in once more, causing him to convulse violently from the pressure. And again came the thick taste of blood mixed with water, water mixed with blood as it erupted from his mouth. He tried to open his eyes with an effort he could hardly afford, but they held fast, so he focused on a single thought. *Breathe!* It was imperative he knew...and that word...that thought urged him on.

He gagged and coughed. Spit and hacked. All the while with a hard pounding on his chest and a muffled voice growing clearer that said, "That's right, c'mon now. Cough it up, Dane, cough it up. You can do it. You're almost there, buddy."

Then he was breathing again. His nose was open. In a final heave, Eric gasped open-mouthed with such agony that he choked on the flood of water that escaped just as a rush of cool air entered. It was two-way traffic on a one-way street. The collision of elements knocked him out completely.

When he cracked open his eyes, Eric lay facedown still, but now on the deck of his pool. The pain in his lungs hurt worse than anything he'd felt before. The only thing he was certain of was that he was taking in air. Oxygen. Life. He focused on controlling his intake before lifting his head, but before he could, again he heard someone say, "Now that's more like it, Dane. Take it easy, bro. Take it easy. I gotcha. Breathe easy, that's right. Nice and slow. In and out. In and out. Just like that. Slow and controlled. Slow and controlled."

The voice sounded familiar. The name "Fanny" came to mind but it came out in a croak.

"What's that, bro?" Fanny asked. "You tryin' to say something? You can do it. C'mon now, Dane, open those baby blues and talk to me."

Eric smiled crookedly. He felt Fanny gently turn and fold him over into an upright but seated position.

"Do we need another heave-ho?" Fanny asked, wrapping his massive arms around Eric's chest from behind and preparing another squeeze to his diaphragm.

Eric choked out a "no."

"Good, so when you're ready, I'm gonna stand you up and throw you over my shoulder, okay? You say when. A thumb's up will do."

Eric raised a weak thumb as Fanny moved around to the front of him to lift him fireman's style into his home. He vomited the last bit of water down the back of Fanny's shirt. Eric was then lowered onto his leather couch only to slip onto the floor. He was lifted again and this time taken to his bed. He heard, "Gotta get you undressed, Dane. Gotta see the damage done."

"Stop," he whispered.

"No? You're embarrassed? 'Fraid I'll see somethin' special? "

Eric grabbed Fanny's arm and held it. "No, Brat..."

"What? What brother?"

"Bratva."

"The Russian mafia? You sayin' that's who shot you?"

Eric nodded weakly.

"You sure?"

"Yes...yes."

Fanny patted Eric on the shoulder and exhaled loudly. He asked, "I knew there was trouble. How'd they know to come here?"

When Eric didn't answer, he then said, "Okay, man. I got you. Now let's see what they did to you. We gotta get you out of all this wet stuff."

Eric opened one eye giving Fanny a half-open glare and whispered slowly, "Be gentle..."

Fanny let out a guffaw. "Now that's more like it. But right now you're one sorry-assed dude, although I do gotta say I'm awfully glad to see you still have your sense of

120

humor, 'cause that means you're gonna be okay, Dane. You're gonna be okay."

Eric smiled fully as Fanny removed his wet clothes and dropped them on the floor. He obliged when his injured chest was examined and he felt Fanny move to his hips, thighs, and feet. Then up to his head that was lifted gently and searched.

"A nice little ear piercing your visitor did," Fanny said as he plucked something out of his hair. "Almost missed it. Looks like a piece of chewed Dentyne gum. Cinnamon."

Eric opened an eye as Fanny presented it to him. A small part of the top edge sliced off.

"You won't need this anymore, so maybe you can just lend me this ear," Fanny joked. "How's that, funny guy? You might need a couple of stitches though."

Eric's head was examined further. Then he was rolled over so that Fanny could get a look at the back of him. Wounds in both his left shoulder and lower right side proved the greater damage.

"We got some trouble here," Fanny told Eric. "So, I'm gonna have to make a call."

He heard Fanny pull out his cell phone and punch in a number while applying pressure to his wounds. He drifted off, then woke to hear Fanny returning from his bathroom. Somehow he was already cleaned up and bandaged.

"Here," Fanny told him. "Take these. Just a couple of Vicodin. It'll help with the pain and force you to rest. Can't have you rippin' Doc's stitches out already, besides, you won't be of much use to anyone until you're coherent."

Eric refused.

"Take 'em, Dane, and don't worry, I'll be right here. Doc'll be back in the morning to check on you."

Eric took them and soon fell asleep.

*

The next morning, he woke groggy but recognized Fanny who sat slumped in the upholstered chaise facing his bed. He called his name but couldn't do anything more than whisper. So he picked up a small pillow and threw it.

"What the?" Fanny grunted as he bolted upright, grabbing at the gun snuggled against his hip.

"Sorry," Eric softly rasped. "Can't talk."

Fanny shook his head and came to Eric.

"What...happened?"

"Found you facedown in a watery grave, my man. Thought you were a goner."

"Yeah...*that* I remember."

"Had to pull you out by the boot straps. Gave us quite a scare."

"Damage?"

"Some. You got a hole in your right side, a nice hit in your left shoulder, and you're missing a sliver of your left ear, but I'll leave the details to Doc. That said, the wounds are the least of your concerns."

"I know..."

Fanny turned away from Eric and yelled to Doc in the next room, "He's awake, Doc."

"Good," Eric heard his uncle say against the sounds of him rooting around in the kitchen cupboards.

Fanny turned back to Eric and added, "They almost got you, you know."

"Yes...tried...to kill me."

"Russian Bratva."

"How'd...you know?"

"You confirmed it last night after I fished you out."

"Oh? Don't remember... anything...except...silenced bullets."

Doc stepped into the room and asked about the silenced bullets on his way to the bed.

"Can't speak above a whisper," Fanny told the elderly man who, while still spry, carried his frame to the right from a small stroke some five years prior. It didn't stop him though, the man still dressed well, lived well, and managed to function at such an excellent level that it kept him in practice as a volunteer for the area clinic. Doc Munroe might have been Eric's only relative, but he was also the island's favorite resident doctor as well.

Eric tried to sit up but his uncle waved him down.

"Just stay where you are, son" he said. "Now what's this about silenced bullets?"

"No sound."

"No sound? You mean like a silencer or piston bullets? The ones that keep the gases inside?"

Eric coughed. Shook an open hand at Doc.

"Silenced," Fanny repeated.

"You're sure?" Doc asked. "Because that kind of ammunition is hard to find."

"Yes," Eric whispered.

Fanny took over the questioning, asking, "How many shots?"

"Five...no, six. Three before ...three after."

"Before and after you fell in the pool."

"Yes."

"And you're sure they were silenced bullets?"

Eric nodded his head yes, adding, "Heard nothing. Glass...just glass."

"You mean from your sliding glass door."

Eric nodded his head yes again.

"Hmmm, well, buddy, there's only one place we know where silenced bullets come from and that makes them Russian for sure. I'm tellin' ya, Dane, it's all this secret sect shit."

Eric looked from Fanny to Doc, allowing his concern to flow between them.

"Don't worry," Doc said. "I've been briefed by Fanny who's been quite instrumental in filling in the details, which by the way, sound credible. So if I were you, I'd embrace for the worse after what's happened here. Go on, Fanny, please."

Fanny continued, "It's got to do with those diamonds and that symbol on that Baikal pistol. Remember when I had a feelin' someone was waitin' for you at the airport? Well, looks like whoever it was tracked you here and they were a lot better at doing that then I was at spotting them."

"Not possible."

"Yeah? Well think again, my friend, because they found you. They've infiltrated your home base. If I'd have come in with you, you wouldn't be lying here with plugs all over your body. I screwed up, Dane, and I'm sorry."

"Sorry? …Apology not accepted. I'm lying here because you saved my life. I was headed for the…bottom of the pool…remember? How'd you know to come back?"

Fanny sighed before answering. "I couldn't shake that feelin' is all. But after I left your place, I saw a white Crown Victoria parked in front of that actor, what's his name? Tom Stockton? Steward? Thomas Steward? Yeah, Thomas Steward's old house. Only there was someone sittin' in the driver's seat. I could only see the person's head because the car was turned away, but somethin' started to click. Obviously not loud enough at the time 'cause I didn't turned around until the golf course. Sorry. But sure enough when I came back the car wasn't there anymore and there was only one place in my mind that it could have gone. So I jammed it over here. By the time I turned the corner, the car was well past me down the street. I could see through your front door that the slider was busted open. That's when I ran around back and found you in the pool."

Eric took Fanny's hand and held it in a still handshake. He pressed firmly. Fanny returned the favor.

"You okay?" Fanny asked.

"Scared."

"Yeah, I would be too, but listen, Doc wants to take another look at you before I move you elsewhere. He put over twenty stitches into you last night."

Eric looked at Doc with gratitude. In return, Doc smiled and patted Fanny on the arm as Fanny continued. "Who else would I turn to in the middle of the night but your very own Florence Nightingale, hmm? He didn't hesitate, either. He even helped me board up your slider and pick up all the glass."

Turning to Doc, Fanny asked, "Hell, Doc, what time did you finally leave last night?"

"Oh, I don't know, around one, I guess."

"Quite the man, Doc."

"Yeah," Eric responded. "Thanks for coming."

"Don't give it another thought, Eric. You know I'm here for you."

"What's… my official damage?"

"Well at the ear, you've lost some cartilage and blood and that's all." Doc reached up to touch his own ear to outline the wound. "The stitches should hold and you'll have no problem there. Fortune followed by missing your head. Otherwise we wouldn't be having this conversation.

"That said, in addition, you sustained a glancing shot to the left shoulder," Doc again pointed to the same spot on his own body. "The bullet entered through the skin lateral to the shoulder and bored through the soft tissue to exit posteriorly. But again Lady Luck was on your side because the bullet spared all vital vessels. Even your rotator cuff.

"The exit wound," he continued by making a small circle with his thumb and index finger, "is only slightly larger and irregular from the entrance wound, but should heal quickly. You'll need the antibiotics that are right there on your night stand."

Eric nodded.

Doc then turned a bit to the side and pointed to his upper right hip.

"The bullet here entered at an angle and deflected off the right illum, or large pelvic bone as you know it, and ended up in the soft tissues overlying the greater trochanter

of the femur. That would be the 'bump' or 'head' of the
bone. Now, aside from any minute bone fragment, swelling
and ecchymosis, you should be okay and able to bear weight
soon."

"Ecchy...what?"

"Bleeding under the skin, you know? Bruising."

Eric nodded his understanding.

Doc leaned over to examine Eric's pupils and to feel
his forehead.

"Love you, Doc," Eric whispered.

"I know. And I do what I can for you, you know that,
Eric. You and the agency."

The two stared at one another for a long minute
before Doc asked, "So what now? You going to call
Oscher?"

"Soon."

"The sooner the better, son, because if what Fanny's
told me is true, you're not out of woods. Tell your boss
whatever you want about your injuries, but I'd play them
down a bit."

"Why?"

"Because they're not life threatening and you'll want
to get back out there. Plus a few stitches won't slow you
down. Eventually they'll be gone and all you'll have left is a
scar or two. But scars tell a story, you know, so long as
you're alive to tell them. Which you are."

Eric suppressed a smile. *Go, Doc, always looking
forward. But what story do I tell Oscher and how soon will I
be assigned fully to Operation Pop Up, because until then,
I'm on my own...*

He figured, first and foremost, he had to leave his
house. The Dane estate was no longer secure. But where
would he go? He needed to heal well enough to carry his
gun. And should he admit that he screwed up? Again? That
he was asleep at the wheel and didn't suspect anyone
following him even though Fanny had? That alone was proof

enough that he wasn't on his game. He needed to tighten the screws and toughen up. Oscher wouldn't stand for this, and more importantly, Operation Pop Up didn't deserve it.

"I hurt like hell," he admitted to Doc.

"I imagine you do," Doc said, pointing once again to the painkillers then stepping out to join Fanny in the kitchen.

Eric twisted in his bed to clear the fog of his thoughts. Russian or French agents, or some other faction of this secret sect, were after him and they wouldn't stop until he was confirmed dead. The question now was whether or not they believed they accomplished it last night. He certainly hoped so. He also knew that there was a Popigai diamond trail that he'd have to follow to its source. And that Arnoult, Oscher, and perhaps even Annette were heavily involved.

He'd have to do some careful navigating and he'd need some good support—someone like Fanny—someone he trusted implicitly and who would give up his life in pursuit of the same goal. He needed to have some answers to the immediate questions that Oscher was sure to have. He needed to heal and be prepared beyond what the CIA expected of him. And, he needed to insinuate himself deeper into Operation Pop Up. It was essential.

In his corner, he had non life-threatening injuries and his presumed death. A death that the CIA would make good use of if he played his cards right, especially since Oscher had already promised more work. From there he'd have to enlist Fanny who, at that moment, was coming back into the bedroom with two pieces of toast on a dinner plate.

"Here ya go, man, eat up."

Eric rose onto an elbow and eyed his breakfast. "No coffee?"

"Water is what you get," Fanny said as he left to go get it. "Truth of the matter is that you need more rest, not caffeine."

"Where's Doc?"

"He left. Said you're fine for now and that I'm to

make sure you take your antibiotics and this sleeping pill, so belly up. He'll be back later. Right now? All's you gotta do is eat, sleep, and be merry."

Eric took the pills and a bite of his toast before looking up to question Fanny.

"What...do we do from here?"

Fanny ran his fingers through his hair and said, "Well, the first thing we do is get you to rest your vocals. Then we go to my place. It's safe and I can take better care of you there. We're gonna have to figure the next step together."

"What about Doc? He'll be offended...you know...if I don't go to him."

"Can't risk it. He's the next link and already more involved than he should be."

"He's managed so far."

"He's a tough bird, that one, gotta hand it to him. But if they come back, I don't think either of us could live with that."

"The Bratva might think...I'm dead."

"Well let's hope so because that would be a very good thing," Fanny responded.

Eric rested a moment while looking Fanny in the eye. "Damned good thing."

"It'll do wonders for your career."

"Covert ops," Eric said before Fanny, as he lay back against his pillows, deciding to take Fanny's advice and rest his voice.

"You got that right," Fanny agreed. "But let's first get through this little matter of your gunshot wounds, okay? Then after that I'm gonna have to get you into the Rover and take you for a little drive. Now won't that be fun?"

"I can...hardly wait," Eric said feeling woozy again. "Just make sure..."

"What, Dane?"

"You slide me in...face down."

17
Fanny's Involvement
Coral Gables, FL

Eric remained in constant contact with Oscher, who
threatened to send a guy down until Eric convinced him that
his injuries weren't as severe as originally thought, and with
Doc's care, he'd soon be back in Washington. Even Doc had
gotten on the phone to discuss it, which had settled the issue.
Eric was healing nicely.

Oscher agreed that the idea of Eric being dead was a
plus for Operation Pop Up and that having Doc tend to Eric's
rehab was the best possible situation for the time being. After
all, Doc had done a tremendous amount of work for the CIA
during the reign of Eric's parents, so why not again?

Still, Eric understood that Oscher was anxious and for
good reason. The gun, the D.C. chase, and the Florida
shooting had cemented the Bratva's spread on American soil.
No one doubted more measures were needed with regard to
their presence. So while Oscher dug deeper in Washington,
Eric focused on himself, his continued research, and
regaining his strength.

"Hey, Fanny, want to get in a little target practice?"
he asked as he looked out the window at Fanny's backyard
that was now covered in red, fallen pine needles that gave it a
soft, thatched appearance. The spread, as Fanny always
called it, was a densely wooded, fifteen-acre flatland of

native trees and shrub species. It was the same woods they'd tromped through as boys.

"Sure," Fanny said.

"Great, let me get my piece."

"What for? Don't I got plenty enough?"

Eric shrugged and followed his friend through the house, one that was deeded to Fanny through a trust, the outcome of a long, family-tied investment to the fortunes of Florida's pioneering railroad magnate, Henry M. Flagler. On Fanny's side came the valued, corporate lawyer.

The house was actually two homes connected by a stretch of lengthy rooms to form a large letter "H". The main floors, still in their original condition, had been laid in colorful, painted ceramic tiles imported from Cuba by families living there well before the two governments had closed their borders to one another. The intricate beauty and artistic touch of those old tiles urged Eric to tiptoe over them, knowing their craftsmanship could never be replicated.

Fanny had converted a third and smaller home on the property into a large den where he invited friends to watch feature-length films or to play billiards, darts, and poker. He'd added a full kitchen and wet bar, a well-equipped gym, a bathroom spa with wet and dry saunas, and along the length of the dwelling, he sported an indoor, soundproofed, two-man shooting range. Behind the booths on the main wall, he'd installed three custom-built gun vaults. Here was where they were headed now.

As they passed the outdoor dining area that blended the space naturally between den and home, and walked beyond the rock-rimmed pool and hot tub, Eric thought of the various stations Fanny had created beyond. There were bow and arrow and crossbow stands. Stations for throwing knives, stars, and even slingshot practice. Fanny also had a full outdoor obstacle course constructed throughout the grounds. It was a virtual paradise for training on all sorts of weaponry and Fanny took great care in its upkeep. The grounds were as impressive as Fanny, not only for its tactical offerings, but also for its lethal properties.

In the quiet that settled between Eric and Fanny, the thought of whether or not he should divulge to Oscher and then to Fanny about Arnoult's confirmation of the secret sect, plagued him. So he turned to Fanny and asked, "How much do you trust Oscher?"

"Why should I?"

Eric laughed. "Yeah, me too, which is kind of unfortunate given that he's our commander. But I can't help but reserve some information until I can put my finger on exactly why. Take the Caribbean for instance, why'd he send me there? Really. What was that all about, Fanny?"

"Don't know, man, but you're right, it's suspect."

"Now I can understand being chased by unknown assailants. After all, the diamond business that Arnoult is so heavily involved in and Oscher is so keen on cracking has a long history. And I hope against hope that whatever Oscher assigns me to in the operation, I can pull it off. But I'd like to have some closure with what's already happened because I'm just too much of a rookie to be rewarded with something like that. I could understand if he told me to lay low in D.C. but to send me off to the Caribbean? I just don't buy it."

"Well, lucky he did because they'd have found you sooner if you'd have come home. But you did okay by it, bro."

"Meaning?"

"Meaning Chambois."

"And your point is?"

"I'm talkin' about the diamond that cougar sported, remember? Even you didn't take it for a mere coincidence. How do you think she really came by it and why do you think she left so suddenly?"

"I don't know, but she wasn't a cougar, Fan. An experienced honey pot, maybe, but believe me, that diamond? It still haunts me. I asked a lot of questions. Fished around, you know? But she didn't bend. Confessed it was a gift. Who knows, maybe it was and I'm just getting paranoid. Didn't they tell us during training that that could happen? I mean that once you realize you truly can't trust anyone, you get spooked?"

"You're not spooked, buddy, not yet anyway, so here's what I think. I think Miss Chambois was part of the package. She was sent down there expressly for you and I think Oscher set it up as sort of a visual clue, you know? Like twinkle, twinkle little meteorite? I'm thinking it was his way of keeping you motivated and to make you ask questions.

"Now she coulda been a honey pot, I'll give you that one. But if you don't come clean with him about her, he knows you're holding back information. And if you're willing to hold back information on a pre-arranged fling embedded with a diamond the size you said it was, then you'd hold back anything. The key to this whole situation is diamonds. You know it, Oscher knows it, Arnoult knows it, and so does this dude who just tried to kill you."

Eric flinched and tried to think of how best to steer the conversation as Fanny led them into the shooting gallery. "Agree," he said backtracking, "But Annette? Maybe I should acknowledge her, although I have to confess that I did buy her story at first. The benefactor, the 'I'm just here to soak up the sun'."

Fanny interrupted with a laugh, "Well you know, good sex can convince a man of anything, right?"

"True, but I tried, Fan, and after she left, it wasn't like I could call her up later and ask. We didn't exactly exchange phone numbers. She was just gone. You'd think if she was working for Oscher, she'd have told me something."

"Just the opposite, man. She'd a done exactly what she did. She's on his team not yours…not yet, anyway. So what'd you do after she left?"

"I did some research on her. Couldn't find a damned thing."

"And if she's with Oscher you wouldn't have."

Eric thought about that and agreed. "Okay then, what about the guy who shot me?"

"Bratva like you said," Fanny answered, opening his bank of gun vault doors.

"Who was after me, not Arnoult," Eric added as his adrenaline surged with bringing Fanny into a confidence from which there was no return. From here on out, there would be no hiding, no omissions or withholding. He reached for a chrome Sig Sauer MK25 and continued.

"Now bear with me, Fan, but Arnoult acknowledged to me and only me that your secret sect really does exist."

Fanny turned to look at his friend who didn't hesitate to add, "Now I know, I know, all your research on Lord Sabaoth is pretty weird, but after what I've learned and seen…well, you're spot on. It's all connected. I mean, I *know* it was the Bratva who came after me and I know Arnoult was telling the truth. I think Oscher knows this too and isn't saying. Just look at the way he reacted to that Baikal when I gave it to him. His demeanor changed in a very suspicious way although he tried not to show it. And that, my friend, is when Oscher switched tack with me."

"Remind me again?" Fanny asked after removing a Walther PPQ and some ammo.

"Oscher went from being angry at me at the start of my debriefing to being surprisingly proud of me. Then, when I showed him the gun, scared shitless. He was paralyzed like a deer in headlights. It was right after that he said I was due some compensation. That's what he called it, compensation, saying I needed a couple of days in the sun because killing is a serious business and there was more work to do with Operation Pop Up. He also said I was just the man for it."

"Or the man to die trying," Fanny interjected. "But, let me guess, you didn't tell him about the hermit kingdom?"

"No."

"Why not?"

133

"Because I just didn't trust him at that point."

Fanny exhaled heavily. "Well, I'm glad you still trust me, although it took you long enough. And I understand, I do, but you've got yourself in a world of shit, Dane. You know that?"

"Yeah but I'm going to get you in there with me."

Fanny asked how.

"I'm going to convince Oscher of it because right now, I'm a dead guy, as in gone. A ghost. My value has just skyrocketed and I'm going to need a live body to shadow. That's you, man. You're my body. You in?"

Fanny smiled broadly. "Man, you're slow to the gate."

Eric laid the Sig Saur on the firing table and asked, "Now, where's my phone?"

Fanny tapped Eric's shirt pocket.

Oscher answered abruptly, "Dane? What's going on?"

"I'm calling to see when you need me in Washington."

"I need you now."

"With caution, I can leave anytime."

"Fine, be here on Tuesday."

"Sir?"

"Yes?"

"Officer Bergan's here and, as you know, he's been with me the entire time. He's willing to assist me to Washington, if that's okay with you."

"You serious?"

"Yes, sir, I am."

"Fine, Dane, just do it Tuesday, capische?"

"Yes, sir," Eric said into the lost connection.

Eric looked at the phone. It was as dead as he was supposed to be.

"Now how's that for coddling?" he asked Fanny who only shrugged.

"Guess the dance is over."

"Either that or another change in tack?"

"Maybe, but he's acting more like a man at the poker table. One minute he's throwing aces out his sleeve and the next he's forcing your call. I don't like it."

"Tuesday will tell, Fan, so how's about we now settle once and for all who's the better shot?

*

They arrived in Washington mid-morning, and by eleven thirty-five, were waiting in the outer chambers of Oscher's office as Sally stole glances between phone calls at the two of them.

"You could be kin," she finally said,

"We're brothers," Fanny offered before Eric could open his mouth. "Different mothers."

"Don't listen to him, Sally," Eric said.

She giggled just as Oscher barked through the intercom to send Eric in. "Well, he'll see you now as you've heard, Officer Dane. And would you like a cup of coffee, Officer Bergan?"

Fanny declined so she returned her attention to the paperwork on her desk as Eric opened the door to Oscher's office.

"Sit," Oscher instructed, throwing open a thick file on his desk.

Eric eased into the chair.

"How's the ear?" Oscher asked, dismissing the bigger discomforts.

"Fine, sir, healing well. Doc did a fine job. I'm grateful."

"Good, good. Now, the ballistics report on the Baikal," Oscher started as he scribbled something across a page in the file. "Everything about it is irrelevant for the time being except the symbol, which you and I did not discuss the last time you were here. Nor did we discuss how this symbol on this particular gun has anything to do with Operation Pop Up, outside of the fact that it was the weapon of choice by the two assailants who died on I-90."

Eric waited in the silence that followed. Then Oscher stopped what he was doing, looked up and said, "How much do you already know, Dane? How much have you been able to piece together?"

"Sir?" Eric asked, as Arnoult's earlier warning about his commanders being part of the hermit kingdom lodged in his throat, causing his response to sound more like a gasp than a question.

"What? Come on now. I know you haven't been waiting around to be informed this entire time. So tell me what you know so that I can tell you how close you are and we can move forward."

Eric weighed his options and then decided on the cautious route.

"I know as much as you and my resources have told me, sir. That I suspect the very brightly studded Miss Chambois was part of my R and R and that the Baikal predates WWI. Its symbol predates even that by some centuries. I believe if what I've learned is true, it represents something more accurately termed a 'caelestis lapis' or celestial stone, and is a symbol originally worn on the cassocks of a rather unique religious secret sect. A society that through the passage of time morphed into the Russian Bratva or today's mafia."

Eric noted two things during his commentary. One, that Oscher eyes had blinked at the mention of Annette, confirming perhaps that she and her diamond were working for Oscher. And two, because Oscher had retained eye contact, the information about the symbol in relation to the Bratva was accurate. So maybe, just maybe Arnoult was right.

After a long silence, Oscher spoke. "What were your resources?"

"Besides you? The Internet, the library, and Officer Bergan's research as I've already mentioned,"

"Yes, Officer Bergan. Anyone else?"

"No, sir," Eric lied as Arnoult's twisted face on the day he brought him in flashed through his mind.

"And what, if anything, did Jacoub Arnoult tell you? Who, by the way Homeland is madly searching for," Oscher asked, locking eyes with Eric as if he'd just thrown a dart between them.

"Arnoult? Nothing, sir. He was wounded." Eric withheld Arnoult's warning again and then banked on Oscher's "if anything" disclaimer to mean that he'd had remained quiet on the subject of the hermit kingdom as well. Instead Eric asked, "Is Arnoult still with us, sir?"

"He is."

"Will you be informing Homeland anytime soon?"

"No, and we won't do that until we're done with him. All he is to them right now is missing and that's how we're going to play it."

Oscher pointed at Eric. "You, however and for the record, are currently dead."

"Yes, sir."

"A ghost."

"Yes, sir."

Again a long silence.

"How much does Officer Bergan know of Operation Pop Up?"

"He's pieced together quite a bit, sir. He's been brilliant, in fact, for what he's been able to assemble without benefit of the parts I know."

Oscher squinted in anticipation as if he was afraid of what Eric was about to ask.

"Can we bring him onboard, sir?"

"Why?"

"Because he'd prove an asset and you can trust him explicitly."

137

"Not enough."

"Because he's ready, willing, and able, and because it would please my parents as much as my being on the case."

Oscher winced. Eric looked away embarrassed by his own audacity and braced for the defeat Oscher was about to deliver.

"As much as I appreciated your parents, Dane, and have honored their request, it doesn't extend to Officer Bergan. That's not how things work around here. On top of that your parents…forgive me but…they're dead. They can't be pleased any more than when they were alive."

Eric nodded in sad agreement as he watched Oscher's chest deflate against what he hoped was a small measure of guilt. The room stilled around them and did not stir again until Oscher leaned over his phone to punch Sally's extension.

"Send in Bergan."

He pointed an angry finger at Eric and said, "You had one chit and it's cashed."

The door opened. Fanny entered.

"Sit," Oscher instructed as Fanny took the seat next to Eric.

"Officer Bergan?"

"Yes, sir?"

"Officer Dane, here, requires your presence."

Fanny looked at Eric then back to Oscher.

"Thinks you'll prove an asset going forward."

"Yes, sir, I think I would…very much."

Oscher stared Eric down until it became uncomfortable. He signed his name on the paperwork in front of him and closed the file.

"It'll be on him if he's wrong," was all he said.

18
The Interrogation
Washington, DC

Seated behind a metal table, Jacoub Arnoult held his head in his hands with his face hidden from view. He'd been imprisoned for days with much of that time spent recovering from the gunshot wound and the remainder under intense interrogation by Oscher and his team. He now felt wounded more than physically.

He had no place to go and certainly no access to the outside world. The only comfort he'd found was in the confinement the CIA provided, something he'd hoped to obtain from Homeland Security through its witness protection program. But now even they didn't know where he was. It wouldn't last, that was a given, for he fully understood that once he revealed what he knew about the diamonds, he'd be worthless to the CIA. He figured they'd either torture him to death, turn him over to France for trial by treason, or cut him loose to be killed by the powers ruling the Popigai diamond trade. So he had retained the most critical piece of the information of the continued survival of the hermit kingdom. Only Eric knew of its existence and he regretted having told him.

At the time, however, he thought he was dying and that the young recruit was too immature to grasp the entirety of the situation. His hope had been to engage the man just

139

enough to save his own life and apparently, he had. He was in fact still alive, although he wasn't where he wanted to be.

He stretched his legs, then stood. The door opened and in walked Eric.

"Ahh," Arnoult said with a slight smile, "Tres bien, so you, too, live. They told me you had been shot."

"Mister Arnoult," Eric replied as he walked toward him, arm extended. They shook hands. "I'm happy to see you."

"Moi aussi," Arnoult replied as he took his seat again, believing they'd be in discussions for quite some time.

"Who's they?" Eric asked without preamble.

"Pardon?"

"They. Who told you I was shot?"

"Oh, yes, your CIA interrogators. They tried to convince me that you were dead. I assume to further isolate me from any and all contacts and familiarities."

Eric laid a blue dossier on the table that Arnoult recognized immediately, and as Eric slid it across the table with his hand firmly planted on its cover, they met eye to eye.

"You know what this is?"

"Oui."

"It's everything you told CIA since I picked you up."

"As you say."

"But something's missing. Can you tell me why?"

"Because it is the only thing I have left to barter."

"How's that when you bartered it with me to save your life?"

"This is true but it is still not in this folder, oui?"

Arnoult studied Eric's eyes for any flinch that would verify what he felt was true. The information about the hermit kingdom was *not* in the CIA's dossier. That meant neither he *nor* Eric wanted it revealed just yet.

"I first want guarantees," Arnoult said. "I want protective custody or to be in your country's witness protection plan along with the transfer of my financial assets. That is the very least your Homeland Security was going to do."

"Yes they were, except that was for information about a false terrorist attack. What we want is something completely different."

"I understand, so for this I will give you a name. One name. A very important name."

"And this name will lead us to the hermit kingdom?"

"Eventually, and when it does you must kill her."

"Her?"

Arnoult felt a line of sweat form on his forehead as Eric leaned in close enough to almost touch his face with his nose. A warm draft fell from it onto his upper lip, making it bead as well. *Eleonore, what am I doing? Should I just tell him I am crazy? That I did not know what I was saying and have been lying to him all along? He might believe that, yes? For I am a liar as he knows. My heart...my heart. It is racing. Mon Dieu. I am afraid that they will kill me for sure. All of them. Any of them, even this boy here in front of me could do it. How in God's name did it come to this? Eleonore! Eleonore! What should I do?*

"Who is she?" Eric asked again.

Arnoult sensed Eleonore was near, holding him. His heart beat loud against her body. He could hear the pounding of it in his ears. He put his hands to them to drown out the sound. He was at the end of his negotiations. *It's time*, Eleonore told him. He squeezed his eyes shut. Thought of the catacombs. Of Tobin Corbett. Of him standing over the man about to die by his own anxious hand. For what? Information? Is this what was happening here? Would Eric kill him for information too?

Arnoult clenched his teeth and tried to breathe. He held tight against the break about to happen. *You can trust this boy,* Eleonore whispered. And he knew it was true. She was right. Through Eric, he would live or die. He banked on

141

living.

"She is la reine des abeilles," he said rather loudly through the gush of air he expelled. "The Queen Bee, n'est-ce pas? You kill her, you kill the entire operation."

Eric's face gave nothing away. In return, Arnoult showed no emotion, not even a budge or blink to reflect what he was thinking. Instead he waited and hoped he'd made the right decision…that there was now an opening in the negotiations. He tried to read the blue eyes looking back at him for an answer, but none came. So again he pleaded with Eric to deliver what he sought.

"We have a connection here, jeune homme. Do you not feel it?" Arnoult asked softly. "You are on the way up and I am on the way out. What I know and what I have taken from it is my life. If I give it to you, it will become your life. In the end, it could kill us both. As you have discovered, I am not a man so easily swayed, so if I give you her name, you must give me what I ask. My life now is nothing in comparison to what I will be giving you and yours."

The glisten of sweat grew on his upper lip as he watched Eric's eyes drop to the minute downward curl at the corners of his slightly opened mouth. He heard the shallow escape of his own breath as if he was again holding it in. Waiting. And he was. Because his own eyes were busy searching. Darting all over Eric's. Probing for something positive in them. Something to confirm that the risk he'd just taken was safe. But Eric gave nothing away. Instead, he once again saw that Eric was now staring deeply into the backs of his. Past the irises. Through the fully dilated pupils. And into their empty, inky black interiors.

"It's Officer Dane," Eric said, stressing his title. "And I'll see what I can do. But I give you no guarantee that anyone here at CIA will feel the same unless this name is as valuable as you say."

"You have my word," Arnoult whispered.

"Which is worth what?"

"My life…and your future."

Eric snatched up the dossier and left the room. It was time to tell Oscher what he knew of the hermit kingdom, but not before doing a bit more research in the CIA's resource center to see if they'd anything on a Russian Queen Bee. When he wasn't able to uncover anything that he'd hoped, he headed to Oscher's office to divulge all that he knew, including what Arnoult had just told him. Oscher leaned back in his chair and with a rising voice asked, "A what?"

"A hermit kingdom, sir. I also thought it was a fantasy when he first mentioned it…"

"First mentioned it?" Oscher asked. "And when was that exactly?"

"In Buffalo, sir, after he was shot. But hear me out because it was all so left field that I didn't give it any credit. He was babbling. At best, I thought he was trying to throw me off any trail, or at worse, he was tripping me up to question which side my commanders really stood. I didn't fall for it. I know where my commanders stand, sir, but now, based on what he just told me and on what facts I've already confirmed, this hermit kingdom does exist."

Eric hoped his earliest fact-finding results wouldn't be questioned of when (weeks ago based on his and Fanny's individual researches) and where (while in the Caribbean) he'd actually done it.

"What kinds of facts?"

"Well, for starters, we have a report on Ashmar Akagriev, Kyrgyzstan's ex-president, sir. And according to it, he was deposed and sent to Barvikha, Russia where he was given asylum amongst several other diplomats and heads of state. Barvikha is a small town in one of Moscow's districts, or rather, oblasts."

"I know where it is, Dane."

"Yes, sir. Well then, you also must know that there's a government-run sanatorium there where certain exiled leaders of pro-Russian countries live in relative comfort and that President Turkov uses as a health retreat. I'm thinking this is where the hermit kingdom is operating from, sir."

"Is that so?"

"Yes, sir."

"And Arnoult told you this?"

"Not yet, sir, but he will. I'm sure of it."

"So what you're telling me here is that our much sought after, much paid for in the way of lives lost with Operation Pop Up's intel about a modern-day, diamond smuggling ring is completely wrong? That Russia's Major General Niembriev is not the one we should be after? That it's a Queen Bee living in a spa-like hermit kingdom in Barvikha?"

"Well, not exactly, sir," Eric answered. "Niembriev, as you already suspect, is running part of the show for sure and he's definitely a key figure in all of this. He may also be the kingpin we need to get to that Queen Bee."

"Arnoult told you that?"

"No, sir, but the hermit kingdom's the bigger operation over Popigai, and as you know, he's only in charge of that one crater. You said that yourself, sir…if you don't mind my saying."

Oscher leaned further back in his chair. Shook his head.

Eric interpreted it to mean that Oscher wasn't accepting that a Queen Bee was running a hermit kingdom nor that she was living amongst exiled royalty and heads of state.

Eric cleared his throat. "I know, sir, bizarre."

"Shut it, Dane."

Eric stopped.

"So you're saying Niembriev is a front man for someone else. A woman. A Queen Bee?"

"Yes, sir."

Oscher sat back to process the information. Eric

watched his mind at work as he appeared to add and delete elements he'd just presented. When finally Oscher showed some satisfaction, he pressed by asking, "And Arnoult won't confirm her name until he's guaranteed complete asylum in the United States?"

"That's right, sir, that and the transfer of his assets," Eric said, repeating Arnoult's request.

Oscher looked at him with sharpened eyes. "Arnoult can kiss his assets goodbye. Because the minute any account is touched he's dead and there's nothing we can do about that."

"But, sir…"

Oscher's face hardened, turned pink. "Now you listen very carefully, Dane. As far as France, Russia, and this hermit kingdom are concerned, Arnoult is officially dead. And since you, too, are walking amongst the deceased, there will be no…not one, not a single solitary move on anything of personal value by either of you. You've been fully briefed on this subject, Officer Dane. What applies to you, applies to him, so do not press me about Arnoult's *assets.*"

"Yes, sir," Eric's face warmed at the verbal slap.

"Now leave. I'll advise you when I have anything further."

"Yes, sir."

Eric left Oscher's office and ventured out onto the street to wonder what would become of all this, including what the CIA might do with Arnoult. The cool air felt good on his hot skin. It had been a long day and Oscher had shaken him. He was ready for a drink. So he walked the streets until he found a neighborhood bar and after laying his cell phone on the counter, ordered a beer. His hand shook as he lifted the chilled pilsner. With all the omissions and lies he'd told Oscher, it was quite surprising that he'd gotten this far. But the many holes in his previous story were beginning to close, and if he could secure Arnoult's identity and get the name of the Queen Bee, then he and Fanny would be on their way to

145

the mission of their lives. Lost in his thoughts, Eric at first didn't hear his cell phone ring.

"Your phone," the bartender yelled from the middle of the bar.

"Oh, thanks," Eric said as he reached for it and saw that it was Glory.

"Well, hello," he answered.

"Hello yourself."

"And to what do I owe this very unexpected call?"

At that she said with some surprise, "Well, first I am very, very happy to hear your voice. And second, I'm in Miami for a few days. Perhaps we could meet, you know, to catch up? I've missed you."

"That sounds doable but I'm traveling right now. Can you hold on until Sunday?"

"Where are you?"

"Not where I want to be, that's for sure."

"I see. Anyway, I leave on Monday, so yes, I'd like that even if it's for just one night. Text me when you land and I'll pick you up. It'll give us more time."

"Will do," he agreed and hung up his phone.

"Now that was unexpected," he said to no one in particular while looking toward the bartender.

"Obviously," the bartender snorted as he walked further away from Eric.

Surprised the man heard him, Eric laughed and said a little louder, "A girl."

The bartender shrugged, threw his wet towel under the counter, and walked away saying, "Lucky you."

Eric finished his beer and headed to his hotel where he supposed Fanny was in the lounge sizing up Washington's social scene. Not much of a fraternizer, Fanny preferred to patiently wait until he caught the eye of an available woman. Tonight had been a success for by Fanny's side was an interesting brunette. He watched the two of them until Fanny flicked his wrist without once breaking his line of sight with hers. Chuckling at being signaled to buzz off, Eric took a club chair in the corner and ordered another beer. This could be fun, he thought to himself. But it wasn't two minutes later that Fanny bounded over and took a seat opposite him.

"Okay, what happened?" he asked, staring into Eric's face.

"Just like that? You'd give up on a beautiful gal like her for me?"

Fanny's laugh broke whatever tension the two were holding inside.

"Sorry," he said. "But I'm the one who's been waiting all day. So fill me in. What happened with Arnoult?"

"Made some headway with an offer and now Oscher's deciding whether or not to accept. Which by the way if he does, you and I are heading to the Motherland."

"Eto khorosho," Fanny teased, meaning *this is good*.

"Nice, Fan, glad you remember your Russian because it'll come in handy. But listen, the highlight of today's events is that I filled Oscher in on the hermit kingdom. I had to. I even told him when Arnoult told me, although I'd have preferred not to. But Arnoult wants a new identity in exchange for a name that'll topple the whole empire. Says it's a Queen Bee not Niembriev like everyone thought. And that once we nail her, we nail the whole shebang."

"Shebang? Is that some kind of new agency code word?"

"That's right and you'd better learn it."

Eric raised his beer.

Fanny chuckled, then asked, "When will we know?"

"I'm hoping by tomorrow. I want to wrap things up with Arnoult and get moving. And right now, he's our only obstacle. "

"It'll happen, Dane. Anything else?"

"Well, I have a lady waiting for me in Miami."

"For real?"

"A flight attendant. Met her a few weeks ago, had

drinks once, and now she's going to be in Miami when I get there. Says we should get together. She's going to pick me up at the airport."

Fanny narrowed his eyes.

Eric cut through with, "I know, trust no one."

"Not now especially."

"Agree, so after this one more time, I'll stop, believe me. I don't want anything standing in the way of this mission."

"But you're dead, remember?"

"She doesn't know that and I'll die for sure if I don't see her again. She's on the up and up. Plus she barely knows me, for god's sake."

"When did you say you met her?"

"On my way to Washington right after our little South Beach celebration with Holdberg and Marsh. I met her on the plane."

Fanny frowned and took another shot. "You sure you're using the right head in making this decision?"

"C'mon, Fan, look at it from my side. Guys like us need a lady rooting for us or else what? We turn into one giant prick, right? I don't want to end up like that, Fan. I want to have someone next to me. Someone who's on my team, you know? And she doesn't have to be CIA either. She just needs to be looking out for me. Understand? I promise, one more date with her and then I'll cut her off. I won't even think about her again until this mission is over."

"You're crazy, Dane."

"You mean crazy enough to have lied to the director of the CIA? Or crazy enough to see the very woman who could be *the one* before my life is possibly over?"

"Both. Just do what you gotta do, but end it, bro, for all our sakes."

"I will, Fan, I promise."

*

The next morning Eric received a call from Oscher. "Get in here, Dane," was all he heard before the buzz of an ended connection.

Eric was in front of Oscher within forty-five minutes. "Here's the deal," Oscher informed him. "Arnoult works for us until we bring in this supposed Queen Bee. We're not Homeland Security. We don't give before we get. We want a name. A real name of a real person. We want to know more about how he and his Prime Minister fit into the network. We also want to know who else is involved besides Niembriev and his Russian crew. We want everything he knows about Popigai Crater and its distribution. And we want him to go over what he's already told us again, and again, and again. Everything. We want to make absolutely certain no stone is unturned."

"Yes, sir."

"You get that name, Dane. He's in room three. Somebody else will take care of the rest. Tell him that he gives you the name or he's history."

"Yes, sir. I will, sir."

"And after you do? Make sure Officer Bergan reports back with you in the Executive Conference room. We've a lot to put into action and I want to make sure everyone's on the same page, capische?"

Eric assured the director he would and then raced to the room where Arnoult was waiting. He hesitated to calm his breathing before opening the door. He wanted to appear composed because he was anything but. After a few minutes, he knocked and stepped through.

"Good morning, Mister Arnoult," Eric said to a stoic Arnoult. "You have a deal but we have conditions."

"As expected," Arnoult muttered with his hands spread in the air.

Eric went over the conditions Oscher had made, and while Arnoult sputtered and mildly cursed in French, he

149

repeated over and over that there would be no other deal. That this was it, take it or leave it. Arnoult looked weary and he wondered if the Frenchman understood that he was out of options. Or that the CIA, after questioning him for so long, was about to hand him a one-way ticket. Would Arnoult accept this final offer? Would he give up this last vital piece of information?

Arnoult closed his eyes and laid his head down on the table. Eric placed a hand on Arnoult's back. "It's you and me, Jacoub. A passing of the torch. Who is she?"

Arnoult rolled his head and when he finally raised it, ignored the bit of drool that had pooled at the corner of his mouth. His watery eyes focused first on the ceiling and then on Eric. Finally Arnoult said, "Officer Dane?"

Eric tilted his head.

"You are un enfant and I am un vieil homme. I will certainly die before you."

"A name, Jacoub," Eric softly pleaded only to hear Arnoult say, "Oui, but you will most certainly die too, you understand?"

Eric pressed his lips into a fine line as Arnoult continued.

"A name? You want a name? Well here it is. Her name is Madame Corrine DuBethonee."

Eric blinked. "DuBethonee?"

"Oui."

"You're sure?"

"Of nothing more."

"But she died over twenty years ago."

"Ahh, mon enfante, we are here and yet are we not dead too?"

Eric removed his hand from Arnoult, recalling his parents' excitement over Madame DuBethonee. They had talked about her at length at many a dinner party. They spoke of her notorious husband, Garamond DuBethonee, and how she had reveled in his political celebrity amongst the highest

150

of French society. But once he'd been shot point blank on the Avenue des Champs-Élysées, she'd gone into hiding.

Rumors abounded over her bitter, anguished loss. Clandestine tales of revenge carried out against Garamond's closest confidantes assumed that she was involved. Unsolved murders and missing persons haunted the closely held circle of DuBethonee's reign. The press and the public alike called her "Le Boucher Pour Bethonee" or "The Butcher For Bethonee," but proof of her crimes was never uncovered. Even her assumed death was never verified. Word of it came in a box containing an anonymous letter that detailed how her body had been dismembered and buried throughout Paris. Included with the letter and wrapped in everyday department store tissue paper was her left breast, flat, shriveled, and dried. The letter called it "la poitrine qui durcit son coeur", "the breast that hardened her heart." DNA testing proved it was hers.

Her other body parts remained at large although randomly collected anatomical specimens fueled speculation. Eventually, death and suspicion within DuBethonee's sphere of influence ended. She was gone, simply gone, and presumed dead exactly as the letter had outlined.

Arnoult coughed. "She tried to kill me once with polonium. The same poison assumed to be used on Yasser Arafat, and she may very well still."

"Except that she's in Russia now. Running the show for the Popigai diamond trade," Eric said without expecting confirmation.

Regardless, Arnoult responded. "Oui, only the Russians call her 'Pchelinaya Matka'."

"Let me guess, that's Russian for Queen Bee."

"Oui, still a butcher but now the bee stands for Bethonee."

Eric patted him on the back before saying a slow goodbye. It felt like a curtain closing between them, but going forward, he'd be forever thankful that they'd connected well enough for him to have this opportunity. Russia was waiting.

19
The Assignment
Washington, D.C.

Oscher sat in deep discussion with several high-level directors from Science and Technology, Clandestine Services, and Support and General Counsel. Strewn about in front of him lay dossiers that by their disarray indicated a fast and furious debate. When Eric and Fanny arrived at the conference room door, he turned with a wave of his hand to say, "Come in. Take a seat."

The two officers settled into side-by-side chairs like obedient soldiers, alert and orderly. Oscher expected some anxiety, not this display of obvious assuredness. He leaned back, and after laying his pen on top of his leather-bound notepad, again pressed forward.

"Operation Pop Up is headed in a new direction," he said. "And thanks to Officer Dane and his successful interrogation of Ambassador Arnoult, we've since made significant discoveries. As a result, we have a clearer picture of what and with whom we're dealing."

He paused for effect before continuing.

"It appears that our previous objective of disclosing how the Popigai diamonds are being transported into the United States is only the tip of the iceberg. Far worse is a woman identified as Madame Corrine DuBethonee who currently presides over a hermit kingdom that's evolved from an ancient empire that first ruled when those diamonds were formed. She's remained undetected for decades, therefore, it's important to realize that our ultimate goal now is to find her and shut her down. This means every person at this table and every operative involved in Operation Pop Up, whether in the field or behind the scenes, will work diligently toward this goal. That said, we'll need to approach Madame DuBethonee as imperceptibly as possible and with someone she'll least expect. Someone she thinks is dead. That's you, Officer Dane."

Eric nodded.

As Oscher turned his head toward the older, well-dressed director to his left, he added, "Director Sidney Edmund of Clandestine Services is highly aware of your contribution to Operation Pop Up."

The man with thin, graying hair and hooded lids that shielded dark brown eyes nodded back without blinking.

"Thank you, sir," Eric said in a way that extended to both men.

"You'll report directly to him and you will, of course, go black. Special Ops. No one outside Operation Pop Up will know of your existence and only a few inside will. I trust you understand?"

Eric said he did.

"Your primary mission is to first locate, then infiltrate and help destroy connections into and out of Popigai. You are also assigned to pinpoint Madame DuBethonee's exact whereabouts. Our team will bring her in unless the situation necessitates her extermination, which you will have full authority."

Oscher turned his eyes next to Fanny. "You, Officer Bergan, will report directly to me and continue the intelligence gathering started by Officer Corbett. We need to know how Prime Minister Jean-Luc Nanterre, through his relationship with Philippe Simone, imports, transports, and distributes those diamonds into and out of France. You are then to help destroy those connections. Do you understand?"

"I do, sir," Fanny replied.

"Good, but make no mistake, gentlemen, your anonymity in the field and Officer Dane's assumed death are the main reasons you're being assigned to Operation Pop. And, yes, your recent discoveries have been pivotal, but some here at the table believe your limited experience will be the Achilles heel. I believe differently. Operation Pop Up, in my opinion, mandates penetration through absolute obscurity and because of your current unique positions, you're the aces in the hole we need going forward. Now it's up to us to provide the additional tools that will support your needs. You've done a good job thus far and I see no reason for not building on that."

Oscher went on to explain the tools involved and over the next three days joined them in brief back, during which the department heads prepared them for departure. They were given recording devices and ultraportable mini personal computers, also called UMPC'S. They were stocked for study with international flight routes, aerial maps, and detailed schematics of underground gas, sewer, and pipelines throughout Europe and Russia. They were streamed with an endless array of data that most had to be committed to memory. Anything else was downloaded onto flash drives that if compromised, served as an explosive device that outdistanced the fastest runner. On top of all this, they were distributed pharmaceuticals: the opiate fetanyl, the pain killer oxycodone, and the antibiotic gatifloxacin.

They were then inoculated and examined. They were given new identities, passports, credit cards, and driver's licenses. Eric's hair was dyed and his eyes fitted with colored contact lenses.

Oscher then instructed both men, particularly Eric, to seal up their homes before reporting for duty. For Fanny, that meant he'd report back within twenty-four hours. But for Dane, it meant thirty-six and not because the CIA had suddenly discovered that Glory Milan was waiting for him in Miami. No. The extra time was necessary for Eric to secure the two Key Biscayne amenities that the CIA had a particular concern. Both were remnants of the disgraced, ex-President Ryan Newcomb's "Winter White House" that his parents had kept on their estate after Newcomb's home was razed.

The first was his helicopter pad. The second was his exit tunnel leading to another home on Hurricane Harbor with a private outlet to Biscayne Bay.

Oscher, however, wasn't aware that Eric had long ago camouflaged the helicopter pad and barred the tunnel, or that the unsuspecting new owners of the second home were unaware of what hid behind the shelving of their pantry. And Oscher did not learn that now. Instead, Eric nodded the affirmative and stated that he'd take care of everything.

*

While waiting to board their flight out of Baltimore/Washington International, Eric tapped out a text on his phone to Glory, all the while sensing Fanny's anger. But having heard his friend's complaints earlier, Eric didn't think he'd have any more to say on the subject. He was wrong.

"This romantic notion of yours about her is either gonna get you killed or take down this mission, so you'd best end it like you said you would," Fanny whispered into his ear from behind. Once stated, the feel of Fanny's presence faded. They would have no further contact from this moment forward except as it pertained to Operation Pop Up. They later boarded and sat in separate sections.

As soon as they landed, Eric looked back at Fanny, who refused to make eye contact. Instead he flicked his wrist. Eric grabbed his bag and exited the plane. What he didn't see was that Fanny had decided to linger behind to watch his greeting of Glory.

Eric found her standing by her car at the curb. How could he not? Glory was a vision in tight denim jeans and white t-shirt, tan boots, and a short caramel-colored leather jacket. Most people considered Miami a winter hideout but it still had its cooler days and this was one of them. She smiled warmly and waved.

"Jump in," she said, which he did as she whisked out of the airport and merged south onto I-95.

"Love the new hair color," she finally said, breaking the silence.

"Do you?"

"Oh yes, very becoming, but why?"

"This?" he asked, pointing to his head to which she smiled. "This is for fun."

Their drive to Key Biscayne took all of forty-five minutes that from her rented convertible presented an unobstructed view of Miami's skyline blanketed beneath a star-studded night. With it came the sharp tinge of salty air mingled with the heady perfumes of woody acacias and blooming yellow ylang-ylangs. For Eric, these images and tropical scents were the embodiment of home, something he looked forward to with each return. They were also the sights and smells he most wanted to take with him to Russia. If only he could.

Glory broke into his thoughts. "Are you okay?"

"Yes," he answered.

"You looked so far away that I thought, maybe I shouldn't have…"

"Not at all. Seeing you only improves things. As a matter of fact, I was thinking of nothing but you," meaning the thought of entering his home with her on his arm now weighed heavily on his mind.

"Good," she said, "Because I brought a bag."

"Oh?"

"And a toothbrush."

Eric put his arm over her shoulder and leaned in to

157

kiss her cheek. "I don't believe I've ever been so uniquely propositioned."

Smiling, he then realized she'd gotten a close look at his ear. Instinctively, he reached up and rubbed it.

"What happened?" she asked.

"Nothing really. A minor accident hardly worth talking about."

"Are you sure? Because it looks like Mike Tyson took a bite out of it."

"Very clever, but it's nothing like that at all. I had a nasty motorcycle spill on some rocks. No helmet. Stupid move, I know, and it's embarrassing, so I'll spare you the details. Besides, I'd much rather talk about what you've been up to."

"Me? Not much but I'm sure something worthy will come up that we can discuss all night long."

The house was dark when they pulled into his drive. There were no illuminating entryway lights at his front door or automatic nightlights shining from inside. So he opened and closed the gate completely before entering the garage and telling her to pull in beside his car. She did in spite of the fact, he noticed, that the garage was dark, too.

He mentioned it might be a breaker, although Eric's concerns had already escalated onto something greater, when after toggling several light switches, nothing came to life. He then asked her to wait until he checked inside the house. He entered through the laundry room and grabbed a flashlight from the wall. He opened the electrical box where he found all the switches flipped off with a note beside them from Fanny-*For your own protection.* Again Eric thanked his friend who, while allowing him to heal at his spread, had taken it upon himself to ensure a safer return. Eric closed the electrical box door and invited Glory in. He guided her to the closed-draped living room and lit some candles, explaining to her that there must be a short in the lines.

"Happens all the time on this island," he said while

urging her to sit on the couch while he went to the dining room table and lit the two large candles there. He next lit several in the bedroom and bath. From there, he entered the kitchen and returned to Glory with a bottle of Krug Clos du Mesnil.

"Shall we?" he asked.

She sighed pleasantly as he poured the wine into glasses.

When their wanting lips finally touched one another's, it was magical. Eric didn't want to it to end, so while still joined, he stumbled with her toward the bedroom. There, he lowered her to his bed where Glory reached up to rip open his shirt. He wrapped his fingers around her wrists and playfully pulled her into the bathroom where he turned on the tap to fill the tub with warm bubbles. He dropped his shirt to the floor while she stood clutching her own at the neckline. Once naked, he stepped into the rising suds and invited her in with the wide spread of his welcoming thighs. She stripped slowly without releasing the hold of her eyes on his before stepping into the tub to sidle up back to chest.

Their lovemaking started with a water-filled sponge that Eric squeezed over her shoulder to watch its soapy trail meander down her spine. He then reached around with his other hand to cup her breast and pull their bodies together. As he did, she slipped onto his lap and began rotating her hips in small, meaningful circles that soon had him groaning with pleasure and pain from the wounds still healing inside.

He pressed his nose into the back of her neck to breathe deeply of her skin and was rewarded with the lightly perfumed scent of gardenias. Sweet, sweet gardenias. This was Glory, who like the blooming ylang-ylangs and salty tang of Biscayne Bay, offered a fragrance he wanted to carry with him into Russia too.

159

20
Wet Foot, Dry Foot
Key Biscayne, Florida

Come morning, Glory rolled over onto her back, stretching as she did to unknot her body from her brief but deep sleep. She hummed softly and ran her fingers through her hair feeling for knots there too. Finding none, she ruffled it to give it that tussled look she hoped Eric would find attractive first thing in the morning. What time was it anyway, she wondered? And just how long had their lovemaking lasted? Eric, she found, was capable of going well into the night. Something she enjoyed too, but given that she had to fly out this afternoon, the night's marathon had left her a bit lifeless.

"Eric," she cooed. "What have you done to me?"

Eric must have heard her from the kitchen because he walked into the bedroom with frying pan in hand. He stood framed by the doorway in a pair of low slung, silk pajama bottoms that revealed the length of his well-defined torso beneath a snug tee.

"The kitchen's working," he announced, leaning against the doorjamb to show his pan's offerings. Just to look at him reminded her of the night's passion and she was once again aroused.

"Thought you might want some protein this morning," he said. "I found some bacon along with some multi-grain bread. There was some concentrate, too, so perhaps a glass of O.J. will help you find your way into the sunshine?"

Glory smiled and stretched long and lean, presenting Eric an offering of her own—a peek-a-boo tease of her breasts from under the sheet that slipped off her chest to just below her hardened nipples.

Eric hummed at the sight of her. "You are sooo bad," he said. "You're also going to be sorry if you don't come join me for breakfast."

"Come join you?" she teased yet again. "Come join me and let me give you a little sunshine of my own."

Eric winked. "You are truly evil." He then turned and went back into the kitchen.

Glory sat up, allowing the sheet to drop fully, and climbed out of bed. She stood for a moment in front of the mirror and took good measure of herself. Tight and tawny. Lean with curves in all the right places. My how she'd worked hard for this figure and with good reason. As a flight attendant, appeal was a minor requirement but for those times when ulterior motives were necessary, fitness and provocative deception were a must.

Either way, the side benefits were good. She liked sharing a bed with Eric, but knew that at the end of the day, she'd still be expected to do her part in something she didn't fully want to do. Not with this one. He was too charming, too alarming even, just the kind of man she adored. And to think he was almost killed. Her people didn't make those kinds of mistakes. But in this particular case, wasn't she glad that they had?

When she'd first received word that he was still amongst the living, her surprise was unimagined. She'd known all along that she couldn't afford to fall in love with this beautiful man. Instead, she was expected to only get close enough for him to believe it so that she could learn what was needed. Her duty was to report the details of every

161

rendezvous they shared—from where they went to dine, to where they slept, and more importantly, what they discussed. But with things moving along so slowly, it was different now. Her collection of information needed to escalate and it was her job to make it happen.

With Eric busy setting the table, Glory dressed, and as she pulled down her shirt, reminded herself that everything she did next was crucial. So it was best she got on with it. Today she needed some understanding of what he was up to and where he might be headed. She also needed to know what escape routes from the island he had, if any, that weren't obvious since he'd disappeared unexpectedly from their radar after being shot and presumed dead. She had only this breakfast to share with him before she had to leave. The wait for him to return from his recuperation and recent travels had been longer than anticipated. Time had been wasted.

When she entered the kitchen, Eric had breakfast served. Coffee, orange juice, toast, and bacon as promised.

Eric smiled. "You look divine," he told her.

"Thank you and so do you. It's just too bad that I've got to fly off. Otherwise, I'd love to stay and play domestics with you for a while," she teased.

Eric laughed and for a few minutes they ate.

So then she asked him, "Have you any plans today?"

"I do" he started. "I have lots of them."

"Oh, yeah, like what?"

Eric wagged his finger while holding a piece of toast to his mouth and with a grin responded, "Well, let's see. I plan to save the world from evil injustice and fly around in a cape to save damsels in distress."

"A super hero, I just knew it!" she exclaimed. "And I like it. A man of true bravado. But you know, I really know so little about you and don't you think a girl gets curious after a while? Especially since…"

"I suppose," he interrupted with a mild laugh, "but

162

like I've been telling you, there's really not much to tell. Simply put, I'm not the copier salesman I told you I was when we had drinks in D.C., although I am in the business of selling commodities. Anything really. Like metals and grains, energy and raw gems. Diamonds mostly. Things that'll trade for some future high price."

"So you're a trader, hmmm? I'm thinking a snob, too, for assuming I would judge you accordingly. But diamonds? Now that really does have my attention."

Eric laughed again, saying only, "Yes, well, as they might any woman."

Wanting to know less of his cover-up and more of the truth but not willing to press it, Glory decided to change strategies. Standing, she went to the window that ran the length of the living and dining rooms, opened the drapes, and stared across the bay at the dazzling Miami skyline of condos, businesses, and banks. From her vantage point she could also see some of Coconut Grove's busy coastline and part of the Rickenbacker Causeway that they'd driven across the night before. She watched as the palm trees swayed and little cars zoomed over the bridge blinking their tiny red taillights like subtle messages of warning. Stop, stop, but she didn't.

"My god, Eric, the view you have is breathtaking. But I just have to ask, have you ever given thought to the fact that there's really only one way on and off this island? Doesn't that ever worry you?"

"Why should it?" he asked, coming up behind her and gently closing the drapes around them both. They stood pressed together this way for a moment.

She finally questioned, "Well what if the bridge was destroyed or something? How would you ever escape to safety? Use the boat I do not see tied to your dock?"

She felt him kiss the back of her neck and linger there.

She tried again by turning to face him. "I mean it.

163

What if you needed to get off this island in a hurry? How would you do it?"

Confusion registered across his face, as if he was wondering why she'd ask that question, so she wasn't surprised when he responded with humor.

"I'd walk on water," he said, letting go of the drapes and wrapping his arms around her waist. "I'd walk from my very own dock to the other side. All on water. Then I'd find some beautiful woman such as yourself to pick me up and we'd go make love in her loft on South Beach."

She reached up to hold his face tenderly between her hands and said softly, "I mean it, Eric."

"I mean it too, Glory."

Realizing the conversation was over but not entirely finished, Glory stepped from his embrace to go collect her things. In the bedroom, she mulled over her failed attempts while Eric cleared the table and whistled a tender tune. She stopped to listen, allowing it to clear her thoughts.

"This one's going to be tough," she told herself.

*

Meanwhile, Eric was busy weighing Glory's efforts to talk about his work and ways off this island. Key Biscayne had always been a haven to him and especially to his parents before him. It's why they'd chosen to live here. But now that an attempt had been made on his life, even he had to implement a more secure escape plan should he decide to remain.

There was, of course, his powerboat equipped with jet ski currently in dry dock as well as his aluminum Boston Whaler hanging next to his kayak in the boathouse beyond the pool. He also still had the tunnel below that he could easily restore, and if all else failed, he had the pad where a helicopter could come in and carry him away. He wanted to tell her all of this but didn't, partly because he didn't

164

understand why she was asking about it and partly because he wanted to control each step they took.

God, this profession can make you suspicious of everyone, Eric chastised himself at hearing Glory re-enter the living room. He turned to see her with overnight bag in hand.

"I'm ready," she said. "Although I do hate to go."

"I hate to see you go, too," he said, surprising himself with emotions that crept in knowing he'd also have to end it right here, right now no matter what until he returned from his assignment.

He walked over to take her bag and guided her into the garage, all the while thinking of how to present it. There he turned her to him and said, "Have you ever heard of wet foot, dry foot, Glory?"

"No."

"It's a little known perk from the Federal Government to Cuban refugees. If a political exile from that island places even one foot on our dry land, they're safe and can ask for US citizenship. No other immigrant from any other country gets this luxury. It's strictly for Cubans."

"And what does that have to do with anything?"

"It's an answer to your question, Glory, because I don't need to escape from here. It's a place I belong."

"You're Cuban?"

"No, I'm home."

Glory looked at him with a measure of sadness that pulled on his heartstrings before kissing him goodbye. She traced his lips with her finger.

"So stay safe, then. Wet or dry, okay? At least until I can see you again." She opened her mouth to say something more but lightly smiled instead and turned to her car.

Eric asked her to wait and went to her. He put her into an embrace. "I've got some bad news. Business, sorry, but I'll be gone for some time."

"Again?" she asked awkwardly. "How long this time?"

"I don't know, maybe a month or more?"

Her lips turned into a pout. "And you're telling me this now as I'm walking out the door?"

"It was unavoidable, I'm sorry."

"You're sorry? So what are you really saying here, Eric? That I might not see you again? Is that what you're telling me?" Her voice sounded edgy, a little angry even.

"No."

She jutted her chin, obviously thinking of what to say next, so Eric spared her. "France. I'm...I'm going to Paris, France. Can I call you on my return?"

"No, I mean, let me think about it, really. Since you'll be gone so long, I think it's better if I call you in a month or two, maybe three. How about six? Does that give you all the time you need?"

Then she insulted him, "And as for last night, I do hope you enjoyed the company."

Eric hadn't expected that. A woman scorned. What? Did she really think she was a one-night stand?

"Glory, please, that's not what I'm saying at all and it's not what you think, honest. I don't want us to part like this. I truly don't."

Glory pursed her lips. Kept her eyes steady on his.

Eric felt the burn of her stare. He weighed what few options he had and then on impulse kissed her lips, her eyes, her chin, and ears. He whispered, "I promise, Glory. I promise this isn't the end of us. It's only the beginning."

He touched her cheek and watched her soften, then break eye contact.

"You can prove it by calling me from Paris," she said. "And telling me when you'll be back. I'm not accustomed to men like you, Eric. I like honesty."

Eric caressed her cheek.

"I do too, Glory, and you'll have it as soon as I return."

She got into her car as he opened the garage door. He

166

wasn't accustomed to someone like her either...or the ache he felt as he watched her car disappear down the street.

21
Fanny's Arrival in Paris
Paris, France

Charles de Gaulle Airport thrummed with the noisy mixture of flight announcements and the hustle of people that gave Fanny the type of arrival crowds he'd hoped for, dense and distracted, until customs where they'd become impatient and glaring. True to expectations, the angered multitudes shielded him all the way to the train bound for Paris's northern station of Gare du Nord. Here he wound through the bustling terminal and boarded another headed south to Gare d'Austerlitz. The switchback was necessary, he felt, for the job at hand. Already Fanny was operable in spite of his need to rest before performing as expected. But assumptions like the one he was taking now could backfire, he knew, the problem was he couldn't help himself. He was live and purposely sent down this rabbit hole to map the terrain, so he felt pressed to move quickly.

Before leaving Washington, he'd been told that the prime minister's assistant, Philippe Simone, frequented the Folies Bergère show, often attending on a Thursday night. That was in two days, giving him barely enough time to surveil the area so that he could determine entrances and exits, security and personnel. Knowing that the Folies Bergère was in the ninth arrondissement to the north, it was natural for anyone watching to expect him to head in that direction. So he'd obliged, until he'd covertly headed in the opposite to establish his home base.

There he spotted the unassuming Grand Hotel des Saints on Boulevard Saint-Marcel and entered through its double doors into a stylish lobby where the jutting front desk replicated the building's angular shape. All seemed perfect. The hotel was just large enough for shift changes by morning and small enough that service should be efficient and swift. He decided to camp here, but try as he might to complete his registration quickly, the clerk was taking his time.

There was much to inquire about and much to advise Fanny of, the clerk said. For instance, "What would you like to see while you are here? What would you like to do? You are very lucky, monsieur, to be here in the most interesting district of all of Paris, the Latin Quarter. Nearby are the many universities including La Sorbonne, l'Ecole Normale Superieure, and l'Ecole des Mines de Paris that should not to be confused with les mines, the underground tunnels for which Paris is so famous amongst so many of its other treasures…" *and where Corbett died*, Fanny added silently while laying Euros on the counter and allowing the clerk's pleasantry to soften his edginess.

Finally the man handed him an encoded plastic card, announcing, "C'est bon! Your key."

"Merci," Fanny said.

"Ah, and what else for you?"

"Nothing but a bath and good night's sleep," Fanny lied.

"But it is early and is outside very nice. Perhaps you'd prefer to walk if your flight was long?"

It was, Fanny thought but answered, "Perhaps."

"Perfect," the clerk exclaimed.

"Au revoir," Fanny said as he walked away from the desk.

"You mean bonne nuit, monsieur," the clerk shouted after him. "Au revoir we will save until you leave us. Oh, and

169

ah, s'il vous plaît, café if you like in the morning will be served here." The clerk pointed to an espresso machine on a small table beside a cascading marble staircase. "And," he continued, "in the breakfast area along with continental breakfast and fresh juices."

"Merci," Fanny said one last time before stepping into the elevator for his third-floor room where he threw his duffle onto the side chair, removed the UMPC from his backpack, and logged in to Oscher, simultaneously marking his location.

Oscher, in turn, reconfirmed: Rende says Folies fabulous 2 night.

Rende, Fanny understood, was code for Philippe Simone. Because Harvey Rende, as Secretary of State in the United States, held a similar position in Washington that Simone held in France and that "2 night" meant in two nights.

Thank Rende for me, Fanny wrote back before logging out. He then stepped over to the window and looked out upon the city just coming to life. It proved, as he'd hoped, that there was still plenty of time to do some early reconnaissance. He opened the folded tourist map on the desk and found the Folies Bergère located on Rue Richer, about an hour and a half's walk or thirty-minute metro ride from his hotel. Fanny chose to walk.

On his way there, he passed the many sites mentioned by the clerk or was at least near them, so he occasionally ticked them off the map as any tourist might. But, what neither the map nor the clerk had told him, and what he didn't know himself, was that he'd also be crossing the bridge at Notre Dame where Simone once stood and dropped Officer Corbett's snipped fingertips into the River Seine.

When he finally arrived at the Folies Bergère, Fanny ducked into and out of the opened shops to his left and right to best determine how these locations might serve him. There was a deli, a cafe, and a bakery where several multi-tiered pastry stands offered an array of fruit-filled delights. This shop was busy enough to allow Fanny to study the streets from inside while being left unattended.

The boulevards were hectic with people riding bicycles, mopeds, and motorcycles dodging obstacles as they sped past. Drivers tooted their horns, shouted "excusez-moi," or let fly the occasional expletive. Their pace was quick and lively. Fanny wondered if it would be the same or worse on Thursday night.

After leaving the bakery, he stepped into a dimly lit sex shop that afforded him the cover of semi darkness to further watch the activity, but once there, the shop's contents snared his curiosity. To his left hung delicate displays of lacy negligees in every shape, color, and coverage. He reached for the tag of an expensive-looking bustier, replete with French-looking ribbons. It read "Made in China". He smirked and let it fall back in line on the rack. Nearby shelves held garter belts and tickling feathers, g-strings and fishnet stockings, as well as various costumes of innocent maidens, nurses, and librarians.

To the right of him, costumes of thick rubber, black leather, and steel-spiked mesh vied for equal attention. Knotted and multi-stringed whips dangled over thigh-high boots and other masochistic-type aides. He spied handcuffs, dildos, and tethers, and in a small container at the end of the counter where he stood, packages of tiny clothespins that, according to the diagram, were for a man's "plaisir sexuel extreme." Fanny could only imagine. From behind him a woman asked in French, "May I help you?" while poking his back with what felt like a leather cattle prod.

"Me? Oh no, madam. I am only...curious," he said as he turned to find a diminutive, red-haired woman. She was dressed in a rather tight fitting suit that allowed the tops of her aged breasts to billow over and appear plumper than they most certainly were.

"Aren't we all?" she asked, switching to English.

171

"American?"

"Oui, and I speak only a little French," he responded with his thumb and index finger held about an inch apart. Her singsong lilt teased him, "No problem, monsieur, sex is a universal language, no?"

Fanny smiled wide.

"Bon, my name est Emerille if you have need of me." she enunciated clearly with a prod to his torso with each word to which he nodded, knowing he would not be in need of her services.

As Emerille walked away, she suggested he follow her to the back of the store where she stopped at the register. She smiled and spread her arms wide across the counter. On display below the glass was an arrangement of men and women in glossy photos and various, suggestive poses. "See want you like?"

Fanny grinned over her misuse of words but then looked up to the wall behind her to stare at another glossy image. This one was of the prime minister and Emerille arm in arm. Happy smiles on both their faces. Was she somehow part of his circle? Was she connected to the Bratva? Fanny pointed to the framed photograph.

"The prime minister."

"Oui, Philippe Nanterre," Emerille said, closing her eyes dreamily.

"A friend?"

"Non, the mechanic…the mechanic est mon friend."

"I see, the mechanic."

"Oui."

A recalculation spun in Fanny's head over the greater odds that the mechanic was involved, so he analyzed the photo's shadow angles for time of day, direction of the building, and its size and contents. He noted, as well, the width of its bay doors and the outfits of both subjects. Nanterre sported casual wear while Emerille wore a flowered dress that kicked up slightly, suggesting a passing breeze

172

from perhaps a nearby ally or side road. The mechanic, however and more importantly, was missing.

"And why is the mechanic not in the photo?" he asked.

"Because, mon amore, he…est…the photographer," Emerille said, throwing out a high-pitched laugh.

"Yes, of course. So, if I need a mechanic, I would go see your friend?"

"Oui."

"Is he any good?"

"He est very, very good, monsieur. Emerille would never lie about a friend."

"And where might I find your friend?"

"La Rue de Bac, ask for Anton."

"Merci, madam, you're most kind. I will go and visit Anton when I need a good mechanic."

She batted her eyes and said, "Bon, say Emerille send you."

"Oui, and I'll visit you again when I am in need of this," he said, tapping the photos beneath the glass countertop.

"Ah bon! Bon!" she exclaimed with much pleasure.

Fanny chuckled as Emerille followed him to the door to hold it wide for him.

"Merci beaucoup et bonne journée," she almost sang. "Come again."

Fanny nodded and turned south but couldn't help to look back at the sex shop where Emerille still stood. She blew him a kiss.

His walk to Rue de Bac took him another forty-five minutes and this was after he'd cut through the Tuilleries Garden and L'Vendome to cross back over the River Seine near the Musee D'Orsay. Once there, he'd ducked into a café called Le Loup Bestiale to sit facing the left front window that from this vantage point gave him a commanding view of the garage while limiting his exposure to the people behind

173

him. He ordered a burger and pomme frites, then focused on the "Meilleur des Meilleurs-- Specialists de L'Automobile."
Best of the Best Automobile Specialists.

The garage was closed, of course, but the office was not, for a single light glowed in its tiny side window. On occasion, someone walked close to it and then away. Fanny wondered if it was Anton and what he was doing.

The server returned with his meal, and as he was putting it on the table asked him, "Do you know, monsieur, that our name is for the beastly, man-eating wolves that once terrorized France?"

"No, I didn't know that," Fanny replied, to which the server said while pointing to the hamburger, "You think if our patrons know, then maybe they get giddy at returning the favor?" He slapped the table at his own joke.

Fanny laughed as he picked up the burger to take a bite. It was dry, just as he thought a wolf might be. Fanny considered mentioning this, but the man had already turned away to the table across the room. There a lone diner sat with his back to Fanny, a curious position resembling his own. What or who was he hiding from?

The waiter and the man laughed, presumably over his own folly, but conversed in whispers. As they did, Fanny deduced that the customer worked at the garage because dark smears of car oil or grease stained the edges of both side pockets of his crisp, white coveralls. Could *he* be Anton? Fanny thought. And what, if by chance, they turned his way? Could he afford to have his own face a recollection in the days ahead? No. It was time for a speedy exit.

Fanny laid several Euros on the table and slipped out the door. His preliminary surveillance for the day was done. He'd studied the streets, connected several possible people to Nanterre's domain, and oriented himself to pertinent locations. The accumulation comforted him and made him feel more grounded. Now it was time to return to the Grand Hotel des Spirits, another hour's walk still, to determine his next course of action.

22
Eric's Welcome
Moscow, Russia

Trees, thick with dark mottled leaves, reached up to a cloudless blue sky with the quiet promise of unloading their foliage very soon. The cool air, made so from pore ice that had already formed underground, expelled a dense, refrigerated smell. Moscow seemed to Eric what Buffalo must be like at this time, although the sights, sounds, and reasons for being here differed. It was a relay point, a destination where someone from the CIA's Moscow station would deliver some necessary hardware for the next phase of his journey, Popigai Crater.

Sidney Edmund, the director to whom he now reported, cast him as Dr. Richard Knudson, an attaché for a large US geothermal company interested more in the area's radioactivity than its diamonds. As Knudson, this new equipment would add to his disguise, but he'd have to rely on M.I.C.E., the agency's acronym for money, ideology, conscience, and ego, to obtain whatever information he could about the operations for distributing the rare stones. He understood, however, that Edmund's team, whoever *they* were and wherever *they* may be, would assist.

"You have my word," Edmund had assured him. "They'll appear as ordinary people. You won't know who they are and they won't know who you are directly. I'm sorry, but it's important to operate in this manner because it's the only way we can protect everyone's identities. Like we said, you'll be on your own but never alone."

Eric accepted the situation with ambivalence and rightfully so, but would put the resulting adrenaline to good use. The only true comfort he found was in his supposed death that at least no one from the Russian Bratva would be actively searching for him, not as Eric Dane, at least. The thread was a narrow one, but it was a tether nonetheless.

From Moscow, the Popigai crater pocked the earth some twenty-five hundred miles to the northeast in the vast Siberian Federal District. Its nearest outpost, Khatanga, was another one hundred and eighty miles more. To get there, he'd arrive by small plane onto its even smaller runway and afterward, be provided additional equipment and transportation. Eric expected an arduous journey. Khatanga's snow and ice was already building. The thought of why he, instead of Fanny, had drawn the short, cold straw of Russia crossed his mind. Briefly. Until he weighed the value of his assignment of finding Niembriev and Madame DuBethonee. And more importantly, that he was charged with bringing in, or taking down, the elusive Queen Bee.

So here he was as a corporate, ball-cap wearing Dr. Richard Knudson, a seemingly innocent geologist sitting on a park bench, drinking a strong cup of grinder, which is what the Russians called coffee that had been cranked. After swallowing his last sip, he tossed his cup into the waste can, walked back up to the kiosk, and asked for another. Inside, the rotund man nodded, making the pink folds of his chin quiver. Another grinder appeared. Eric paid in rubles, laying them on the narrow counter, and returned to sit again on the bench.

Who's who? he wondered as he studied those walking briskly by or stopping themselves for an after-hour's beverage. His mind's eye alighted on one person and then another. *Are you CIA? You?*

It felt like a sick game to have unsuspecting people support him but to not know whom they were or where they'd be. He supposed he'd get used to it and eventually assured by it when the time came. That's what the director had told him. "It benefits you to not know who these people are."

Really?

He finished his coffee and given that it was almost six p.m., wondered if he'd missed his contact or if the contact had missed him. He'd have to message the director at some point, but not now, because there was still time left. But when no one had approached him by seven, he decided it was time to go to his hotel and grab his bag. The last flight out was in three hours.

Whatever had happened, he'd followed Edmond's instructions to the letter and would continue to do so. If the opportunity for the transfer had been delayed or missed all together, perhaps it could be rearranged in Krasnoyarsk during his layover to Khatanga. He calculated another ten hours of travel time, assuming of course everything else went according to schedule.

When he returned his hotel key to the cherubic, older woman behind the polished desk, she asked in clipped English, "Leave now?"

"Da," he answered.

"We serve well?"

"Yes, yes, of course."

"You have no complaining?"

"No."

"Good, I have package." She reached below the desk and pushed a dark leather briefcase toward him.

Eric felt a rush of relief.

"Come one hour ago for you."

Eric turned it away from the woman, broke the plastic seal, and flipped open the lid. Inside were schematics and charts, land surveys, and a collection of measuring gadgets.

Things an attaché for a geothermal company might need. Edmond had come through. He closed the case and laid extra rubles in front of her.

"For you," he said. "Buy your boyfriend a lovely dinner."

"Boyfriend?" she giggled, placing her hands on matronly hips and thrusting her ample chest forward. "I am babushka!"

"No," he demurred.

She giggled again and deftly scooped up the money with a slap of her hand. "You good man," she said, leaning over the counter with a smile that must have surely won over her husband so many years ago.

"You good babushka," he said in return, leaning into her.

She squealed with delight and banged repeatedly on her little gold desk bell. She yelled to the doorman, "Avtomobil!"

Outside a tan car pulled forward to take him to the airport.

"Spasibo!" they yelled to one another.

Eric slipped into the four-door Lada Priora after first placing his black duffle across the seat and the briefcase at his feet after. After a mile or two, the driver presented a wrapped package over his right shoulder. The action alarmed Eric and forced his shoulders back. It could be a bomb after all.

"For your journey. A gift," he said with a broad smile and spoken with a long, hard "e" as in "geeft", something he'd continue to do with every "i" he spoke.

Without responding, Eric studied the driver in the rearview mirror, who added encouragingly, "A man give to me. Say he is friend."

Eric fixed on the two eyes that again flicked in the mirror. They were brown and clear. Young. But when the man finally grew uncomfortable, he broke from Eric's stare and pressed harder on the gas pedal.

"What's the rush?" Eric asked as he felt around the top of the package. It was crushable with something else hard underneath.

"No rush, crazy people is all. Crazy drivers. Like America, no? Sit, I get you to airport safe, okay? No problem."

Eric gave a slow nod but continued to gaze at the man's reflection.

You? he wondered. "What did the man look like that gave you this package?"

"Look? Ahh, you know, like you. Baseball cap," the driver answered with a nervous laugh. "Da?"

"Da," Eric said.

"Good, good, then I drive. You sit back. Enjoy."

Eric turned to look out the window and asked, "How much further?"

"Ten minute top, okay?"

"Okay."

Eric watched the city of Moscow blow by as the Vnukovo airport signs started to appear. The two men said nothing more to one another, although the uncertainty of everything that had just transpired, gnawed at Eric. His journey had only just begun and although expected, Edmond's unknown persons connecting to him felt eerie, not reassuring. He needed to get to Khatanga, if anything, just to narrow down the number of people with whom he had to deal. There, real people waited, people he had to study and question, and he had a job he'd been assigned to carry out.

At the airport, he took the package into the first bathroom he found and unwrapped a small backpack containing a portable spectroradiometer used for measuring radiation. His cover was complete.

By the time he boarded his plane, they were already behind schedule by an hour. Seems TSA in Russia was a lot less trusting. Everyone's questioning had been long but congenial. The inspection of Eric's duffle, briefcase, and small backpack was thorough but his cover had worked well. The next thing he knew he was flying off to Siberia's third largest city of Krasnoyarsk. He'd land around nine a.m. and be off again by ten. He'd arrive next in Khatanga the following day.

*

It was the older Japanese-Russian man seated beside him on the twin-engine plane to Khatanga who elbowed Eric awake. He was saying something apparently very funny, because he kept laughing while pointing out the small window. Eric realized they were about to land. He shook the old man's knotted hand and said, "Spasibo, ya vizhu." *Thank you, I see.*

Upon exiting the plane, the site of the river town threw him. The ground was arctic white, broken only by bricked buildings and sheds overstuffed to the point of littering. The tiny mounds moving toward him were people in heavy, hooded coats, ready to claim loved ones and co-workers. The closer they got, the more he could see of their expectant faces. One in particular caught his attention...a rugged, ushanka-hat-wearing man of about sixty years of age with clear green, steadfast eyes that beamed at him from an etched face. The man tromped toward him with a gloved hand extended and asked, "Docktor Knudson?"

"Da," Eric answered.

The man opened his arm to a waiting sidecar mounted to a stitched up Russian-made Ural motorcycle about as vintage as the driver.

"Is it safe?" Eric asked in Russian.

"Da," The man said curtly.

"Do you speak English?" Eric asked, hoping that he did.

"Yes," the man said just as curtly before walking

away.

When Eric didn't follow, the man turned back and said, "Comez, not far," which was about as much as Eric would hear him say for the next sixty seconds or so as they drove, smoke billowing from the broken muffler, to the Khatanga Hotel.

The man cut the engine in front of what looked like a hospital. He stepped off the motorcycle and removed the ushanka from his head and handed it to Eric. He removed his gloves and did the same.

"What's this?" Eric asked.

"Keep, you need."

And then he held out an open palm. Eric first tried to give the hat and gloves back but the man refused. Instead, he broke loose and wiggled his fingers and said, "Tip".

"Oh, I...I'm sorry," Eric stuttered and reached into his jacket for a couple of rubles. "But you know I could have walked here, right?"

"Da, so, I give you this, too." He reached into a saddlebag and handed over a half empty bottle of vodka. "For warmth. Drink plenty."

Eric waved it off as the old man shrugged and put it back in his pouch. Stepping out of the sidecar, Eric tried again to hand back the hat and gloves but the grizzled man had already sputtered off. Eric watched him leave, then pointed himself toward the hotel.

Inside, Eric found the lobby full of loud and on-the-way-to-being-drunk groups of explorers. Everywhere, backpacks, tents, and supplies lay strewn about the small reception area. Bottles of Russian vodka were being passed around as fast as the jokes were being told. More bottles stood or sat empty on the coffee table between the two sofas. Seems the travelers were congregating at the Khatanga Hotel from several different expeditions before heading up to Taymyrsky and the North Pole. And, by the sound of the different languages Eric heard spoken, they were from

182

around the world.

"Is it always like this?" he asked in Russian of the pleasant-looking woman behind the desk.

"Yes, there's much to do out of Khatanga. Mostly treks and explorations, you know? We've had our share of famous people come through our little hotel. Are you American?"

"Yes."

While looking at his passport, she switched over to the same broken but earnest English he'd heard since arriving in Russia and asked, "What brings you, Docktor Richard Knudson?"

"Radiation in the crater west of here."

"Ra-di-a-tion," she sounded out. "Da, Popigai?"

"Yes, Popigai."

"Maybe why my hair white."

"Perhaps but doesn't nature take care of that on its own?"

"Da, nature can be good, can be cruel, especially in Khatanga. You must be careful, Docktor Knudson, to keep on hat and gloves. In winter, you could lose fingers or toes if not careful. Fall off like this." She held up her right hand with a bent index finger, teasing him and said, "Suggest you drink good Russian vodka always to stay warm. No? Summer, winter, no problem."

"Like these guys?"

"Oh, all good guys leave today. We take bottles, clean, refill. You want maybe?"

"Maybe, yes. I'll take one."

"Good, here, I add to bill." And with that she proffered a full bottle of the elixir along with his key and told him to go to the second floor.

As he did, he tripped over a man sprawled by the stairs wearing a red parka and yellow bandanna. Eric said excuse me as the man, who suddenly appeared very sober, winked at him, and said, "Welcome."

183

Eric studied his face. *Are you?*
And then just as suddenly, the man fell asleep.

23
Glory Be
Paris, France

"La Grand Vie rue Roissy d'Anglais," Fanny told the taxi driver, who grunted at the command and then cast an air of disgust after he saw Fanny track their progress on his UMPC. Fanny ignored him until a block prior when another grunt escaped after he asked to be let out early.

"Nothing personal," Fanny admonished while stowing the device inside one of the many pockets of the black vest he wore over a dark shirt and even darker jeans. For Fanny knew that slipping into the bar restaurant on foot was far more effective than showing up curbside in a shiny, new cab.

As expected, La Grand Vie was busy, both indoors and out, upstairs and down, making it advantageous to survey the room from the shadows along its northern interior wall. His intent was to reach the upper deck in the rear for its panoramic view.

On his pass through the main salon, Fanny recognized no one. So after climbing the staircase, he entered the men's restroom, spent a few minutes there, and then stepped out and approached the railing. He saw no one familiar still. As he descended, he caught sight of his mark flanked by three other men. Simone, with drink in hand, was comfortably settled on a sofa tucked in by the bar and listening intently to the man closest to him. The other two were leaned in from adjacent club chairs. The hands of the one speaking flew in several directions to make his point, all of which appeared negative.

Fanny chose a plush stool at a nearby counter and ordered a cognac. Then turned an ear toward the archway that separated him from Simone's group. They spoke in hushed tones about a shuttle service or something like it. He heard "ground transport" and then "baggage" or "paquet." Soon they quieted and a newer, lighter, and happier voice floated through the air like a perfumed scent.

"Bonsoir, messieurs," she said in cheerful greeting.

"Ah bon, she has arrived," Simone said to the other men and, who by the sound, was noisily kissing the backs of her hands.

"Glory Milan, messieurs. Our beautiful flight attendant."

Fanny's interest perked. *Glory Milan.* He resisted turning to verify her presence and instead shook his near empty glass at the Englishman beside him and said, "Hey, have you seen the bartender lately?"

The man turned to him with a boozy smile, raised his own glass, and mumbled a "jolly oh, mate" before signaling the barkeep for attention. Fanny coaxed him into some light banter and after a few minutes, excused himself to again climb the stairs. On the wall between the men and ladies restroom doors, stood a bank of decades-old telephones and it was here where he lingered. He knew that at some point most of the women would need to escape, if only to get away from all the testosterone for a moment or for the opportunity to make a smaller, but still grand, re-entrance into the lounge.

In time, Glory came lightly up the stairs, placing one high-heeled designer pump in front of the other. Fanny took in her graceful rise before putting his own cell phone to his ear as if on a call. He watched her open the ladies room door, and without ever taking a glance at him, disappear inside.

Fanny waited. It was indeed Glory Milan, the very

woman Eric had embraced at the airport. He mouthed a profanity and returned to his seat. Presently, she returned to her group as well, and although Fanny couldn't make out much more of what was said due to the increased noise of the lounge, he could nurse another drink until they disbanded.

When they did, he followed them toward the front door and jostled into position behind the three men who now guarded Glory and Simone. Glory asserted that she must sleep. The trip had been long, he heard her say, and since it had also been on such short notice, she'd barely had the chance to recuperate.

He stuck close to the group at the taxi stand where Glory and Simon were first to step into the next available cab, after which the three men walked away into the night. A young couple grabbed the second, but Fanny was quick with the third and once inside, pointed in the direction of Glory's cab while pressing several Euros into the right shoulder of the driver.

The man reached up and took hold of them, exclaiming, "C'est trop!"

"No, no," Fanny argued. "It's not too much, son parfait." *It's perfect.*

Simone and Glory's route took them to a glamorous, older apartment building where Fanny had his driver motor past, then allow him out after taking a right at the corner. He peered around it in time to see Glory wave from outside her front door to Simone, whose hand extended above the roof of the cab and waved enthusiastically back as the car sped away.

From his vest, Fanny pulled a small monocular to peer through as she punched the security panel with a four-digit code: upper left, middle, upper right, lower something. And after she was gone, he ran to the entrance. There, he sprayed the keypad with an aerosol powder. The darkest, most recent fingerprints glowed brightest: one, five, three, eight. *Voila.*

On the way to the stairs, he took note of the elevator's stop and after reaching her fourth floor level, opened the door to a black marbled corridor where from beneath the third door down, a sheen of indoor light glowed in its high gloss. This was it. This was her place.

He put his ear to the door and listened for the click of her stilettos. There were none. He tried the handle. It was locked. He picked it and stepped inside. A small chandelier cast a soft light on the foyer although the living room beyond was dark. He stepped to the foyer's edge in time to catch a view of her from behind in the back bedroom donning a long silk robe. He then waited until she switched off the lights to address her.

"Glory, it's me, Eric," he whispered. He heard a muffled gasp. She must have put her hand over her mouth. He waited as her movements suggested she'd reached the bedroom door again and was fumbling for the hallway's light switch.

He flicked them on for her from his end.

She froze. Her eyes grew wide in fright.

He raised both hands and said, "It's okay, Glory, I'm Eric's best friend, Fanny Bergan. Listen, Eric's in serious trouble. I'm sorry to have followed you here but we need your help…I mean, Eric needs your help. He's asking for you because he knows he can trust you and its true, I know, because he's told me everything about you, even how you picked him up at the airport in Miami in your convertible. Remember doing that?"

Glory pressed her hands firmly over her mouth. Fanny had not eased her mind with his intimate knowledge. She spotted the block of chef's knives on the kitchen counter. So did Fanny although he decided not to stop her if she ran for them.

"Glory? Really, I mean no harm. Take a knife if it comforts you, but please, please know that I'm not here to hurt you. I'm here because Eric thinks you can help him. And

I…I think he's tied up in something very dangerous. Someone tried to kill him a couple of weeks ago. Are you aware of that?"

She still didn't move.

"Now he's hurt again. In the hospital. He might die," he lied.

She raised her eyebrows that suggested, *"die?"*

"He needs you, Glory. Can you help him?"

Glory's eyes opened and closed as Fanny came in for the close. "I know he'd appreciate it very much to have you by his side when he wakes."

"Wakes?" she asked, trembling and covering her face with splayed fingers. "How…how bad is…?"

"It's bad, Glory. He's heavily sedated right now and like I said, he might die. But before he went under, he…well...he asked me to go back to Miami or D.C., if necessary, to try to find you. By chance, I stumbled onto you tonight at the Grande Vie."

"You were by the telephones."

"Yes, I went to the bar for a shot of courage, you know? I was calling people, trying to figure out what to do and how to go about it. But I couldn't approach you because you were there with some business men, so I followed you here…to your apartment."

Glory slid her hands to the base of her neck, exposing the rigidness on her face. He understood how the shock of seeing a strange man in her Paris apartment might do that. But he hoped by now that he'd convinced her his reasons for it were valid. His efforts, however, failed and as a result, she turned and ran back into the bedroom.

Fanny dashed after her and tackled her to the floor. They wrestled. She scratched and clawed. He grabbed her wrists, a move that gave her some leverage to flip their bodies over with a strength he didn't expect and to knee him in the groin. He let go.

She leapt off him to throw open the bedside table's

drawer, forcing him to heave himself at her and to land across the bed. He grabbed again at her right wrist. She jerked it away while the drawer banged to the floor. Her .22mm glinted in the semi-darkness but he was quicker than she to grab it. With a raised hand, he held it away from her reach.

"Now, Glory," he said with as much calm as he could muster. "I'm not gonna to hurt you. I just need information, that's all. Help me help Eric and I'll leave you alone, honest to God. Eric's my man and I'll do anything for him, even if it means sneaking into your apartment. But you and I both know what we're dealing with here. I'm not gonna to lie anymore. It's diamonds, big diamonds."

Glory flinched.

"But just so you know, Eric's fine, Glory. He's fine. You're fine. I'm fine. He's not in any hospital and he's not gonna die. And we want to keep it that way, don't we? You can help us and we can help you. We just need to work together so that everybody wins. Eric agrees. If you help, then you're helping Eric. Should I call him, Glory? Should we ask him? I can do that."

Glory turned her face away from his pleading.

"I'm sorry, really," Fanny continued. "I understand. You need a minute to take it all in. That's cool, but Glory, we don't have a lot of time, you know. Every day shipments are moving and every day hundreds of millions of dollars are being made by someone else. You know what I'm saying? People in big places. We're in little places, the three of us, but we make big things happen for those people. People like Simone and the other three men you were with tonight."

"Stop," Glory commanded, "and get off my bed."

Fanny looked down the length of himself stretched across her silk comforter.

"Watch the belt buckle."

Fanny rolled onto his back and sat up, scooted to the edge of the bed and reached down to smooth out the

190

covering.

She smiled for the first time…barely.

He then beckoned, "Glory, c'mon, let's talk in the living room. I promise to behave. I promise to be honest about everything if only you'll do the same. We could do a world of good for Eric as well as each other."

She moved past him with caution as he dropped her .22mm back into the drawer on the floor. Once in the living room, she sank into a chair. He chose the couch opposite.

"We good?" he asked.

The look on her face told him differently.

"Okay…."

She interrupted, "Why are you here and not Eric? He said he was coming to Paris."

"He was and he did. We came together, but why are you here?"

"To surprise him of course. I care for him, if you really must know."

Fanny smiled at her lie. Hadn't she told her friends at La Grande Vie that she was here on short notice? Notice from whom?

"He had to go back to Miami."

"So soon?"

"Part of the job."

She took a deep breath that he hoped calmed her, which was good. She needed to relax so that he could better deal with her. He took a deep breath himself and moved the same foot forward to mirror hers in a show of emotional alliance. He'd learned that in the presence of familiar company or someone in similar pose, at least, people were more receptive to another person's presence.

"And now what?" she asked.

"Those men you were with tonight, who were they?"

"Acquaintances."

"Simone is an acquaintance?"

"A family friend."

"Who deals in diamonds," Fanny said flatly.

She pressed her lips and lowered her eyes.

"I said we needed to be honest didn't I, Glory? Well, here I am, now what about you? I think you might know something about diamonds too, am I right?"

Her lips parted.

"Popigai diamonds," Fanny added for impact.

She held him in a long, surprised stare.

"We really can't beat around the bush," Fanny said after a respectable wait. "Eric is smack in the middle of this whole chain of events and it's gonna cost him his life. If you have anything to tell me, tell me now because you could save him, Glory."

"Yes, but it would get me killed."

"I won't let that happen. You help me help Eric and I'll keep you safe."

"You don't know what you're talking about."

"Yes I do, Glory, and I can do this for you. I'm part of an organization. Eric, too. We have ways of protecting people like yourself. We have an entire world to hide you in. Wherever you want to go."

"Even the moon because you are *that* powerful?" she asked with sarcasm.

"Yes, if that's what you want."

She bent her head in thought. When she looked back up at him, her eyes glistened with early tears.

"I've heard that before, you know, from other men, from other….oh, forget it. You understand it's not just Simone who will kill me? There are other people out there. Dangerous people. People who will hunt me down anywhere in the world, including the moon until they find me. They will never stop, ever, and I hate it, I hate it. The whole lot of it," she whispered, head bending again. "I always have but what could I do? I was raised, you see, to help my uncle get whatever he wanted from this world."

"Is Simone your uncle?" Fanny asked, accepting that

only a close, domineering relative could command such allegiance. The thought soured in his mouth.

"Oui," the first French word uttered from hers. "And I do whatever it takes."

"Including falling in love with Eric?"

"No, my feelings for Eric are real even if it's not yet love. He's a good man. A beautiful man. He's not like him."

"You mean Simone."

"Yes."

"And what have you told Simone so far?"

"Everything that's expected of me. Everything I know. Everything we did."

"How's he gonna use the information?"

"I haven't the slightest idea."

"So you were sent only to learn what you could from him."

"Yes, and to seduce him."

"Which you did."

"Of course, with pleasure."

"And what did you learn from him?"

"Nothing much. He hardly talked about his work, saying only at first that he was a copier salesman. But later, he admitted to being a commodities trader in metals and grains. Also energy, diamonds, and raw gems. It was a lie, I know, but then…"

"Diamonds and raw gems?"

"Yes, that's what my uncle wanted to hear."

"So he knows?"

"Yes."

"And you knew Eric was lying to you but…."

"But I still fell for him, if that's what you're asking."

Glory bowed her head that allowed a tear to drop onto her robe. Fanny remained silent, knowing that if he uttered another word, it would ruin the progress he felt was at hand. Finally she spoke in a voice barely above a whisper, "I thought, maybe he would…that he could in some way…"

193

She sighed heavily and resolutely and fiddled with her sash. She was weakening. It took a few minutes more for her to again look up and ask in a final, quiet surrender, "Exactly what is it that Eric wants and how can you help me?"

A ripple ran through Fanny's chest as her words opened the wider chasm. Time, now, was critical. He had this one night only to coax from her what he needed and he was determined to not waste a moment of it.

24
On The Gulag Trail
Siberia, Russia

Day two at Khatanga and Eric was tense. Already he'd discovered that the ushanka hat was wired. It had happened when he'd put the frosted sheepskin on his head for a laugh in front of the mirror. But when he'd tied the strings under his chin, he'd felt a small, hard disk press against his ear. He'd squeezed it and suddenly everything around him had grown loud. He could better hear the elevator binging midway down the hall. He could hear the people outside his window two floors down. He could even hear someone cough from another room. He'd later run outside to search for the rugged man with the Russian motorcycle, because if anyone was one of Edmund's men, it was him, but he couldn't find the guy.

Since then his lack of progress had continued. Not even the money he'd spent to appeal to anyone's ideology, conscience, or ego had gained any useful information on Popigai. Neither did the sharing of vodka. Perhaps the lingering darkness had upended all their sensibilities, allowing them to party from early afternoon until midmorning. Whatever the cause, he'd find the same people wasted at four in the late afternoon as at seven-thirty in the morning on the next. His efforts had proved futile.

That evening, however, he met Dr. Marty Landers, a

British writer and historian on his way to the Popigai Crater. He was after first and second-generation accounts of the Japanese who'd lived and worked there since World War II. Eric had learned of the people's unusual situation through Operation Pop Up and decided to question Landers over dinner as if he hadn't a clue.

Landers assured him, "It's quite surprising, Dr. Knudson, how little anyone knows of what happened to them."

"Call me, Richard," Eric said. "I certainly had no idea, especially since Japan entered so late, but doesn't everyone pay a price for war?"

Landers squirmed in his seat while twisting a gold pinkie ring around on his left hand and said, "Certainly, but Japan paid it in ways not many other countries did. And, as for late entry, I believe your atomic bomb took care of that. No, Richard, the under-annotated atrocity was what happened to them *after* the war was over. Some went to Siberia and never returned. Others waited years until Japan was finally healthy enough to support their homecoming. Japan had been devastated, of course. So it's no wonder they accepted the reparation agreement, figuring perhaps what the bloody hell, they're being fed, housed, and given work every day, how could we do any better?"

"What numbers are we talking about?" Eric asked as their drinks arrived.

"Japanese slaves? Oh my, there were thousands. There were so many that if they'd returned to Japan at the end of the war, they probably would've died on the streets of starvation. Japan, you see, simply couldn't support them. It also certainly didn't want to deal with whatever these men might have resorted to otherwise. No, Japan was in no position to take on more problems. To them it was clearly a win-win situation. Russia, of course, wanted the labor, but I can't imagine that the individual slaves preferred it over going home. No, no, the Russians were quite brutal."

"How so?"

"Well, some died of starvation anyway because food in Russia was also rather meager, but most of them died in the mines. Hard work and a stiff backhand, if you follow. There were the coalmines of course...and the diamond mines, particularly Popigai, which is why I'm headed there. Seems there's some issei who never left and some nisei who didn't care to leave since they were born there and consider it their home."

Eric knew of the issei, or first generation Japanese. Some *were* still living; their average age over eighty-five. But why they'd never returned to Japan when they could have was complicated. Either they'd found a new home or were brainwashed. Some probably married someone who wanted to stay. A more probable reason, Eric believed, was that they were profiting directly from the diamond trade, something he'd prove once there.

"I met a guy once, a couple of years past called Johnny Tang," Landers said without pause as a waiter placed an elk steak dinner in front of him. "Nice chap. Worked at a golf course on Maui of all places. Drove a cart around with a big orange cooler of Tang on the back, offering cups to thirsty golfers. That's how he got his last name, 'Tang'. Real name's Jonoji Igarashi.

"Anyway, he was born and raised in Hawaii but was conscripted at age eighteen by the Japanese Army because he and his parents were Japanese citizens. He had to fight for a country he'd never known. But he went through his training anyway and given a rifle. Then he was sent off to battle. Never even fired the bloody rod, mind you. Hell, he was only out there about three months before the war ended and he was captured on his way to Nanking. Can you imagine? Nanking, another dismal chapter in Japanese history. But, no, the lad ends up in a Siberian prison instead. I don't know which would have been worse.

"For the next two and a half years he ended up

working for the Russians. Sorry, but it's the damnedest after-the-war story you'll ever hear and partly why I'm pursuing it today. He inspired me. Says he was a changed man after that and I don't doubt him.

"Now think how angry you'd be if it were you. A life lost and at whose expense? Japan's, Russia's, or maybe America's even? Hell, if it had happened to me, I'd be all tied up in knots and out for revenge, if anything just to set the record straight.

"But all I saw when I met him was the kindest, old soul you'd ever want to meet. Thin as a reed and always a big smile. You'd never know he'd been a slave unless he told you."

"That's pretty amazing," Eric said truthfully, repeating the same words he'd spoken to Oscher during his briefing. "And no one's ever written about them?"

"Well, a few have but there's really not much out there. So I'm going help by putting them in print. Maybe land a movie deal. People need to know about these chaps, especially Jonoji. He's a good man. History's full of Hitler and his extermination attempts of the Jews and all that, but it doesn't document piddle about those Japanese slaves. It's a real blight in the annals of history and needs to have a little light shone on it. That's where I come in. That's what I'm going to do. Expose it and broaden their story."

Eric nodded firmly, then asked about the diamonds.

"Oh, the diamonds, well, once the war was over Russia went silent on them. There's not been a word since, no sir. Well…not until recently." Landers stopped and shifted his eyes toward Eric and again twisted his pinkie ring.

Eric addressed the cliffhanger. "What do you mean?"

At that Landers covered his mouth in a sign of secrecy until he finally asked, "Why, what's your interest, your real interest?"

"None, I mean, I have no interest in the diamonds. Mine's strictly radiation. I'm just curious since you've certainly sparked my imagination."

"I see, well, you can't blame a guy for asking, can you? I mean it is diamonds we're talking about, mate, and diamonds can do something to a man."

"Like what?"

"Make him greedy."

"You greedy?"

"No, but I'm concerned."

"Why?"

"Why? Because not less than a couple of months ago, Russia put out a press release saying there were so many diamonds in there that they could flood the market for the next three thousand years."

"Three thousand years, that's what the press release stated?"

"To the letter, mate."

"And when do they plan to do this?"

"*That,* they didn't say," Landers said leaning in to Eric, a move that caused his napkin to fall to the floor. "But I'm betting such news will attract all sorts of people."

"Like who?"

"Are you serious? Poachers, claim diggers, and all sorts of nefarious opportunists. The Queen is rather disturbed by the news, you understand."

"Which queen?"

"What? Why the only one that matters, of course."

Landers smiled in a way that made Eric uneasy.

"She's putting together a delegation, joining three other countries to send some experts out there to verify what they've got."

"And you're part of that delegation?"

"No, no, I'm not under the Queen's authority," he answered, sipping his drink.

"Authority?" Eric pushed. "But you're already here."

"True, but I wouldn't dare. Too dangerous. I'm just writer of biographies you see..." he trailed off.

Eric wondered if Landers was waiting for him to probe deeper, so he reverted to Landers' research. "Come now, Marty. If I were in your shoes, interviewing Japanese ex-prisoners of war who'd once worked in the Popigai diamond mines, I'd surely want to extract some valuable information, if not only for my Queen, then at least for the sale of my timely book."

Landers drained his glass with eyes fixed on Eric. Then moved a piece of elk around his plate. "And if I were you, Richard, looking at any purported radiation emanating from the Popigai Crater, I might assume the same thing."

The air suddenly shifted as if Landers had realized that Eric was someone other than represented. An awkward moment lagged as the waiter brought a second round of vodkas.

"We should stay in touch," Landers told him. "I think we could be helpful to one another at some point in our journeys."

Eric sat forward in his chair and said, "I agree." *Because I need to know if you're MI-5 or Scotland Yard or some subgroup of SO14's Protection Command. And I need to know what you've got on me.*

Landers felt around his lap for the missing napkin. As he did, the pinkie ring he'd kept twisting throughout their meal was now upright, revealing a large, clear stone. And then it hit him. *You could be Bratva.*

His heart skipped a few beats.

Landers is tailing me or is up to something worse. I need to get out of here.

By the time Eric regained control, he found that his fingers had already pinched open the small packet in his pants pocket. It gave him a measure of assurance to refocus on Landers and confess, "It's on the floor."

"What?"

"Your napkin, it's under your chair."

"Is that so?" Landers asked, smiling thinly and

turning in his seat to bend over and retrieve it.

As he did, Eric ran offense. Things were adding up. The ring, the Queen, Popigai. He took advantage of the situation by emptying the small packet of ground powder into Landers' drink.

Slowly Landers sat upright and went again about spreading the retrieved napkin out on his lap. He looked first at his food and then his drink before leveling his eyes on Eric.

The two men measured each other in silence until Landers broke the spell by saying, "Certainly, Richard, shall we keep in touch then? I dare say, it would be rather good for the both of us. Mighty dangerous territory we're headed into."

"Could be," Eric replied, registering the warning as Landers finished his drink.

"Good," he said, placing the now empty glass on the table. "Then it's settled. You go and record any radiation you find and I'll record what little known history I find. Sort of puts us on level playing fields, don't you think?"

"Near enough," Eric replied. "But I don't work for a queen, only looking for one."

Landers winked sleepily while patting him on the back for what seemed too long and said, "Oh, yes, I see, or at least I think I do. But fret not, Richard, because when you shake the hive, you expose the queen. Watch out, though, because I happen to know she's got one hell of a stinger, mate."

Eric shrugged the hand off his shoulder as the drug took effect, making Landers relaxed.

Once in his room, he removed his shirt, put it in the bathtub and soaked it. Having Landers touch him could have meant anything. Micro-powders, dust, tracers, and he wasn't taking any chances.

25
Popigai Bound
Siberia, Russia

Eric sent a message to Edmund requesting an investigation of Dr. Marty Landers and stating that he was ready for Popigai. In return, Edmund replied with, "Landers clean. Depart 0700, Mi-17."

He'd be leaving Khatanga by transport helicopter, Soviet made and as reliable a bird as the director was proving himself to be, which is why Eric resisted sending a second request for an update on Fanny's progress in Paris. He figured if anything needed sharing, Edmund would have already mentioned it. As a result he was unaware of Fanny's discoveries, including those that centered on Glory and her relationship to Simone. Nevertheless, thoughts of this new light in his life never strayed far from his mind. His last words to Glory had been, "I promise this isn't the end of us. It's only the beginning" and he hoped to prove it as soon as possible. Good thing he was moving forward.

At dawn, Eric ventured out to the airfield without spotting Landers and kept his fingers crossed that he was still deadheaded enough to give him the opportunity to leave unnoticed. So far, so good. He stood there until a barrel-chested pilot brushed past, so anxious he was to load boxes that Eric assumed were necessary for his survival. Eric gave chase.

"Excuse me, but are you my pilot?" he asked, shouting to the man's back while he shoved items through the helicopter's hatch.

The pilot turned to look him up and down. "You Knudson?"

"Yes, you American?"

"Yep, by way of Texarkana. Name's Trenton Carroll. We'll hightail it outta here in about fifteen. Got one more load to stow and then we're off. You okay with that?" The pilot slipped his big paw of a hand into Eric's.

"Yes, of course."

Trenton cocked his head. "You ever been out to the crater, Doc?"

"Nope, first time."

"Well let me give you a piece of advice then." He pointed to the items Eric held in his other hand. "You put that there ushanka and gloves of yours on and you keep them on. Gets mighty cold out there. You get one touch of frostbite on either of those two spuds growing outta the sides of your head and they'll fall right off."

Eric smiled, thinking, *now why would he specifically mention the hat unless he's with Edmund?*

"Those are a hat and gloves, ain't they, Doc?"

"Yes they are. Ed, a friend of mine, was kind enough to gift me with them," Eric answered, hoping Trenton recognized the name as Director Edmund.

The pilot gave no inclination, instead he simply stared at Eric with his hands on his hips waiting for him to put them on and climb aboard. When finally Eric did, he left to go back for the last stack of boxes.

Eric tried again inside the cockpit to engage Trenton into admitting he was CIA or at least associated with the organization by asking, "So, how does an American man like you end up in Khatanga flying a Russian transport helicopter? You ever in the military or do any work for the government?"

203

"No, Doc, I did not. Military wouldn't have me…flat feet. Had to learn it all on my own. Found work through Camburton. *That* took me to Afghanistan. Quit after being shot at one too many times and I didn't have the legal right to answer back, can you believe it? Here we are workin' in a war zone and couldn't even protect ourselves. Hell, it was against the law and the company's policy to carry a gun," he answered through the micro-phoned headset. "Spent two outta five years of my contract damned near gettin' myself killed for someone else's profit. Never did quite add up, so's I hitched myself to a couple a guys headed here to find another line a work. Turns out Khatanga was too tough for 'em, so here I am last man standing."

Eric changed tack to tie the pilot to the diamond business.

"So now you're the one who profits way out here in Siberia? How do you do that?"

Trenton chuckled but didn't connect.

"Hell, I barely make ends meet but I did fall in love with a local gal. A real Dolgan. We barely communicated 'cept in the ways that mattered. Married her seven years and five kids ago. She keeps me busy, plus I fly Myrtle, here," he said petting the joystick fondly. "Anyways, got lots a side jobs, too. Need an engine repaired? I'm your man. Fix your icebreaker? Call me and I'll get 'er runnin'. There ain't a machine I can't coax back to life, no sir, not even a kitchen toaster."

Together they laughed with Eric feeling less and less sure he'd crack him in any way. The guy was either very good or just didn't have anything to do with the crater and its diamonds, aside from taking people out there to solve whatever curiosity interested them. So he figured he'd go take stock of the boxes Edmond had provided.

As Eric removed his headset and excused himself to the hold of the helicopter, Trenton instructed, "Help yourself. Look for the blue tape but be sure to hook up before you start pulling things out, ya hear?"

Eric did as asked and maneuvered around the cargo. He found four blue-taped containers, laid them side-by-side on the floor, and opened them for inspection. Inside he found what he expected: an arctic tent, down-filled sleeping bag, dehydrated foods, canteen, water purifying tablets, maps in plastic Ziplocs, and surprisingly, a laptop, remotes, and two tubes containing small black drones.

"Now isn't that special," Eric said as he studied one of the photographs mounted on the tightly packed metal containers. What he saw looked like an elongated bubble but was instead a specialized six-inch, five-pound explosive flying machine called a Night Spyder T-2000. The CIA had equipped it with pinhole laser beams beneath the belly and a fisheye lens at both front and rear.

He tore into the sealed diagram of the remote and its panel. As expected, the roller bar moved the drone left, right, up and down. And the "fire" button? Self explanatory. He could clearly put these drones to good use, especially with the expanse he'd have to cover that couldn't be done as well on sled or Humvee. Neither of which he had anyway. No, loaded drones in possible hostile territory would be very handy.

"Edmund, you're amazing," Eric said aloud only to have his voice drowned out by the whirling din of blades above his head.

After another hour, the sight of the not-so-distant crater consumed Eric. It was bigger than he'd imagined. At about sixty-two miles in diameter, Popigai was the smallest of Siberia's depressions, amounting to seventh in size out of its eight craters. But even at that, it was hard for Eric to absorb the size of the meteors that had struck some twenty million years ago. Bolides of that tonnage and circumference, he figured, most certainly would have scared any ancient, religious sect into believing that their fabled god was indeed extracting revenge.

"Yeah, hard to imagine it until ya see it, right, Doc?" Trenton piped.

"You're not kidding. It's amazing, but have you ever been to Vredefort in South Africa?"

"No."

"Heard it's three times the size, but, what the heck, right? They're all big as hell."

"You ain't shittin'," Trenton said before banking the helicopter to the left and adding, "Not far now."

They landed about forty minutes later on a flat plateau only a couple of hundred feet from a river and with a thumbs up, Trenton said, "We're down.

Eric looked around at the desolate landscape that included, at about three hundred yards away, a small building from which two furry beings waddled out. Their light brown faces were as golden as the pelts that lined them. Both looked enthusiastic.

Trenton popped open the door to yell to them, "Preevyet, Nesutak! Rebe!"

"Preevyet!" a female voice yelled in return as she picked up her pace.

Turning to Eric, Trenton said, "Rebe's a hardy gal. Nesutak's daughter." And then he raced to her and put her in a wide embrace. They spoke in a language Eric only partially understood, so he turned away to unload the cargo.

Finally they joined him with Rebe showing as much strength as the men, although her father finally stopped to inspect the labels and to nod his approval. Afterward, Trenton again spoke to the old man in his native tongue. In snippets, Eric believed he was asking if the "uncle" was happy.

"Yes, yes, very happy," he answered in return, appearing genuinely pleased.

Eric next heard in English "caribou" and "happy with tofu?"

"Yes, yes." And the question "lamplight?"

Again, "Yes, of course, uncle, I wouldn't forget lamplight." But then Trenton said something that made the man dance, "cabbage."

Rebe patted Trenton's back in a motherly way and said, "Thank you, T. We make salad with aronia berries. Very healthy. And spork, huh? Oh my, you really a very good boy."

"Rebe, darlin', you forget who you're dealin' with." The both of them laughed as Trenton placed his arm around Rebe's shoulder and began a private conversation with her all the way to the building. Her giggle, familial and trailing back to Eric, spoke of their closeness.

Eric looked at Nesutak who was now prying open a box and shortly found what he was looking for in a bag of spiced beef jerky. The old man laughed a "tee, hee, hee" while offering him a piece. It reminded him of the times sailing on Biscayne Bay when he'd shared similar leathery strips with Fanny. It *was* delicious. Rich and smoky...and tasting of salt.

They sat gnawing their treats until Trenton returned with some new bundles.

"Just like my wife," he said to Eric. "Keeps me busy, that one. She'll keep you busy, too, Doc, if you hang around long enough. Best keep to your own chores or she'll have you nailin' the roof down, if you know what I mean."

"Thanks, Trenton, I'll keep that in mind."

"All right fellas. Nesutak?" he reverted to the old man's language, telling him to take care of himself and to do as Rebe tells him.

Nesutak giggled and nodded, giggled and waved.

Then turning to Eric with a long look, he advised, "You take care now, and if Rebe gives you too big of a honey-do list, tell her she'll just have to wait for me. By the looks of you, I'm guessin' it won't be too terribly long."

"Will do," Eric said with a laugh.

Trenton gazed back at Nesutak. "Always a happy

fella that one. You're in good hands. They can radio me anytime there's a need. I'm only a couple of hours away."

"Thanks, man," Eric said shaking his hand. "I'll be fine."

"Right, that's what the last fella said, but see that trail right there? Follow it and you might just find his bones in the river. Try not to do the same, ya hear?"

Trenton nodded and winked a goodbye just as Rebe came back out of the building. She arrived in plenty of time for the three of them to wave Trenton off. The Mi-17 lifted, hovered briefly, and then whooped off into the distance.

"Come," Rebe sighed to Nesutak and Eric. "Hot tea."

Nesutak shuffled forward with earnest, waving to Eric to leave the boxes. No one would take them, the motion suggested. Look around. No one's here except us. Eric followed, knowing it wasn't entirely true because it wouldn't be long before he'd find Niembriev's mines or Landers would lead Niembriev and his men directly to him.

26
Oscher's Dilemma
Washington, DC

During training, Oscher had always harped that the hallmark of an exceptional CIA officer wasn't in the elimination of a target, it was in the gathering of vital intelligence. So when Oscher's assistant received Fanny's communiqué from Paris about Glory, she squealed with excitement. It read, "New asset: Glory Milan/Simone's niece. Flight Attendant, US Falcon Airways. Confirms: PM directs shipments. Simone transports. Arnoult negotiates airline/shipping contracts. CDG primary outlet using GCL personnel."

"Wow," Sally said. "He did it!"

Fanny had tapped through Glory Milan into the very resource they needed to disable the movement of Popigai diamonds out of Paris. It was, of course, something Arnoult had yet to confess and whose cooperation now waned. Surely with this new information, derailing the portion out of Charles de Gaulle Airport looked close at hand. She proudly entered Oscher's office to place the document firmly under his nose. Oscher read it slowly.

"Get me the names of all General Confederation of Labor personnel at de Gaulle, Sally."

"I'm on it."

"And we need Arnoult. Get him in here at fourteen

hundred hours."

"Yes, sir."

Arnoult was secreted away at a condotel where he enjoyed limited privileges. They included escorted walks with CIA handlers through the nearby park, which he did every day, and the use of the gym and saunas. Sally figured he could be anywhere at the moment, so she decided to contact one of their team directly.

She first phoned Officer Connie Sayles and got her message center. Then she dialed Officer Albert Chun and received his. She next rang Arnoult's room. No answer. She placed a call to the gym only to have the attendant tell her that he hadn't seen Arnoult all morning, although it did seem a little strange given that he was usually there at this time.

"Nice fella," the attendant told her. "Always updates me on the weather."

Sally thanked him, then drummed her fingers on her desk before calling the team's division head, Frank Ludwig.

"Hi, Frank, it's me Sally in Oscher's office. I'm looking for two of your officers, Sayles and Chun. Have you heard anything from them recently?"

"Let me see…"

She heard Ludwig flip through some paperwork on his desk, then say, "They were supposed to check in again at ten o'clock but there's no confirmation of them doing that, and it's what, ten-fifteen?"

"Correct. Do you have their dawn report handy?" she asked him.

"I do, at oh seven hundred it says, coffee delivered and no change. That's it."

"And nothing since?"

"Nothing since, but like I said, it's only ten fifteen. Not quite red-zone territory, Sally."

"It's Arnoult, Frank."

"That it is. I'll go investigate it myself."

"Thanks, we appreciate it. Oscher wants him brought

in at fourteen hundred hours."

"No problem, he'll be there. Which room?"

"I'll save number four for you, Frank, but listen, call me back as soon as possible, okay?"

"Roger that."

Sally buzzed Oscher with the news.

"We're having difficulty connecting with Arnoult's handlers, sir, but Frank assures me he'll have him in house by fourteen hundred hours."

"What kind of difficulty?"

"Neither Chun or Sayles is answering their phones."

Sally heard the halt of his breath.

"Sir?" she asked. "Frank says they're mid-morning report is only fifteen minutes late."

"Is that right? Well we don't have fifteen minutes when it comes to Arnoult, Sally. So tell Ludwig he'd better haul his ass over there and find out what the hell's going on."

"I did, sir. He left a minute ago."

"Good, update me every five."

"Yes, sir, anything else?"

"The GCL names, Sally, and stat."

*

Ludwig, meanwhile, pursued his officers through the same channels Sally had only to meet with the same results. So he tapped Officers Fleuter and Yearwood on the way out the door and sped with them to the condotel, confirming with Sally along the way that he'd keep his lapel mic on at all times. Twenty minutes later, he walked past a front desk under normal operation and directed his men to room twenty-two thirty on the second floor by instructing them to take the stairs while he took the elevator. Something was terribly askew. He felt it in the air and in the prickle on the back of his neck.

"Check everything along the way," he said. "Exits,

rails, windows, fire escapes. Eyes open."

Inside the elevator, Ludwig did the same by inspecting the camera, control panel, ceiling, and walls for tampering. He checked the maintenance hatch. Again, nothing out of the ordinary. He reconvened with his team in the hallway to find Chun missing from his post. They walked slowly down the corridor, examining the carpet, walls, doorframes, and handles of each apartment until they reached Arnoult's door.

Ludwig examined its exterior. There were no scratches or signs of illegal entry. He pressed his ear to it. No noise. Nothing. He knocked and got no response.

Pressing his mouth to the doorjamb, he whispered, "Sayles, Chun, you in there?"

Once more no answer came.

Ludwig handed Officer Fleuter a duplicate key as he and Officer Yearwood moved to the opposite side with arms extended, Glocks loaded. Fleuter knelt on the floor, inserted the card in the slot, and pushed open the door. For a moment, no one spoke until Ludwig quietly moaned, "Holy shit."

Back at CIA headquarters, Sally had updated Oscher every five minutes with whatever she'd heard from Ludwig's open mic. But when his expletive sounded, she'd stopped. "Frank, what's going on?"

"It's bad, Sally," he answered. "Best you call me because I need to talk to the boss directly."

Sally dialed him and transferred the call. Oscher jabbed the speaker button on the videophone and sternly asked, "What's going on?"

He heard Ludwig suck air through his teeth, then say, "I'm sending a stream now, sir, so you can see for yourself."

Oscher switched to video and what he saw was a massacre. Officer Albert Chun laid twisted facedown on the floor with a possible gunshot wound to the abdomen from which a pool of blood seeped into the beige carpet. Officer Connie Sayles was sprawled on her back with her gun thrown

212

some eight to ten feet. Her upper body bore a gaping chest wound.

As Ludwig panned the room with his camera, Oscher asked, "Christ, Frank, what the hell happened?"

"It seems room service delivered more than just breakfast and this is only the half of it."

"What?"

"One minute, sir, while I hand off this camera. Take it, Fleuter, and stick with me."

Ludwig now appeared in front of it.

"Sorry, sir. Ah, yes, as far as I can surmise, it appears that at oh seven hundred coffee was indeed delivered. As instructed, Officer Chun would have been at the door in the hallway and Officer Sayles in the room with Arnoult. Chun would have opened the door and followed the server in."

Ludwig and camera moved to the table.

"Sayles, if she'd been standing here, would have supervised the server's actions. Arnoult may or may not have been seated there. It's hard to tell because of how we found him."

"Meaning?"

"Meaning? Better to show you, sir."

Oscher followed Ludwig through an open door into the connecting bedroom. There, face down but half on the bed laid Arnoult. He'd been shot in the back of the head at point blank range. His skull was split open and its milky gray contents were strewn across the quilted coverlet. Blood was splattered everywhere.

"I believe Arnoult fled the dining area, sir, and made it this far before being terminated."

Oscher studied the scene, asking to have the camera held on Arnoult for some time. He then commanded Fleuter to move around the room and return to the living area.

"What can you surmise about Sayles and Chun?"

"Well, here...," Ludwig said. "Fleuter, can you hold it over Sayles's body please? We need a close up. Thank you.

213

As I was saying, here the attack is frontal, suggesting she stood in stance, arms extended, weapon up. It looks like the force of the shot knocked her back. Raise the camera, please? This would have thrown both arms wide with the right hand hanging onto her weapon until floor impact."

Ludwig pointed. The camera panned.

"Okay," Oscher said. "But that would have been one hell of a blast, Frank."

"Definitely," he agreed while stepping up to the dining room table.

"Now it's highly probable that while Sayles was being attacked, Arnoult shoved the table forward to run for cover, causing the coffee pot to fall to the floor because you can see from the carpet's imprint that the table's moved. Close up, please, Fleuter."

"And what about Chun?"

"Well, I'm thinking he was eliminated first, then Sayles as she approached from the bedroom or bathroom, and last Arnoult at the table. I say that because Chun appears to have been in motion at the time of impact. Perhaps he was moving toward the shooter when hit, forcing his body to rotate. Here, let me see if we can show you how he landed. Yearwood, could you raise Chun's right hip? Careful, just like that, thank you."

Oscher watched as the camera moved in.

Ludwig continued, "As you can see, sir, his weapon is still in hand suggesting that as he rotated, he brought his arm across his body and fell on top of it."

"Let's go back to the blasts. There had to be at least three. Surely someone heard something."

"They did not. It was business as usual down in the lobby. The stairwell, elevator, and hallway all empty on arrival. No one even peeking out their door. This was stealth. Clean and quiet with a maximum of three high-powered shots, because neither Sayles or Chun returned fire. The shooter must of used a silencer."

Or silenced bullets, Oscher said to himself.

"Find any casings?"

"No, sir, but then we've only just gotten here. We'll do our sweep and if anything shows up, I'll let you know."

"Thank you, Frank, but dig deep, okay? These are *our* people. Document everything. Photographs, particles, etcetera. You know the drill."

"Yes, sir."

"And Frank? Fix it so Homeland has a chance at finding Arnoult's body. They've been ripping the city of Buffalo apart ever since he disappeared. We owe them that much for our interference."

"I will, sir.

Oscher disconnected from Ludwig and sat with his head bowed, allowing himself a moment of silence to pray for his team. Already he knew who killed them and ballistics would prove it yet again. The Bratva, he was certain, had found Arnoult.

Where the hell are you guys coming from? Oscher wondered. *And how many of you are out there?*

Oscher rubbed his forehead, thinking that Dane and Bergan had better complete their missions and fast. One more officer lost or silenced bullet showing up on his turf was more than he could stand. He needed this operation shut down fast.

27
Folies Bergère
Paris, France

Fanny slipped mid-show into the Folies Bergère's theater as an assemblage of bare breasts, visible amongst the feathers and rhinestones of a dozen or more of Paris's most beautiful women, paraded across the stage.

"Yip! Yip! Lee! Lee!" the adorned ladies sounded, their outstretched arms linked one over the next and their legs kicked high in unison.

Their squeals grew louder until a bosom much more voluptuous and decorated emerged onto the stage. The star had arrived. She raised her arms and slid down into a full split. From there she laid back and kicked her legs wildly in the air to expose a pair of ruffled, ruby-red panties before somersaulting to stand as regally as before, much to a riotous applause of the audience.

Fanny enjoyed her antics, then set to scanning the room for Simone. He found him seated next to Glory, who was wearing a chiffon halter dress in the richest shade of teal. Her shoulders brushed Simone's on occasion as they smiled to one another. He found a seat nearby. Within minutes, Glory excused herself. After a short wait, Fanny followed suit into the lobby to wait until she reappeared. When she did, she hesitated, perhaps from surprise, before gliding toward him.

"I can't stay because he's probably timing me," she announced, stirring the air around him. "But I do have something. There's a shipment tonight. FTA France."

"What time?"

"Ten-fifteen."

"That's in an hour, Glory."

"Yes, I just found out. But if you check your phone, you'll see the number of this place."

His first impulse was to challenge her but he said nothing, putting his hand to his heart instead to express that he was touched by her efforts.

She looked away. "I suggest you go. My uncle is leaving as soon as the show is over, so you haven't much time. I can create a delay if you need it."

He nodded and moved his hand to her shoulder.

"Don't," she said sadly, shrugging him off. "I am as much a traitor as a fool."

Fanny couldn't argue, so grateful he was for her treachery. "You won't be sorry," was all he could say to comfort her.

She stared at him with what now appeared only as sorrow. "Will you contact me after? You know, to let me know what happened?"

"Yes, but I don't have your number. You called from a house phone, remember?"

She reached out to him for his cell phone, palm up, fingers wiggling.

He handed it to her and watched as she dialed her own number and held it toward his face. From the interior of her clutch, her cell rang as the number registered on his display. She ended the call and handed it back to him. "And what if I don't hear from you, what then? You never told me where are you staying."

"No, I didn't."

"I just gave you my private number, so the least you can do is give me the name of your hotel. What if I can't reach you by phone? What if I need to see you? Or is this strictly a one-way business we're running here, you and me?" she asked growing angry.

Fanny thought about lying to her yet again, but in the awkward silence regrettably answered, "Grand Hotel des Saints."

She took a final look at him and parted without as much as a backward glance.

At the curb, Fanny removed the battery from his cell phone, rendering it useless to any tap she or anyone might soon initiate. He then hailed a cab.

"Transport Services, Charles de Gaulle airport, please."

En route, Fanny dismissed the flurry of nerves growing in his stomach and instead checked from his UMPC the flight schedule and gate location for the outbound ten-fifteen FTA carrier to be sure it hadn't changed. He then reviewed, again, the CIA's aerial maps of its baggage claim and loading zones. Once there, he talked his way past the gate as if late for work and ran to the carrier's transport hangar. He found the employee storage room, grabbed a cargo-loader's jumpsuit, and put it on. He next stole a badge hanging from a corkboard and slipped it over his head. He sprinted across the tarmac, catching up with a struggling transport worker.

"Ah, bon, let me help you," Fanny offered as the two of them aligned one of the crates on the trolley. "Are you going to verify this last shipment so we can clear the runway?"

"Not me, that would be Marcel," the man said, pointing to the slender man who was leaning against a stack of empty pallets while smoking a cigarette.

"Bon," Fanny said enthusiastically and then helped him load the crates onto a waiting plane before lightly sprinting back to the man, who grew increasingly nervous with his approach.

"Marcel, my God, sorry I'm late. Simone sent me," Fanny apologized.

Marcel nodded, saying, "I see" in a way that undermined the casual comfort in which he expressed it. It might have been the narrowing of his lips but Fanny sensed he'd raised the man's suspicion. After a long drag on his smoke, Marcel grumbled, "I need help before he gets here. What time is he due?"

Fanny checked his watch and told him within the half hour.

"Shit, we barely have time." Marcel looked at the transporter. "What is taking that lug so long to clear out?"

The worker wheeled the trolley back into the hangar and disappeared.

Marcel flicked his spent cigarette onto the tarmac, turned to Fanny and ordered, "Let's go, but you carry the ladder."

Fanny grabbed it and followed him out to a sleek Cessna Citation to set it up at the wing where Marcel indicated, watching as the Frenchman climbed up and opened the inspection panel above the fuel tank. From his coverall, he pulled a rubberized package, dropped it inside the tank, and attached its tether securely to the fuel cap. He then instructed Fanny to follow him to the other side where they did the same.

Marcel gave the pilot a two-thumbs-up as Fanny retreated with the ladder. The pilot, however, did not engage the engines. Instead, he sat with a look of suspense on his face.

Fanny looked to Marcel. "What's happening?"

"I don't really know but we will soon find out," he said, pointing as Simone, with another man trailing, walked briskly toward them.

Simone jabbed a finger at Fanny. "Who are you?"

"I was sent, sir."

Marcel's mouth drew into a thin smile.

219

"By whom?"

The man behind Simone stepped out with his gun raised to Fanny's chest to stand between them. Fanny put his hands in the air. "Now hold on. I was sent here by someone you know, a certain heavily invested party."

Simone glared at him while addressing the man, "Riland."

As he did, Fanny lowered his arms into a defenseless posture, daring Riland to take the shot against him. Riland released the safety of his 9mm. It made a soft click.

Simone reached into the pocket of his suit coat and, to Fanny's surprise, removed a small ball-peen hammer. He placed his other hand on Riland's shoulder and gently moved him aside. "There is *no one* who would have sent you, so I will ask you one more time, who are you and why are you here?"

Fanny swallowed.

Simone twisted the hammer around in his hand, waiting. But when Fanny failed to reply, he let it slide down his palm to swing it loosely from the sway of his wrist and said, "I can kill you with this in any number of ways."

Suddenly the hammer flew upward. Fanny ducked to the left but failed to keep it from hitting his jaw. He then dove to the ground, pulled out his own weapon, and fired. Riland growled in pain as Simone shouted for him to finish the job, but he was slow to react, which allowed Fanny to pop off a couple more shots while rolling toward Marcel. His first bullet missed the man entirely but his second found Riland's throat. In his final rotation, Fanny turned his weapon on Marcel, who dropped without hesitation.

Fanny pulled himself up the pallets as Simone came at him with the retrieved hammer in hand. He threw it again and the next thing Fanny knew his Glock was flying up in the air. Simone had expertly pried it away from his grasp with a flick of the small tool. Simone then landed penetrating jabs to his cheek, nose, and jaw. Fanny tried hitting in return, but his right hand was smarting too much, so he decked him in the chin with the heel of his left while thrusting a knee into his groin. Simone doubled over. Fanny pounced on him by folding himself over Simone's head and back to lift him upside down from around the waist and pinning his head between his legs. He then pile-drove Simone headfirst into the tarmac.

The pilot looked on in horror as he engaged the Cessna's engines. Fanny ran for the ladder to race back to the wing. He opened the panel as quickly as he could and removed the fuel cap, taking with it the attached package. The pilot banged on the window as Fanny scrambled down the ladder and ran back to Riland. There he retrieved the 9mm and a set of car keys and sprinted off the tarmac.

Fanny tore through the empty transport hangar to look for the other worker but couldn't find him, so he headed outside to where Simone's luxurious, dark green Citroen Metropolis waited. He slid into it and spun away, throwing Riland's 9mm and the diamonds onto the passenger seat.

About ten miles outside of the airport, Fanny pulled off the A15 onto the shoulder of the road. He took a deep breath and rubbed his right hand, hoping it wasn't broken. He then reached over to the weapon to see, once again, the familiar engraving. Bratva. Riland was Bratva. They were everywhere. Had anyone other than the ones he'd killed seen him come or go? Had he been followed? Time was no longer on his side of that he was sure. He needed to contact Oscher immediately.

Through his UMPC he typed, "URGENT. Simone + 2 dead. CDG grd transport. Shipment delayed. Have sample. FTA Flt 808, aborted at 2215. Pilot involved. 9mm Baikal in hand/Bratva. Orders?"

Within seconds, Oscher responded, "Find Nanterre."

Fanny panicked, not really knowing how he'd find the prime minister at this hour or where he'd be tonight of all nights. He soon realized the answer was right in front of him. He rolled down all the windows, hoping the traffic noise would mask his voice as he hit the Bluetooth button of the car's phone, and said, "Nanterre."

Nothing happened.

"Prime minister."

And again, nothing.

On the third try, he said, "PM."

The phone rang, a man answered and then paused, but Fanny didn't recognize the voice as Nanterre's so he proceeded with caution. "It's me, Riland," Fanny said as the wind and cars pass by. "There's been an accident."

"What kind of accident?"

Fanny cleared his throat. "Simone's hurt. I need the prime minister."

Fanny tooted the horn as another distraction and added, "Hurry."

Somewhere behind the man on the telephone, another person asked about the call to which the man told him. The other person barked instructions.

"Come to the garage," the man said and hung up.

Fanny then knew the bark belonged to Nanterre. But which garage? There were hundreds of them in Paris. So he again flipped through the car's address book. Nothing. And then he remembered. "Best of the Best," he said aloud, then corrected himself to "Meilleur" and up popped the automobile specialist. He followed the directions to the now familiar garage on Rue de Bac and pulled Simone's car up to its bay doors where a man stood on either side with them opened wide. Fanny shielded his face with a stiff wave to the man on his left.

"And here we go," he whispered.

In the back of the garage and beside an official

222

looking Renault, stood Nanterre now bathed in the harshness of the Citroen's headlights. Fanny eased the car forward as the doors closed behind him and the two men walked up on either side of the car. The prime minister shielded his eyes and with the other signaled at Fanny to shut the lights off. Fanny did not, even after killing the engine. As the two men approached, Fanny lifted the Baikal with his right hand, his Glock with his left, and crossed them over his chest. When they reached the driver's and passenger's windows, Fanny pulled both triggers, taking them out simultaneously. The prime minister squatted and did his best to crawl to safety.

Fanny lost sight of him momentarily, but once out of Simone's car, found Nanterre scrambling to the other side of the Renault. "Stop right there," he instructed with the Baikal pointed at the prime minister's backside.

Nanterre, still on hands and knees, straightened to raise both hands.

"Get up and turn around."

The prime minister obliged with hands still raised. "What do you want?" he asked, not recognizing Fanny as one of his own.

"You're moving shipments in and out of Paris," Fanny answered, stuffing his own gun into his coveralls. "I know because I just witnessed one and have evidence to prove it. So tell me...how many shipments a day do you make?"

"You are joking," Nanterre answered defiantly.

"Hardly, and to prove it, let me tell you from where your diamonds come. Popigai. You understand Popigai?"

Nanterre's eyes darted around the room in search of help or to find something, anything, to use in his defense.

Fanny held his stance, bearing down on him with Riland's pistol. "How many?" Fanny growled through clenched teeth.

"It depends," Nanterre answered.

"Ballpark it. Fifteen? Twenty?"

223

The prime minister wheezed.

Fanny sidestepped around Nanterre, and from behind, pressed the Baikal into the prime minister's right temple. "Do you recognize the feel of this gun? It's Russian and very, very special."

Nanterre squeezed his eyes shut and squelched a nonverbal response. Fanny sensed that he was about to make a desperate move at grabbing the gun, so he shifted to the left, confusing Nanterre and thwarting his actions.

"Nice try but you aren't going anywhere."

Nanterre reached out again, only this time he grabbed the Baikal with both hands. As he did, Fanny lifted it above their heads. The prime minister, however, was strong and brought the barrel back down, jamming it into his own mouth. They struggled. The prime minister tightened his grip. He then overlapped his trigger finger with Fanny's and squeezed. *Fzzpt.* The sound of a silenced bullet escaped. Fanny fell back in surprise, knowing that if he hadn't had his head over Nanterre's shoulder, he too could have been taken out.

"Holy shit!" he shouted as his mind skittered. What just happened? Nanterre killed himself? And because of what? The Baikal? The Russian mafia? The Queen Bee? Fanny looked at the prime minister and then at Riland's gun, making a decision. Suicide it is.

In a rush, he wiped the Russian 9mm of his prints before pressing Nanterre's back to it and then removed a few parts from Simone's Citroen to make it look as if it was in for repairs. After that, he removed his bloodied jumpsuit with the intent of disposing it in butcher shop's waste bin next door, and headed for the train that would carry him back to the Grand Hotel des Saints.

His adrenaline shifted into a lower gear as soon as he entered his room, that is until he saw the shake of his hands, a clear reminder that guns like the Baikal belonged to the Russian Bratva. To Fanny, nothing spoke more clearly.

224

Simone and Nanterre were more than deeply involved. They were near the helm. He needed to go out again to find Glory for she would surely be dead before night's end. But first he needed to see what was in the package he'd taken from the plane and notify Oscher.

He ripped it open over the bed. Diamonds of every hue and size spilled out. Their value overbearing. Fanny moved them around before logging onto his UMPC again to contact Oscher.

"URGENT. Have samples. 2 dead, including Nanterre by suicide at garage, Rue de Bac. All Bratva. Must secure Milan."

He collected the diamonds along his other things while waiting for Oscher to respond. The wait wasn't long. "Sending Bac team now. Abort and come home."

"But I'm not done here," he shouted at the message, knowing however, that he wasn't in any position to argue. He then added, "Okay, okay, Oscher, I'm outta here. But you better find Milan or she's as good as dead."

He tapped the top of his device closed and slipped it into his duffle bag. Grabbing that, he threw it over his shoulder and opened the door. There, the hard nose of a gun pressed into his forehead.

28
Drone It
Popigai Crater

"You show me?" Rebe asked Eric. "You show me how to do, Doc Knudson?"

"Da, I show," Eric told her and invited her out into the open field as they tromped over thinly-iced ground, listening to the crunch of it under their feet as they ventured further away from the narrowing river.

Rebe tried to keep up but her thick coat and heavy work boots slowed her and made her giggle. Regardless, Eric pressed on because of how she'd responded earlier to his help with her canoe. Any assistance he gave her now would only embarrass her again.

His previous blunder had happened very early when she'd indicated she wanted to show him some old mines. They'd taken her canoe, a simple dugout of sturdy wood, and while going down a lesser-known tributary of the larger Reka Anabar, she'd stopped to collect tiny, copper-colored fish for their night's dinner.

She'd stood to step forward so that she could tie a rope around a large boulder that she laughingly called a Siberian anchor. As she did, the canoe shifted and Eric, quick to grab at her hips, found her slapping at him with a series of quick flicks. Her face red.

"Doc, Doc, no, Rebe fine! You sit. I catch food."

And so he'd sat as she proceeded to tie the canoe, tipping it as before, but steadying it with her other and more obviously practiced left foot. Now, several hours later, she wanted to learn how to fly the drone. How could he have resisted?

He removed the Night Spyder T-2000 from its tube, unfolded the blades, and set it on the ground. He next configured his laptop so that the Spyder's front and rear lenses projected its images on the screen, picked up the remote, and handed it to Rebe.

"Okay, Rebe, take this. This is the roller ball. You move it this way to move it right and left, forward and back."

"And this one?" Rebe asked.

"Don't touch that one, Rebe. It'll self destruct," Eric showed by throwing his fingers wide as if it had exploded.

"Fire button," Rebe said as a matter of fact.

He watched her work the controls as the drone lifted and fell, crashed, then lifted and fell until she had a modicum of command over the craft. He stepped behind one of the boulders with the laptop so that she couldn't see him and made her do it all again. This time she flew it over his head as he watched the shaky images jump around his screen. Finally she steadied it, before diving it into a soft pillow of snow.

They spent the early afternoon together while he did maneuvers, took photos, and sent them to Edmond. He wanted to document the terrain he'd be traveling the next morning that would then be in near darkness. With the light fading, he decided to pack it up.

Rebe, he figured, must have had enough, too, because she suddenly asked, "Hungry, Doc? Nesutak make special meal for you. Good protein. You like."

"Yes, I am hungry, Rebe," he told her as they crunched their way back to the canoe and rowed to their cabin.

Inside, Nesutak stirred a large pot of broth that boiled

atop of a stovepipe oven in the center of the room. The top plate glowed as Nesutak called Eric over and dropped in a block of tofu.

"Watch, watch," he indicated to Eric, who peered into the boil just as the old man released the school of tiny fish that Rebe had collected earlier. While the hot broth churned, the fish swam in spastic desperation and bumped and thrashed against the block of creamy, white tofu to burrow inside until their tails twitched to a stop. A few hardier fish crawled into the same hole.

Rebe explained. "They find cool place to go inside tofu. We eat. Very special."

After several more seconds, Nesutak scooped out the tofu with a large ladle and placed it on a worn cutting board. Here, he cut it lengthwise and wrapped each finger-long stick inside steamed cabbage leaves. He placed two cabbage wraps into a bowl and spooned broth over them. Handing Eric a set of chopsticks and his serving, Nesutak smiled his toothy grin. Eric hesitated only to hear Rebe giggle.

"You no like?" Rebe asked shyly.

Eric smiled and said, "Oh, I like very much. Like you said, good protein. It makes me very happy."

They ate quietly, slurping their broth and biting into the cabbage wraps until they were gone. After dinner, Eric excused himself and ventured outside to a rustic table where he sat staring up at the starry sky, thinking of how Fanny was in Paris, probably eating foie gras while he was eating tofu stuffed with live fish. His thoughts were broken by Nestuak's and Rebe's laughter from inside the cabin through the microphone in his ushanka. They must have been discussing the night's meal. He squeezed the snap head off, then booted up his UMPC, and logged on to find a disturbing message from Edmund. Seems Fanny had indeed been busy.

Simone was dead. Nanterre, too. By suicide? How the hell did that happen? Plus Fanny had killed four others, Bratva no less, just to save himself and now he was told to abort and come home? Edmund didn't elaborate, he only asked for an update from Popigai, so Eric responded with "Preliminary run today. Will begin morning survey of mines. Drones handy. Any more on Bergan?"

Without word by early morning from Edmund, Eric busied himself with the inspection of the backpack he'd prepared. Inside was one of his laptops and a drone. Nestled around them was the other necessary equipment he'd need, along with a few new items that Rebe had added: oilskins filled with sardines, dried fruits, a fishing line, and instant coffee. He left by way of the Pakboat he'd found inside one of his crates. The kayak, when assembled, measured thirteen feet, five inches and was light as air.

He rowed for several miles, checking every now and again for voices through the microphone in his hat. Nothing. He rowed some more. Finally he came upon the embankment where Rebe had taken him and that led to the first of several old mines nearby. He pulled his kayak ashore and walked the quarter mile toward its location. Nothing. No sounds. No motion of any kind detected. He decided that the mines were indeed abandoned and went back to the water to travel a few more miles. As he approached the next set of mines that Rebe had mentioned, he started to hear some scraping noises. He stopped again and walked cautiously toward the sound. When he closed in, he hid behind a boulder. It sounded as if someone was pounding the hardened earth. There wasn't any digging, just some scraping and the dull thud of a repeated thump.

Eric pulled out the drone and released it high above the area, filming as he did to watch from his laptop. There was other movement further away. Headlamps. Many of them, perhaps thirty or more, coming from single beams attached to the heads of men that looked like they were going into the mine.

He picked up Russian orders being shouted through the earflap of the hat, "Davay! Poydem! C'mon!" *Let's go!*

There's work to do!

Eric raised the drone higher and thanked the darkness for its cover. He followed the men's march down to the last man to disappear. He was in the process of bringing the drone in when he heard a crunch behind him and turned as the sudden drop of a wooden shovel handle crashed into the side of his head.

When Eric woke, two men were dragging him toward a small flatbed truck. His hands and feet were bound by tape. Inside his mouth, they'd shoved a bandana and tied it in place with a second. He was tossed like a potato sack into the truck and landed with a thud and muffled groan. One man got in the truck bed with him, the other started the engine and sped them away from the mine.

They drove for some time. Eric wasn't sure of the duration because of his repeated nodding out, delivered from the butt end of a baton. But he did happen to open his eyes when they finally stopped near what appeared to be several rows of buildings. Eric figured this was where the Japanese must have once lived, worked, and died excavating the mines during the war. Again the two men dragged him. They then deposited him face down on the floor of someone's office.

They said in Russian, "Colonel, we found this man. He had this."

Eric heard his backpack being dropped on the desk.

"He had this too, sir," the second man added, depositing what Eric believed was his drone.

The colonel cleared his throat and asked the men, "Where did you find him?"

"Behind a boulder," the first man answered.

"At the mine?"

"Yes, Colonel. We'd just dropped off the crew. Vlad went for a walk to piss, maybe, I don't know, but he found him and brought him to me."

Finally some names, Eric said to himself. But was this man Colonel Rabokov? The one who partnered with

Niembriev?

Vlad spoke up, "I was looking for mosses, sir. For tea."

"And you found him instead?"

"Yes, sir. I saw a light from behind the boulder and when I went around it to see what it was, there he was with his computer. So I hit him with my shovel. That's when that device fell from the sky near Yugov."

Yugov joined in. "It almost hit me."

"Did you question him?" the colonel asked.

"No, sir," they answered in unison.

"He was unconscious, sir," Yugov added.

"Good, good," the colonel said. "Put him in the chair."

They followed orders by picking him up and pushing him into a chair to face the colonel.

"Remove the gag."

They did.

"And the hat and gloves."

They removed them and laid them on the desk near his backpack.

"So," the colonel said to Eric. "What brings you here?"

Turning to his men, he squinted his eyes and asked, "What is that, gentlemen?"

The two men looked at each other and shrugged.

"Don't you hear it? Where is it coming from?"

Yugov picked up the hat and held the earflap to his own ear, saying, "Here, Colonel Rabokov, it's wired."

Bingo, Eric registered. *Rabokov.*

Rabokov snatched the hat from Yugo and looked at Eric. He placed his hands flat on his desk. Sarcastically and with a tip of his head to his men, he said, "He's a spy."

Yugov agreed while picking up the backpack. "And he has all of this."

Rabokov crossed his arms over a firm chest. "Yes, he

does, Yugov."

"Who are you?" he demanded.

Eric weighed his options before telling them that he spoke only a little Russian. And then in English he continued, "My name's Dr. Richard Knudson. I'm an American mineralogist and I've come here to verify radiation levels in the soil."

"Radiation," Rabokov flatly repeated.

"Yes, sir, radiation. Your men have made a serious mistake."

"You have identification?" Rabokov spoke slowly in English.

"Yes, sir, in my jacket."

"Vlad, bring it to me."

Vlad rummaged through Eric's pockets and produced a plastic pouch containing Eric's papers. He handed it to Rabokov. Inside, Rabokov found his passport, corporate identification card, and other various travel documents that verified him as Knudson, although Rabokov appeared to not believe them.

"Your Russian good enough to understand 'kol'tso smerti', Dr. Knudson?"

Eric indicated he didn't but the guards did and they chuckled.

"No matter, you will find out soon enough."

He then addressed the two men in Russian, "Take him to K Barrack."

They again lifted Eric and dragged him out the door. When he was deposited in K Barrack, they removed the tape from his hands and feet and replaced it with chains. They pointed to a bed for him to lie down on and chained him to its frame.

"No worries," Yugov said to Eric. "Breakfast, lunch, whatever you like. We bring like nice hotel, no?"

Eric watched as Yugov slapped Vlad on the back. They both laughed and turned to leave the building.

"I have to go to the bathroom!" Eric yelled at their backs.

"The bathroom!" he said louder, pointing to his groin.

Vlad turned back, pointed to the pan under the bed, and then walked with Yugov out the door.

29
Kol'tso Smerti
Popigai Crater - K Barrack

Eric remained chained to the bed all day, having had only a single meal of creamed potatoes with bits of what looked like chipped beef, until the men he'd watched earlier go into the mines returned. They entered K Barrack exhausted but already showered. Some staggered by Eric while others peeked at him in passing. The men to Eric's immediate right and left looked at him at length but didn't speak, as if waiting for him to break the silence.

A guard walked up to Eric and shouted "Mind your own business!" He then pointed his rifle first at the one man and then the other and said, "You know the rules."

Both men laid back and pulled their blankets up to their chins. The man to his right rolled over but the man to his left faced Eric with apologetic eyes then pulled his blanket over his head. Within the hour, a buzzer sounded that abruptly woke everyone who'd fallen asleep and greatly disturbed the rest. Tension in the room rose as Colonel Rabokov framed the doorway. Eric didn't know what to do, so he simply laid there, attentive.

Rabokov, meanwhile, walked down the center aisle and rapped the side of the bed frames of about fifteen men, including Eric's. "Take him, take that one, and this one. This one and this one," Rabokov said in Russian as he banged and ventured deeper into the barrack.

The guards wrestled the men up and out of their bunks, forcing them to stand near the aisle. Some trembled visibly.

Rabokov stopped in front of a frail Japanese man who was holding his stomach. "What's the matter, Shenji? You don't like our little game? You maybe want to see the nurse instead? Are you sick Shenji?"

The man shook his head no, keeping his head down as he choked back tears.

"Maybe you'll get lucky again tonight, huh, Shenji-san? Because you are one fortunate guy," Rabokov teased wickedly before he commanded his men to line up those selected, place black hoods over their heads, and shackle them together.

"Let's go," Rabokov said.

They exited the building with their right hands placed on the right shoulder of the man in front of them. Eric's blind fear intensified, and from the grip of the man behind him, he understood there would be reason for it.

They walked several hundred feet before entering another building and stepped over its threshold. He could hear and feel the guards shoving some of the men ahead, telling them, "Here! Here! You, hold here."

When one of the guards touched Eric, he jumped slightly but was slapped and ordered to back up against what felt like a hand railing. He complied. The hoods were removed and Eric could now see that they were in a large room and that the railing, as he had correctly identified, formed a circle in the center of it.

Rabokov watched as his guards chained them to a central lock in the rail. Then Rabokov pointed to a burly one who up until now had only stood at attention by the door and said, "Okay, let's do this."

The man stepped forward and pushed a cart that held many types of pistols as the other guards aimed their own at the chained men. The man walked by and handed out one gun per man. When Eric was given his, he looked at it and saw that he held a Gsh-18, a Russian invention forceful enough to penetrate Kevlar. He considered aiming it at Rabokov and shooting him point blank. Then rethought his options, wondering what the hell was about to happen.

"Gentlemen," Rabokov started. "Some of you already know the rules but we have a new member, a Docktor Richard Knudson. He does not know this game."

Rabokov walked over to Eric and smiled.

"It is called kol'tso smerti, Docktor, or in English, the ring of death. It is a simple game of roulette, you see. There are fifteen of you and each of you has a loaded gun. Yes, loaded, but only one of you has an actual bullet. We will see who that is in just a moment."

Eric held his eyes at Rabokov's back as he walked away, thinking, *is this for real?* But when he looked beyond the colonel, he saw that the guards, all five of them, were now placing bets on the table and calling out numbers and names. The gun suddenly felt very heavy in his hand. He understood it was possibly live and that he could kill the man in front of him just as easily as he could be killed from the man behind. Eric calculated the odds against the turn of the day's events. He felt fairly certain that the gun behind him would not be holding the only bullet because they had yet to fully question him. This had to be pure posturing on the part of the great colonel. It just simply had to be. Or was it? Was it more possible that these Russians were crazy enough to think, "What the hell? Get rid of the doctor and get rid of our new problem." Simple as that?

Oh, it is definitely possible, but will they?

Eric placed a bet of his own that they weren't so willing to remove him. Instead, their brazenness would be better served by putting the only bullet in his gun to kill the man in front of him either as a lesson or a warning. He felt certain that if someone had to die today, it wouldn't be him because any other scenario just didn't compute.

The guards finished placing their bets as Rabokov counted the money and said, "This is good." He waved the stack of rubles in front of the chained men then laid the money on the table.

Several prisoners began to weep.

"Come now, ladies," Rabokov derided as he stood. "This is no time for hysterics. Someone could get hurt unnecessarily. Now, please, calm yourselves."

Laughing, he looked to his men, who on cue joined him. He stopped them with an open palm and commanded, "Your weapons, please, gentlemen. Raise them high."

The men raised their guns to the head of the man in front of them, some of them shakily, others with resolve.

"On the count of three, you will fire. Anyone who does not will be shot. Are you ready, moi deti?" Rabokov told them by enunciating each word slowly and calling them children.

Eric felt the cool nozzle from behind press into the base of his skull and understood immediately that whoever was holding that gun was doing it with confidence. Best he did the same. This was do-or-die and he'd be damned if he was going to show even the slightest sign of weakness. So much had come to pass and here it was, the defining moment. *At least it'll be a quick death,* he told himself. And, to the man in front of him he apologized, *I'm sorry, but an even quicker one for you.*

No other thoughts formed as the sound of his own breathing consumed the black void. He braced himself with his eyes glued to the back of the head of the man in front of him. He gritted his teeth and as Rabokov counted down, his growl grew louder. At the count of three, fifteen guns sounded but no one fell, although a burst of blood sprayed out from a man about six spots ahead of Eric. Slowly Eric moved his eyes to witness the scene while Shenji, three men behind him, wailed. The guards hooted as Rabokov checked the betting sheet.

"Well done, Tomas!" Rabokov announced.

The chained men, however, were hardly aware anymore with most now either squatting on the floor or bent over the rail in tears. A few were vomiting. Eric was the only man holding his position and the last to lower his gun. His stare was hard and it took him a while to simply close his eyes as a flood of questions engulfed him and his body shook from the strain.

How insane is this? Have you no decency at all? he asked of Rabokov. *Is this for your betting amusement and torture only? And what has become of me? How could I have survived pulling that trigger on an innocent man? It would have been better to pull it on myself. This can't go on. I've got to figure a way out of this because this…this…is barbaric! What kind of animal are you, colonel?*

Eric turned to look into the eyes of Rabokov, who was now surveying the room. His answer came from the enigmatic smile that beamed back. The colonel had accomplished his intended goal. Every person present was and should be afraid of him. He had the power to do as he pleased and he did. But Eric knew that every man, including Rabokov, had a master. *Who is it, colonel? Who's yours? Major General Gregor Niembriev? Madame Corrine DuBethonee? And when, where, and how can we meet?*

The men were marched back to K Barrack with some having to be half carried, especially Shenji, who flopped in his captor's arms after falling unconscious. The smell of vomit and urine permeated the night air. Eric walked half dazed, so deep in thought he was, following the man in front of him. When they returned to the barrack and were locked in, another guard entered and stood by Eric's bed.

"I believe this is yours," he said in perfect English as he handed Eric the ushanka hat that was now ripped apart, its leather torn and hanging in places where the microphone had been removed. "Very ingenious, you mineralogists. But we

238

wonder what noise does radiation make that you would need such a special hat?"

Eric took the hat and laid it on his chest. They eyed one another. The guard then turned and bumped into the bed behind him. The man lying there reached up in self-defense, brushing the guard's left hip with his hand. The guard turned back to Eric. Eric shook his head but the guard hit him in the stomach anyway. As Eric grimaced in pain, the man again reached up and then quickly laid back down, throwing his blanket over his head. The guard left.

When everything quieted, the man peeked from under his blanket at Eric. Their eyes locked as the man slowly stuck out his tongue. On it was a key. He plucked it off and unlocked and relocked his bed chain. He smiled and handed it to Eric.

"You're a thief," Eric whispered.

"And a good one," the man replied with a heavy accent. "But even I am too afraid to do anything more. You keep it. Use it when you can."

"You don't want to escape?"

"Certainly, so maybe you'll find a way for that to happen. But I am a thief not a killer. I watched you. You didn't blink pulling that trigger. That means, you're not as afraid as I am to take a life. I can only hope that you will find a way out of here soon because I do not wish to be the man in front of you the next time they put a gun in your hands."

Eric watched the man disappear again under his blanket and wondered just how much trust he should place on him. Was this a set up? Was he a snitch? Eric decided there must be some truth to the honor amongst thieves, so he stuck the key like a chaw of tobacco between his cheek and gum. There it rested, unlike Eric, who slept with the caution of a soldier at war.

30
The Rude Awakening
Somewhere outside Paris

The air was hot and thick, like the stagnate kind you find inside a hotel's laundry room. Its dry, mustiness cast Fanny into a hacking spell that as he coughed, muffled against the wide tape covering his mouth. When he finally caught his breath, he dropped his head to his chest to retrace what he could remember.

I was taken by gunpoint. Check.

Russian Baikal to be exact by a goon much bigger and meaner than me.

I was put into a car, back seat, and blindfolded. Hands, feet, mouth duct taped and pushed to the floorboard.

I was driven approximately forty-five minutes at what? About forty miles per hour, for how long? About twenty minutes.

We stopped twice for traffic lights. The first time turning left and the second right. And there were three more for stop signs.

Which way from there? Think, Fanny. Any turn at those stop signs? Yes. Left at the first and then straight at the second and third. Check. No, wait. There was a roundabout somewhere.

Then we were on a highway of some sort, going, say, sixty miles per hour for fifteen or so. Okay. Then off and back into a developed area. Where again we turned right, left and then left.

That all took about another ten minutes or less at maybe forty miles per hour. No, probably thirty-five and puts me roughly thirty-three miles from my hotel to either the southwest or northeast.

Fanny blamed the blindfold for his disorientation and bucked again against his restraints until the sickening squeak of someone rising from a metal chair opposite caught his attention. He wasn't alone. The approaching footsteps fell: one, two, three, four, five, six. Whomever it was had traveled from about eighteen feet away. He raised his head, throwing his nose into the air as the smell hit him, that dank waft of cigarettes that permeated everything from his black leather jacket and saddle-soaped boots to his breath. It was the goon.

Fanny immediately tucked his chin so that the guy couldn't get an easy shot. The goon, instead, ripped the tape from his mouth, taking with it some stubble. A painful tingle took its place. Fanny's heart pounded in his chest, his ears. He yearned to kick out but couldn't.

"What the hell?" Fanny snarled through the hurt.

The goon turned and shuffled toward the door.

In the darkness of his blindfold, Fanny counted his steps while returning to recapture the events up to this point. *How did the goon look? Big and square. And the driver? Bald. What was he was wearing? Also leather. And the blindfold after it was put on? Soft, like a necktie.*

How many steps has the goon now taken? Five.

How did the four-door, black sedan smell? Cigarettes like the goon. And the carpet? The seat? Like filthy fiber and old cowhide.

Eight steps.

What did I hear along the way? Trains? Trucks? Cars. Lots of cars. What about horns or bells and whistles? Think, Fanny, it all means something. It all adds up.

Ten.

241

The sound of a deadbolt slid open, the door swung in.

No fresh air, making it an interior door about thirty feet away.

The room was taking shape.

Fanny asked, "Where the hell am I?"

He got no answer except for the sound of two sets of feet. The goon with the heavier boot step. And the other?

Oh, I know the other. Sure, stilettos and the only person who knew where I was going in the first place.

The goon removed Fanny's blindfold, but before making eye contact with either of them, Fanny squeezed his eyes shut, pursed his lips, and asked, "For god's sake, Glory, why?"

A hard hit landed across his chin. Spittle flew from his mouth and his head swung wildly into his right shoulder. Caught off guard, Fanny realized that if it hadn't have been for the padded shoulder of his own jacket, his neck would have snapped. He dropped his head again to his chest, letting the blood drip onto his shirt and willing his breathing to slow. The thump in his head, however, grew.

Glory spoke with disdain. "You killed my uncle, Fanny, and the prime minister. Six men, six! But not one of them, not even the prime minister, was as important to me and my family as my uncle."

Fanny kept his head down.

"Do you understand?" she asked, her voice escalating. She commanded the goon to lift Fanny's head to her. "Do...you...under...stand, Monsieur Bergan?"

Fanny peered into her angry brown eyes. "No, Glory. I do not. Why don't you help me?"

She exhaled heavily, throwing her arms into the air. "You know exactly what I am talking about. You came to me remember? You stalked me. You tricked me!"

Fanny interrupted. "Yes I did, Glory, and you gave your uncle up to me, do you remember that? Or was that some sort of trick of your own?"

"I gave you nothing. My uncle was there to kill you, you idiot. What do you think, hmmm? That we are so weak, my uncle and me? My family? Or do you think it's just me who would fall for your clumsy charm or be so much in love with your friend that I'd defy everyone so completely, huh?"

"I guess not, Glory, which means you played the both of us."

"Ah, so now you see the bigger picture of the much larger world out there. Of course I played you but then you underestimated us, didn't you? We're far more strong and determined than you can imagine. We are people descended by gods," she declared.

"And ruled by a Queen Bee…Madam DuBethonee," Fanny stated, underscoring her rising anger.

Glory hissed through clenched teeth.

Fanny continued, "Oh, I know about her, Glory. Madame Corrine DuBethonee a.k.a. the Butcher for Bethonee. We all do. But you? You outsmarted us, Glory. You're no pawn, no damsel in distress, are you? No, you're as involved in the Popigai diamond trade as your uncle."

Glory stood with her back to him, nodding her head repeatedly.

"So what's your part in all of this?" Fanny asked. "Do you bring the diamonds into Paris and then fly them into the United States hidden inside wings and cavities? Do you bring them into New York? D.C.? Miami? Of course you do. But where else do you have ties besides Russia, Glory? Geneva? London? India, maybe?"

Glory squinted her eyes at Fanny. Her growl was low. "Who are you?" she asked, "and who do you and Eric really work for?"

"Just like that?"

"Just like that," she said, snapping two fingers.

Fanny licked his bloody lip and sucked the blood into his mouth to mix it with new phlegm. He spit the wad toward the goon. The goon took two steps forward and clocked him between the eyes. Fanny's head snapped a second time.

"Stop!" Glory yelled. "I need him conscious!"

The goon held his knuckled fists midair.

Fanny groaned. *That fuckin' hurt! But I ain't gonna stop now, so c'mon, give me your best shot. My chin's out. I'm tied to a chair. How much easier can it be?*

"Look at me," Glory demanded. And then to the guard, she screamed, "Make him!"

The goon opened his palms to slap Fanny's face between them, and in a singsong voice said, "Open your eyes, my little friend. Madame is not through with you..."

When Fanny batted them open, the goon spat some mucus of his own between them and whispered, "And neither am I."

Fanny gritted his teeth and delivered a head butt with enough force to send the goon staggering back. They yelled curses in unison. Glory screamed again, coming between them. The goon swayed from the assault and rubbed his forehead.

Glory consoled him, "It's okay, Mika. You're all right, yes? Yes? Tell me."

"Yes, madam."

Turning to Fanny, she scolded, "You're not playing nice, Fanny. You forget that Eric wants me and I will find him. I will make you both pay for what you've done here in Paris. You killed my uncle and the prime minister. Big mistake. But you also killed Gerard, Marteen, Riland, and Marcel. Oh yes, they had names. They were our people and they cannot be so easily replaced. Your stupidity will be dealt with."

Fanny snickered.

Glory stood defiant in front of him, her anger rising. With clenched fists, she beat him on top of his head, his shoulders, and across the face and screamed, "You will pay for this! You will! I will send you to hell for what you've done!"

244

The goon lurched forward to grab her fists in his giant mitts. "Allow me," he said.

Punch after punch zapped all reality. Fanny remembered crashing to the floor and being kicked and stomped. Glory screamed something primal. Evil. And then everything turned black. Mercifully, blissfully black. Fanny floated. The pounding in his head, his heart, his feet, thrummed in unison. He became transient. The world around him grew mute. He had no thought. He heard no other sound. There was only darkness.

31
Nyet Again
Popigai Crater, K Barrack

Guards rousted the men early the next morning for a march. Everyone except Eric, that is, who remained shackled to his bed and waited to see what would happen next before pulling the key from his cheek and nestling it inside the ushanka. Eventually a new guard arrived to release him, while another stood by a flatbed dolly that carried a large canister.

"Up," the guard motioned after unlocking his chains.

Eric rose and was pushed forward as the guard pointed to the pots under each bed, telling him to get to work at dumping them into the canister and then stacking them on the dolly. He was then shoved outside to hose them down and given the same treatment by the other guard who soon walked away, pushing the dolly over the dirt road. Now wet, he was forced back inside to mop the floors while trying his best to redirect his thoughts from the shivers that held him so that he could hatch a tentative plan for the next round of roulette. As darkness fell, the men returned. They were excited, but it wasn't until the arrival of the thief in the bed next to him that Eric learned what had them chatting.

"A new visitor's come," he informed Eric. "They seem to be everywhere these days."

"You saw him?"

"Yes, he was calling them arseholes while they dragged him into the colonel's office."

Eric thought of Landers. "A Brit, maybe?"

"Or Irish."

"Can we find out?"

The thief shrugged. "If you wait long enough, he might just show up in the bunk next to you."

Eric settled back against his pillow, wondering if it was Landers and whether or not he'd come to K Barrack. If so, he first wanted to know what Landers had done to get captured and then how they could collaborate. An English agent, if he was as Eric suspected, could be useful. The man, however, never arrived.

In the meantime, Eric shared his plan for the next kol'sto smerti with the thief, asking him to pass it along to the man beside him, who, in turn, did the same. An hour later he was again released from his bunk and ushered inside Rabokov's office. On the desk, Eric noticed his drone, the UMPC, his flash drive, the microphone wires from his ushanka, as well as his various identification papers still inside the plastic pouch. He swallowed dryly.

Rabokov was seated at his desk rapidly tapping the pen he held in one hand between thumb and forefingers with his head resting in the palm of his other.

"So what do we have here besides spy equipment?" Rabokov asked, looking up at Eric for the first time. "Because I now understand that your hat and microphone were just the beginning."

Eric didn't answer.

Rabokov stood and picked up the flash drive to toss it into the air like a coin. On its third rotation, Rabokov palmed it tightly in his fist.

"I have asked you a question, Docktor Knudson."

Eric stared at him blankly.

Rabokov waited a full thirty seconds before probing further. "You know how to use a gun, Docktor. Where did you get your training? Was it in the military or are you CIA?"

Eric took a breath before answering, "The military. I was in the Army."

"But you are too young to have *been* in the army, Docktor. Does this mean you are still a soldier?"

"No, I served four years to get an education."

"An education?"

"Yes, our government will pay college expenses if you serve."

"I see, and yes, I forgot how your government spoils you. May I ask why you did not want to stay in your military?"

"I wanted to be a mineralogist."

"To study stones, am I correct?"

"Yes, well, no, that would be the job of a geologist. I study minerals and as I've been telling you, my specific interest here is radiation."

"Radiation, da, Docktor, I understand."

Rabokov turned away from Eric to drop the flash drive on his desk. He next leaned over to Eric and announced, "I believe you might know someone we picked up today. Like you, we found him where he should not have been."

Eric felt a spurt of adrenalin at the hope it might indeed be Landers, and if it was, that he might have an ally in the Englishman after all.

Rabokov instructed the guard to bring in the new visitor.

The guard left to quickly return, shoving Landers into the room. Landers looked haggard. He'd obviously not slept and was recently beaten. Both eyes were nearly closed. His jaw jutted to the right with a swelling the size of a small plum. His cheeks bore bruises and cuts while his left arm hung dead, without the control of his shoulder. It must have been dislocated.

"Have a seat, I believe you might know Docktor Knudson," Rabokov said.

The guard took hold of Landers' shoulders and wrestled him into the chair opposite Eric. Landers groaned from a pain so intense that he ignored Eric's presence.

"Now, gentlemen, if you tell me who you really are and why you have been snooping around my mines, you might live long enough for a final meal." Rabokov waved his hand toward a sideboard that up until now had gone unnoticed. Arranged there were several trays of sliced meats, pickled vegetables, and crusty breads.

"Well?" Rabokov asked.

Neither man spoke.

"So this is how it will be, hmmm? But gentlemen, please, I beg you to not upset me today for I am in a happy mood. I am a new grandfather. Panimayete?"

Only the guard smiled to indicate that yes, he understood.

Rabokov strolled away to make a sandwich. As he did, Eric reassessed his situation to include the arrival of Landers and what he'd have to confess in order to survive this ordeal. The options seemed so limited that they choked the air out of the room.

With his half-eaten snack in hand, Rabokov removed the engraved Baikal from the guard's holster and stood behind Landers. Slowly he placed the revolver angled up into the base of Landers' skull.

"I'm waiting," he said.

Landers steeled himself in silence.

Rabokov, who was now sucking soft bread from between his teeth, continued, "This is like the kol'tso smerti, no, Docktor Knudson? Except only now I hold the gun."

Eric's mind was awhirl with possibilities. On the desk lay his explosive flash drive and UMPC. If he could only leap for it, jam it in, and trigger it, he could blow the place up taking Rabokov and…and…and…

What the hell am I thinking? And me and Landers with him. So what else can I do? Grab the gun? Wrestle the

guard? What, man? I don't know but I gotta do something!
Bah...lam!

The explosion was so close that for a second or two, Eric lost his hearing....but not his sight. No, for Landers was dropping to the floor after first knocking his head against Rabokov's desk on his descent.

Eric jumped out of his chair to brace himself against the desk's edge; the shock of the colonel's actions had catapulted him into a new reality. Rabokov next pointed the pistol at Eric with a cold, calculated eye traveling down the gun's front sight to land between his own.

"Panimayete, Docktor Knudson? You understand now? We are not joking here at Popigai."

Eric stammered. Coughed. Tried to catch his breath. The guard came at him, thrusting his hands around his throat. Eric clawed at the vise grip cutting off his airway but failed and then passed out. When he woke, groggy and unsure, he found himself back in his bunk. He lay chained with a painful ache in his neck, shoulders, and throat that when he swallowed, felt as if his Adam's apple had been crushed. He dared not speak. He looked to the thief asleep on his back and then listened as the barrack's door opened and the lights were thrown on. Again a buzzer sounded. Men groaned and covered their eyes as Eric slipped the key out from the ushanka to place it painfully into his mouth while massaging his jaw. Another night of games was about to commence.

"Up!" the guard yelled.

Once more they were hooded and marched to the chamber where they were pushed against the circular railing. This time, however, when the guard came to Eric and removed his head covering, he was disconnected, and another man, hooded and stumbling, was shoved between them. Again he was shackled. Eric noticed first the Levi's and then the familiar shape of the man's now hunched back and shoulders. It was Fanny.

Are you shitting me? Eric screamed to himself until

250

finally, amidst the all noise of shuffling, tears, and coughing in the room, he managed to whisper Fanny's name.

Fanny squared his shoulders slightly.

He whispered again, this time carefully abbreviating what he'd told the other prisoners earlier in the day.

Fanny straightened.

Rabokov entered and looked directly at Eric with eyes colder still. But nothing confirmed more than when the corners of Rabokov's mouth rose ever so slightly that this day would be his last. He watched the colonel joke with his men, take their bets, and then walk purposely over to Fanny to remove the hood. Once freed, Fanny turned toward the colonel, exposing to Eric the smear of blood from a broken nose on his face. His right eye was swollen shut and his lips were cracked open. Still Fanny managed a weak smile.

Rabokov smiled back. "You Americans have no idea how capable we Russians are. I will break you. I will break you both." He spit onto the floor and ordered the guns distributed.

Eric now figured Rabokov's true intent was a double murder...his and Fanny's...and that the only way he could avoid it, was for his plan to be executed perfectly. But would the other men follow his instructions when he'd yet earned their confidence, if in fact a bullet or two were elsewhere? He hoped so. He scanned the room to gauge their preparedness but someone in uniform had entered the room. Someone important looking enough to further tip the scales against him.

The man, decorated with a single star, ignored the five guards placing their bets. He even ignored the cigar smoke that filled the already breathless room. Instead, he chose to half-sit upon a stack of wooden crates with one arm resting comfortably over his muscular thigh. His eyes were heavy looking as if almost napping, but from the way he smiled, Eric sensed he was very much awake.

Meanwhile, the guards pointed at and pushed

251

prisoners in passing in order to slap their faded rubles onto the table. Colonel Rabokov counted each one and then laughed at the man who bet against him.

"You're a fool, Nikolas! Have you yet to learn?" He shoved the guard away to take rubles from the next man. When all the bets were placed, Rabokov showed them to the man on the crates and laughed. "It should be an easy win tonight, eh, Major General?"

Major general? Is it Niembriev?

The major general looked at Rabokov from the corner of his droopy eyes, before taking one last look at Eric and an even longer, more satisfying look at Fanny, who stumbled slightly into the man in front of him.

"It remains a happy day," he said as he stood and left the room.

The words careened inside Eric's head because there was no room for error. The men had better come through. He figured that after Rabokov was killed, he'd need to remove the cuffs with the key now wedged in his mouth, reach for a new firearm provided he survived the hail of gunfire that was sure to follow, and then kill enough guards so that he and Fanny could leave the building.

How much time would that take? A minute? Ten minutes? No…probably more, and I don't have it.

With the support of the other men, however, it was the only plan he had.

Rabokov stood and adjusted his uniform, telling the chained men to raise their weapons. And to his comrades, who huddled over the betting sheet, he addressed, "Gentlemen, a man will die today by the hand of another. Who will it be? We will see. But make no mistake, all these men are traitors and spies. Each deserves to die but I can give you only one. One that I promise is richly deserved."

Rabokov looked toward Fanny.

After several excruciating minutes, Rabokov finally yelled, "Fire!"

32
The Escape
Popigai Crater

Eric's peripheral vision confirmed that the other prisoners had done exactly as he'd asked. The men along the front half of the railing were on their knees, while the men in the back had remained standing. More critically, all had pointed their guns at Rabokov, who now smiled but looked unsure as to why. In the tense few seconds that followed, the air stilled...even the five guards froze to decipher the scene before them and then Rabokov, along with his smile, faded.

Meanwhile Eric had used the time lag to unlock the central chaining mechanism in the rail. Chaos ensued. Some prisoners fell to the ground while others ducked or crawled behind other men. Everyone, however, joined in the fracas. Screams and orders battled above a volley of gunfire, but nothing tamed the beast now unleashed inside the chamber after Rabokov went down.

Eric leapt upon the guard closest to him to wrestle away his weapon, while Fanny scrambled for the easy pickings of Rabokov's that remained holstered to his dead body, and together they blasted their way toward the exit.

"Where're we headed?" Fanny asked as they jumped into a truck that Eric hotwired.

"Got a Pakboat."

"Where?"

"I don't know at the moment but we're out of here!"

Eric swerved around obstacles, making Fanny cringe in pain and him take notice. Neither, however, acknowledged the obvious. Instead, they continued south out of the complex, keeping the headlights off until they were safely out of range of the madhouse.

"Where are we?" Fanny asked through battered lips.

"Popigai."

"You're kidding me."

"Wish I was, partner, but unless you have some real purpose for staying, you'd better tell me how the hell you ended up here."

"I wasn't. I was headed for Washington," he answered with a grunt as he pulled the truck's headrest from the seat mount. "But before I could leave my hotel, I found myself at the end of a barrel."

"Bratva?"

Fanny pressed the foam cushion against his abdomen.

"You're shot."

"Maybe, but if you stop on my account, we don't stand a chance."

"How bad is it?"

"Not too."

"So tell me about Paris then."

"It's a long story, okay?"

Eric looked over to his friend who'd laid his head back in the space of the missing restraint. The man was a wreck.

"Take a break," Eric comforted him. "There's nothing more either of us can do anyway until I find that damned boat."

Fanny agreed and after a short while slipped into a fitful sleep while Eric followed the one-track road further away from K Barracks. Eventually it ended at the mine where he'd been captured. Things were looking familiar. There was the rock behind which he'd been clubbed, and better yet, there was the path he'd taken from the river.

Excited, Eric jumped from the truck and ran around to move Fanny onto his shoulder. Fanny opened his eyes and together they trekked their way to the river for a canoe Eric hoped was still tethered between the two Siberian anchors he'd pinned it between. It was. He settled Fanny on the floor and rowed well into the night until he reached the bank nearest to where Rebe's cabin stood.

She, not Nesutak, was first to throw open the door with a shotgun held high. But when she saw who it was, she screamed, "Doc Knudson! Doc Knudson! Come! Where did you go? We tried find you!"

Eric waved to her from the shore for help while trying to lift a semi-conscious Fanny out of the canoe.

She ran as she cried, "We been so worried. Where did you go? Where you been? And who? Oh my…" Rebe stopped mid-sentence to stare at Fanny. "He hurt."

"This is my friend, Fanny Bergan" Eric told her. "I think he's been shot."

"In face?"

"No, in the abdomen."

"Okay, I try fix," she offered quietly.

Between them they hauled Fanny inside where Nesutak had already begun to boil water for tea, but when he saw what they carried in, he knew it would be used for other purposes. So he pulled the warmed kettle from the fire, carried it over to Rebe, and ran about the cabin grabbing first-aid supplies, towels, and an assortment of herbs and ointments.

Rebe went into immediate crisis care. First she removed Fanny's shirt to find a half-inch puncture wound from either a gunshot or sharp object, she couldn't tell and wasn't about to root around it to determine. So if it held a bullet, it would have to stay. She next cleaned it with the tea water, then numbed and sutured it. She topped it with a wad of herbs her father had carefully rendered and gently dressed it in gauze. She then poured a small glass of whiskey and set it next to Fanny and went about working on his broken face. The last thing she did was set his nose with a quick snap of it between her two palms. The sickening pop filled the room. Fanny gasped awake from the suddenness of it, at which time she placed the whiskey to his lips and made him drink.

Eric, meanwhile, had been rummaging through the rest of his belongings for the laptop he'd left behind. He needed to contact Edmund with his news and to arrange for their departure...all four of them.

He typed, "Urgent. Popigai disrupted. Bergan here and wounded. Need pilot, medical care, protection for four."

Within minutes Edmund responded, "Sending pilot for you and Bergan only. Report upon stabilization."

Edmund's message was clear that he wasn't going to help Rebe and Nesutak. So if they stayed, they'd surely die or end up in prison themselves. It would be up to Eric to convince them to leave.

As Rebe tucked Fanny under some blankets, he told her, "Rebe, you and your father have got to go. There's some very bad men from the mines who might try to find us as soon as they realize we've escaped. So you've to start gathering your things."

"But your friend..."

"Trenton's coming for us."

"Good, he bring supplies. I radio."

"No, don't, because these men I'm talking about? They're probably on their way right now, Rebe, so you two need to get out of here pronto."

"We go when you go," she said, patting his arm with assurance.

Eric held her hand there but she resisted and moved away, saying, "We ready, Doc, always ready."

Eric watched her roam about the room busying herself and was amazed by the confidence she exuded in every aspect of her life. Nesutak, too. Here they were living in a near-barren wasteland, yet through their nomadic existence, they'd made it their home. He felt useless to them. He didn't know the territory or the terrain. He also didn't know what shelters they traveled between. So how had they come to be here when he needed them most?

Eric dismissed the thought that they might be CIA, too, and tended to his own packing.

Sometime later the whoop of Trenton's helicopter could be heard in the distance. Eric looked at Fanny and noted how much better he appeared now that his nose was realigned. The skin around his eyes and on his hand, however, had blackened to the color of purple eggplants.

Suddenly Nesutak ventured in gripping his binoculars.

"Mans," he huffed in English.

"Yes," Eric answered him. "Trenton's coming for us."

"No," Nesutak shook his head and by using several fingers indicated more than one.

"Mans," he said again pointing north beyond the hills.

"How many?" Fanny asked weakly.

"Mnogiye," Nesutak answered nervously.

Rebe translated. "Many."

"We've got to get out of here," Eric urged Rebe. "And you're going with us."

"No, we head south, no problem," she answered. "They no find."

"But, Rebe, there isn't time!"

"Yes, time."

Eric spun her around toward the heap of belongings she'd packed earlier, before running out to the landing helicopter. When the blades slowed, Eric opened the door and yelled, "We've got a medical issue so how quickly can you turn this bird around?"

"Nesutak?"

"No, a buddy of mine."

257

"Man, you need to leave right now 'cause there's a heap of trouble headed this way, and believe me, they saw Myrtle. They were wavin' for me to do a fly over, which I did not do. I know Russian soldiers when I see them."

"How many?"

"Ten at least. So let's get your buddy on board so's we can hightail it outta here."

Eric ran back to the cabin where Rebe was already assisting a more clear-headed Fanny to the door.

"This our means?" Fanny asked, looking grateful.

"Yep, from Edmund, now get a move on. You, too, Rebe unless you've changed your mind about Trenton's helicopter."

Rebe giggled as she gave Fanny a gentle push onto Eric's shoulder and Nesutak bristled past toward their waiting canoe with their bundles.

"We fine, Doc."

"I know, Rebe, the finest."

They said their goodbyes at the helicopter but only after Eric had loaded Fanny into its belly and he'd dug through his duffle to remove the second drone and its remote. He handed her the equipment.

"Here, Rebe, for you. You know what to do with this thing, right?"

"Yes," she giggled. "Hit button."

"You got it Rebe, hit the button if you need to," Eric hugged her and then Nesutak before climbing in. Through face and hand gestures he mimed, "Get going, you don't have much time."

Trenton handed Nesutak a few necessities they'd need, climbed into the cockpit, and said, "See you next time, Rebe. And Nesutak? Eat good meat. Stay healthy, ya hear?"

Still they appeared in no hurry.

"Why don't they go?" Eric asked Trenton.

"Oh, they'll squirrel outta here fast enough. Look, they'll be okay, trust me. They know what to do better than anyone and will take only what they need and nothin' more. The rest they'll leave behind for those Russians, who'll be mighty grateful 'cause there ain't nothin' else around for miles."

"Nothing except a stolen truck."

"A stolen truck?"

"Yeah, we left it back about twenty miles or so. That's probably how they found us. We led them right to Rebe and Nesutak."

"Maybe."

Eric shook his head at the disgust of his own doing.

"What's your story?"

"I'll fill you in on the way to Khatanga."

"Okay, but you ain't goin' back to Khatanga 'cause those guys know it's the only way out. So, if you're gonna to try and do that, you can't be anywhere near that town until it's safe."

"Then where do we go?"

"Well, if you like rustic, you can use my yurt. It's got some provisions, canned meats and stuff. Nothin' much else but it's plenty enough to get you through a day or two. Plus it'll give your friend a place to catch some shuteye."

Trenton flipped switches and grabbed the joystick. "Got me a bit of the wife's potato bread and borscht in the cooler back there. Take it. You're gonna need it," he added.

Eric thanked him as he lifted the bird above the heads of Rebe and Nesutak and hovered. They waved from the river as they stowed the rest of their belongings in the canoe. Trenton tipped the blades left and right before whirling off far to the west. He then began a slow, wide bank back toward the east. Trenton's yurt was only hours away, but in spite of it, the pressure in Eric's chest mounted.

33
Return to Moscow
Moscow, Russia

Trenton's yurt provided Fanny a blessed place to sleep while Eric arranged for new travel documents so that they could leave from Khatanga on the most immediate flight out to Moscow. When Fanny's eyes opened some twenty-four hours later, Eric went to him. A strong glare stared back.

"Whoa, what's up besides you?" Eric asked to lighten his mood.

"Your girlfriend," Fanny snapped. "She's got a mean right hook."

Eric tried to suppress the chuckle that rose in his throat.

"Oh, she didn't do all this," Fanny said, circling his face with an index finger. "But she's responsible for it."

The ridiculousness of the accusation had him moving back from Fanny's bed. He knew Fanny had never favored his involvement with Glory, but how could he possibly connect her to the bruises on his face? As Fanny planted his feet on the floor to stand, the shaky attempt had Eric stepping forward again to assist.

"Back off," Fanny scoffed.

"What wrong with you?" he asked as Fanny gave him a hard shove that put him off balance. His friend's fists were now balled and moving toward him.

"Shit, Fanny!"

"I told you, didn't I?"

"Told me what?"

"That that woman could hurt this mission!" Fanny took a swing and a miss, due mostly to legs that teetered on his approach. Eric tripped him to the floor and then landed on top of him to pin back his shoulders. Fanny continued to struggle as they wrestled like the teenaged boys they'd once been. With Fanny wounded, Eric had the slight advantage, so he eased up a bit and whispered into his friend's ear, "Give it up, Fan, and just tell me what's going on."

Fanny gave one last jerk as Eric released his hold. Slowly they rose to their knees and then stood facing one another. Fanny, still on tender legs, said, "She's one of 'em."

The words hit Eric's ears like a foreign language. The thought of Glory having anything to do with Popigai made no sense. She was a flight attendant in America, no less, so how could that be possible?

"She is, Dane."

Eric took a deep breath. "Okay," he whispered. "Where's your proof?"

"It starts with the dude and his gun in my face," Fanny said as he wobbled over to the pot of freshly brewed coffee on the table. He poured two cups and lifted one to his lips, leaving the other there. After a sip he said, "He threw me in the back of a car and took me to some kind of commercial laundry on the outskirts of town at which point your girl showed up."

"And why would she have been there?" Eric asked, walking over to take a seat.

"She was there to force me into telling her where you were and who we worked for."

Eric put both hands around the warm, second mug. "But she doesn't even know you, Fan, much less that we're connected, so tell me again why'd she go to Paris."

"You told her *you* were going, remember?"

Eric said he did. "And somehow she mistook you for me?"

"Don't be a smartass," Fanny said, his glare returning. "I was on Simone's tail who happens to be her uncle. They're family, Eric. I followed them to her apartment and made my way inside after he dropped her off. It took some convincing, but she finally gave in and agreed to help me with Operation Pop Up because of you."

"You told her?"

Fanny paused. "The next night she was with him at the Folies Bergère where she set me up to intercept one of his shipments, only she double-crossed me. I handled it... and him...he's dead. After that, Oscher sent me out to look for Nanterre, which I also handled. Went out rather spectacularly, I might add, and after that? Well, my hotel and then, bam, off to the laundry where she and her goon had their way with me. Later on I was tossed onto a mail-carrier out of France and delivered to Niembriev."

"The muscular one at Popigai?"

"Correct. He put the finishing touches on my face and asked a lot of questions. I didn't mind so much except for the needle, because I thought maybe it was truth serum. But turns out it was something else. Slept like a baby until I woke up inside a cattle bin in Khatanga. Rabokov tried to pick up where Niembriev left off."

Eric looked down.

"Guess I'm still under the influence a little. Sorry, man."

"For what?"

"For that," Fanny bobbed his head toward the floor where they'd just fought.

"You're kidding me, right?"

Fanny sighed. "I coulda nailed you, you know..."

Eric let out a snort. "You took your best shot and missed, Fanny, but okay..." He held up a hand. "Let's just

262

get back to Glory and Niembriev."

"Let me just say something first."

Eric met his eyes, waiting again to be surprised.

"It was pretty smooth the way you handled Rabokov."

Eric relaxed. "Yeah, well, we all pulled the trigger on that one."

Fanny extended his hand. "It was inspiring."

Eric put his in Fanny's and shook.

"So Glory," Fanny continued as he let go. "She was hell-bent on getting me killed and then tracking you down to do the same but I got the first shot in."

Eric twitched in his chair.

"Settle down. I wasn't in any position to actually shoot her but I would have and you gotta know that, you understand me? Which is *why*," he emphasized, "I'm here and so is Niembriev. This is the end of the line."

"And Glory? Where's she now?"

"Why would you care after what I just told you?"

"I don't know, except that if she's still out there…"

"If she's still out there, she's still a threat."

Eric covered his mouth to think, then looked back at Fanny, "Just tell me about the last time you saw her."

"She and the goon were checking out my UMPC."

"By way of the flash drive?"

"Yeah, but think about it. It couldn't have gone off because I'm still here, right? Besides, Niembriev told me I only cost him one good aide, not two."

"Then there's a chance we could still bring her in."

"Are you serious? Bring her in? I'm sorry I couldn't take her out."

Eric blew air from his mouth as Fanny continued. "She played us both, man, so you'd better come down to earth with this."

After a long, quiet standoff, Eric pointed toward the sound of an incoming helicopter.

"Trenton," Eric stated as he went to the window to have a peek. Fanny followed him.

"He's not CIA," Eric told him. "But I trust him and so should you."

Fanny squeezed his eyes into slits that questioned whether either of them should.

"He's been vetted by Edmund. If you don't believe me, you can check it out for yourself."

"I might."

"Well do it fast then because without him, we're toast. He's our only way out of here."

Fanny placed a firm hand by way of apology on Eric's back. Upon Trenton's landing, they stepped out to greet him.

"Got word your major general left awhile ago in a private P2006," Trenton shouted at their approach. "Twin engine. Woulda liked to seen it."

"Me too," Eric quipped. "Seeing Niembriev leave would've been a lot better than hearing about it."

"How reliable's your source?" Fanny asked.

"About as good as you're gonna get around here...the wife," he answered, handing them a canister of her meat and cabbage pie.

"Thanks, man," Eric said. "Lucya's a lifesaver."

Trenton smiled at the compliment. "That she is and her fixin's sure beat huntin' and fishin' for them, don't they?"

"Amen to that," Fanny responded.

"So how much of a lead does he have on us?" Eric asked as they entered the yurt and Trenton hung his heavy flight jacket on a door-side hook.

"'Bout nine hours."

"He headed to Moscow?" Fanny asked.

Trenton shook his head no. "He's goin' to Barvikha."

"To be with his pals, I guess," Eric said, referring to DuBethonee and the other exiles.

Fanny turned a conspiratorial glance toward Eric.

"I said we can trust him," Eric countered before continuing, "There's a sanatorium there that we need to get inside of."

"Won't be easy," Trenton offered. "But it is heavily connected to the Village."

"How so?" Fanny asked.

"Well, for one thing, the Village supplies the entire town, meaning anyone staying in the sanatorium goes there at some point in time or another. And if it supplies the town, there's sure as hell a lot of delivery trucks goin' in and out. You get your hands on one and you got yourself a free ride anywhere you wanna go, especially if it's a Mercury."

"What's Mercury?" Fanny asked.

"Mercury supplies companies like Mikimoto and Harry Winston. The jewelers, you know? You name a top seller and Mercury supplies it."

Fanny turned to Eric. "It's a thought."

"And a mere one at that," Eric added.

Trenton added insight. "Mercury's what built that town and has carte blanche. No one'll question a couple a drivers. Not even one as beat up as you, Mr. Bergan."

Fanny cocked his head at the jab.

Eric turned to him. "Guess we have some shopping to do."

Fanny's shoulders dropped.

"We good?" Eric asked.

He answered with the familiar flip of his wrist.

*

The next day, Trenton transported them to the airfield, from where hours later they landed under a dark, dense fog, at Moscow's Vnukovo International Airport. To Eric the scene before him felt as if he'd stepped into a WWII postcard when the airport was one of Russia's premier

265

military airbases. Its VIP hall, dead ahead, was empty, although normally it was manned whenever the president was in the city. Still, he felt an unseen eye upon them.

They grabbed a taxi and were taken to Odintsovo, a small town about seventeen miles south of Barvikha. There they entered the Radisson Park Inn where two rooms had been secured for the Americans traveling on business. Fanny, however, had some explaining to do at the front desk about his face. Fortunately check-in was effortless with Fanny offering the excuse that while test-driving the latest Lada, a deer had run across the street, forcing him to brake so hard that the airbags deployed to cause all the damage but saved him from killing the animal.

"Too bad," the clerk had told him. "Venison is most excellent this time of year."

Thirty minutes later they were back in the lobby posing as tourists ready to board a bus headed for the Barvikha Luxury Village.

"Why the gaishnik?" Fanny asked when he noticed the traffic cops.

"They want to make sure we rich Americans don't get robbed on the way," Eric replied. "At least until the price of things does. Spend a little and they'll be happy."

"Yeah, well, is it normal for them to carry a gun?"

"Don't know, but listen, we're just out to buy a few souvenirs for the wives back home. And, you know, to find a truck."

"Sure, but maybe we shoulda taken a cab."

"Fan, we agreed that getting bagged and tagged as tourists was our best disguise, didn't we?"

"We did but..."

"But what?"

"Nothin'," was all Fanny said.

Eric wondered if Niembriev's drug was still playing havoc with his pal's system.

Fifteen minutes later, the bus turned left into the

Luxury Village, it's entrance indicated in towering neon letters nestled in the landscape. The upscale mall was stark but softened by a surrounding pine preserve. Its parking lot was dotted with expensive cars. After stepping from the bus, they heard the first traffic cop tell everyone to return in exactly three hours, no more, no less, while the other cop walked over to inspect an expensive Maybach Exelero. Eric and Fanny strolled the grounds and peeked inside store windows. At a small boutique, Eric patted Fanny on the chest with the back of his gloved hand and said, "I'm going in for the wife."

"Spare me and buy two," Fanny replied.

Eric ducked inside. Even the ventilated heat smelled pricey. He wandered up to one of the displays and touched some of the items there. He then picked up a bottle of nail polish. The clerk sauntered over and asked him in Russian if he'd like the small bottle of black lacquer she held in her open palm.

"It's lovely," he told her.

"It should be. It's Azature, you know? One of your American Hollywood companies."

"I don't know that one," Eric said, wondering at the same time how she knew he was an American when they'd just conversed in Russian.

She pointed to his badge. "Wild guess, but too bad because we love Azature here in Russia. Notice, please, that this bottle contains real diamonds. Like stars in a night sky, no?"

Eric took a closer look.

"The ladies go crazy for them, see?" She extended her other hand so that Eric could admire the sparkle of her fingernails.

"Interesting, how much for the bottle?"

"Oh, one should never ask how much, just how many," she answered with a coy laugh.

Eric pretended not to notice. "Then how about a

scarf?"

"Oh a scarf would be much more expensive than this nine-million-ruble bottle."

"Nine million? You must be joking."

She shook her head slowly while moving the $150,000 bottle of polish in front of his eyes as if it were a tiny bell.

Fanny popped his head through the door and asked Eric to step outside, which he did while still shaking his head in surprise.

"What's up?"

Fanny led him to a bench. "I just saw someone we know. Someone you, at least, will be very happy to hear is alive."

"Glory?"

"Yeah," Fanny said.

"Where'd she go?"

"Dolce & Gabbana."

"Was she alone?"

"She was."

"How long's she been in there?"

"One minute, ten seconds, and counting."

"And did she see you?"

"No, she was busy rummaging through her handbag while the doorman held the door open."

Eric stared at the shop, wondering why she'd come to Barvikha and whom she'd come to see. The questions must have played across his face because Fanny answered with, "Niembriev?"

"Maybe."

"Or DuBethonee. What do you think?"

"I don't know," Eric said, "But there's only one way to find out."

Fanny looked at his friend.

Glory emerged twenty-five minutes later carrying a large shopping bag and made haste for the valet's kiosk.

There she handed a ticket to the attendant who also took the bag from her arm. Soon a cream-colored Bentley arrived. She nodded before settling into the back seat as the valet gently placed the bag into the trunk.

Eric and Fanny watched the car glide toward the mall's north exit and turn on its right blinker.

"Where do you think she's headed?" Fanny asked, cupping a leather-gloved hand to his mouth.

"Can't be the resort, so I'm betting on the sanatorium."

Fanny pointed to a cab but Eric shook his head no and nodded to an unattended motorcycle nearby with its key still inserted.

"You're kidding me."

Eric smiled.

"That's a hell of a death wish, Dane."

They stuffed their badges into their pockets, mounted the bike as naturally as possible, and left the parking lot.

34
The Hermit Kingdom
Barvikha, Russia

Barvikha's pine forest wrapped the highway in a tight cocoon of primordial green. And as such, its density softened the motorcycle's sputter while Fanny and Eric gave chase to Glory's Bentley. They followed well behind her car until it turned into the sanatorium through a gate that restricted their entrance. So they turned, instead, in the same direction onto an earthen road that ran along its southern border. Neither man knew where it would take them, but after rumbling past opulent dachas, up small hills, and deeper into the preserve, they discovered it ended at a small lake.

The lake bordered the sanatorium as well, so they hid the motorcycle, and ran to the wall where a small hole offered them a limited view of its expansive lawn. Walking about were several patients. Many had either their heads and faces or chins and noses bandaged, although several others, perhaps visitors, were ensconced in conversation beneath the building's gazebo-like roof. Fanny and Eric struggled to see more as the sound of a siren cut through the woodland.

"Hear that?" Eric asked Fanny.

"Think they're onto us?"

"Could be, so let's move."

They worked their way along the wall until another crack revealed itself. This one gave them a view of the well-preserved medical facility that was originally built for Russian leaders and the treatment of their digestive disorders but now offered complete medical and plastic surgery services. However, its height and a bank of trees blocked their view of the deluxe apartments where Eric suspected all along that Madame DuBethonee lorded over her domain.

Fanny pointed to the building's patio and asked, "What do you make of that group over there?"

Eric moved in. Three men in trench coats stood, as one woman wrapped in white mink, remained seated. The men seemed agitated and as a result, the woman soon began tapping her cane to the floor. At first she did it lightly, but as the conversation escalated, she banged it, making it glitter in the light.

"Trouble?" Fanny asked.

"Soon enough because these guys are totally ignoring her."

"That'll cost them."

At that they heard her command them to shut up and to bring the conversation down a few notches.

"Listen to him," she demanded.

"No, Madame, I will not," the man closest to her sternly replied.

Fanny and Eric cocked their ears to hear more but the sounds of the wind, birds, and the clattering of leaves muddled the conversation. Shortly, their attention turned to the sanatorium as Glory stepped out.

Eric watched her every move. Fanny studied his. "You hoping she's headed somewhere other than the patio?"

"Maybe."

"But what if she is?"

"Then she is," Eric answered.

Fanny said, "You already know what's what, so let it go, man."

Eric didn't respond.

They watched her step up to the group, and after

politely greeting the men, bend down to kiss the woman on both cheeks. The woman patted the bench next to her. Glory accepted and then rested her hand on the woman's arm. The men left shortly thereafter but Glory and the woman stayed. So did Fanny and Eric.

"You got it now?" Fanny asked.

"Unbelievable," Eric answered with a deep sigh.

"Then the fur is DuBethonee."

"Yes."

"And Glory?"

"I'm sorry to see it," Eric said with pursed lips and his focus still on the women.

"And the men....Bratva?" Fanny asked.

"Probably their top guys."

"Thought one might be Niembriev."

"The one with his back to us."

"Yep and that tells me we've nailed them in the beehive."

"Not yet. We've still got to get inside without getting stung."

"Then we'll have to use a little honey."

"Meaning what exactly?"

"Glory."

"I don't know."

"You got something better up your sleeve?"

"Not yet, but if I find it, we could be out of here by tomorrow."

"You're dreamin', man."

Eric turned to stare at him until Fanny conceded with a shake of his.

"It's now or never, Fanny."

Fanny left with an annoyed gait to retrieve the motorcycle. He drove them back through the forest to the rear entrance of the Barvikha Spa and Resort. There, they ditched the bike and ventured out its front doors to give the impression that they'd been inside for the better part of the allotted three hours. But as they crossed the parking lot toward the Village shopping center, they noticed their group was now lined up for the bus and a few gaishnik were busy interrogating them.

At the end of the line, a portly man and a much younger and much more expensive-looking woman, evident by the red leather soles of her black stilettos that showed whenever she crossed one tired foot over the other, waited anxiously. And it was behind these two that Eric and Fanny slid in while reattaching their badges. The obese man gave them a cursory look.

"What happened?" Eric asked him.

"You heard the sirens and then they go and lock us in. My god, it was horrifying."

Eric exchanged a knowing look at Fanny. "That's too bad but we didn't hear a thing."

"How could you not?" the man retorted.

"We weren't here, we were in the resort enjoying a cognac. But I've got to tell you, the price I paid would've bought five bottles back in the States. Think they'll tell us what happened?"

"You could ask," the man said, referring to a cop headed their way.

When he stood before Fanny, the officer held out his hand until Fanny presented his passport and visa. The cop looked them over carefully; then studied Fanny's face.

"American?" he asked. "Please remove your sunglasses."

Fanny removed them. The officer looked at him again with a wondering expression.

"An airbag, sir," Fanny indicated through hand gestures in order to explain his face.

"Automobile?"

"Yes, sir."

"Ferrari?"

"No, sir, a Lada."

"La…da," he repeated with a tsk, tsk, tsk but looking satisfied over something he mumbled about Americans.

He presented Fanny his papers with formality and as he withdrew his hand, he mimicked a big "boosh!" as if an airbag had gone off. And then he laughed and turned to Eric where he once more stood wiggling his gloved fingers to request identification. Eric obliged.

The officer held the photo of Dr. Richard Knudson up to Eric's face and asked, "What kind of docktor? Medicine, animal, or psychiatry?"

"I'm a mineralogist. I study radiation."

"Radiation. Da."

"In the soil, sir."

"Da, radiation is everywhere in Russia, no? You find any radiation, Docktor Knudson?"

"No, sir, not yet."

The officer looked up as if offended his country would be so lacking, so Eric added, "I'm here on business, sir, not to look for it. I'm in meetings only. On radiation."

"And your hotel?"

"The Radisson Park Inn."

The officer handed Eric back his paperwork. "You Americans are very funny. Radisson? Radiation?" The cop pitted one word against the other with each hand. "You no see?"

"Yes, sir, I think I do."

"We are very funny too, no?"

People in the line giggled but no one relaxed, especially Eric or Fanny.

The officer gathered himself and looked at them both. "Shopping?"

Eric answered first. "Yes, sir, for the wife in America."

"Da, the wife," he repeated, raising his brows.

He then turned to shoo the other officers along, saying, "Okay, we are done here."

274

Eric and Fanny took a collective sigh and followed the others like a herd onto the bus. The portly man turned to Eric and asked, "Shopping for the wife? Didn't you say you were in the resort having a cognac?"

Fanny laughed, "Well, what do you think drove us to it?"

The man tilted his head, nodding his agreement. "I wasn't aware there was a radiation meeting at the hotel, Dr. Knudson."

"It's private, just me and a couple of possible new contacts."

"Yes, of course," the man responded as he hurried his female companion down the aisle. Then after taking their seats, he leaned across and continued, "I'm a doctor, too, Dr. Knudson. A veterinarian. Perhaps you'd like to join me for lunch tomorrow so that we can have a professional conversation. I'll show you the Meyendorff Castle."

Eric swirled the man's offer around in his mind with what he and Fanny had yet to do and answered, "But I don't even know your name."

He needed more time to think.

"Of course. I'm Dr. Allen George and this is Lydia Saunders."

"Happy to meet you both and this is my associate. Will Miss Saunders be joining us?" Eric asked, purposefully omitting Fanny's name and deciding Dr. George might be useful after all to get him onto the sanatorium's grounds.

"Ah, no, Lydia's going in for a minor treatment, but if we play our cards right, we'll finish lunch in time for me to check in on her. And would you care to join us as well?" he asked, looking at Fanny with concern that he might actually accept.

"Thank you, no, Allen. I've other plans although I do appreciate the invitation," Fanny replied with an unintended disrespect.

"Fine, but there's a hospital there, you know, where

they could check out those eyes."

Fanny glared.

Dr. George smiled and without losing a beat asked Eric, "Shall we meet at noon, then, in the lobby?"

"Noon it is. Thank you."

After stepping from the bus on their return to the Radisson, the doorman approached to say in near perfect English, "Excuse me, Dr. Knudson, but a package is waiting for you at the bell stand."

Eric thanked him and acknowledged how it was a pleasure to hear his native tongue spoken. The man bowed, saying, "It's my pleasure" and walked away. For an instant Eric fought the nagging feeling that he might be one of Edmund's men. Then dismissed it and picked up the package that had surely come from him. He tucked it under his arm and invited Fanny up to his room.

As they entered, Fanny asked, "A drink first?"

"Yeah, neat, two fingers."

Fanny poured snifters of Russian Standard and set them on top of the dresser as Eric opened the envelope to remove driver's licenses, a registration, insurance card, and other necessary paperwork for traveling in Russia.

He next held up two fat Harley Davidson fobs. "Check this out."

"Good for fast exits, shoulders, and weaving only," Fanny said as he rubbed his thumb over the logo. "Otherwise it's a waste of good chrome here."

"Yeah, well, at least the helmet will hide our faces and nationality," Eric added.

The fob's logo slid open. Inside were several pellets. Fanny removed one and held it up in front of his eyes. "Well hello there, little darlin'!"

Eric laughed at recognizing the BB-sized explosives, then walked over to raise one of the snifters to Fanny and said, "Here's to fob bombs."

"Cheers," Fanny said, clinking his glass.

As Eric lowered his, the smile on his face disappeared into a grim line. "You realize that we're close to getting our hands on DuBethonee and can finally go home, don't you?"

Fanny threw the vodka back in one gulp but Eric wasn't done talking.

"Seriously, Fan, if things don't end up the way we hope, for me at least, get the hell out of here."

"No way."

"Think about it. Going forward, if it comes down to me or you, cut the cord and save yourself."

"Like I said, Dane, that ain't gonna happen because neither of us went through all this shit just to leave the other behind. We're gonna get outta here together no matter how pissed I am at you, so you'd best understand that once and for fucking all."

They stared at one another for several seconds, neither wanting to break the connection.

Finally Eric raised his snifter, as Oscher's words slipped from his lips. "For God and country."

"And the mission," Fanny saluted.

35
The Luncheon
Barvikha Sanatorium

Fanny rose first, hoping to be gone by early morning.
He buzzed valet and asked that the Harley be brought around
to the front of the hotel. When it arrived, he took stock of the
dark beauty before him--a black-on-black rod with dual heat
shield. Fanny whistled.

What is it about a Harley that makes it so beautiful?

"Nice pipes," the valet said when he handed Fanny
the full-face helmet.

"Yeah," Fanny responded.

"Did you buy it at the Village?"

Fanny answered no, and then as both valet and
doorman watched, Fanny mounted the hog. He revved the
engine and then rumbled more than pulled away from the
Radisson. As he did, he checked his side mirror and saw the
two attendants still watching in awe.

Now on the road, Fanny felt the freest he'd been since
leaving America, although he was conscious of the opposite
being true. Police were everywhere and the episode of the
stolen motorcycle from yesterday remained unsolved.
However, those problems paled in comparison to what the
day might bring. Right now he wanted nothing more than to
test the bike to see what it could do. So he took it up and
down the hills all around Odintsovo and then into the city of

Moscow where he tended to the details of their expected departure from the larger Domodedovo Airport. Afterward, he took the Harley on some trails where he could test how the wide tires handled the rougher track. Satisfied, he reluctantly returned to the highway and headed toward Barvikha.

Meanwhile, Eric had gotten up early as well and was in conversation with Edmund. Everyone at CIA was anxious about the impending faceoff with DuBethonee and was now placing equal emphasis on its success and failure. Oscher talked strongly on strategy, while Edmund stressed survival.

"We won't rest until we know you're coming home," he said.

Eric appreciated it but knew that the axe was falling. The question was on whom?

By eleven forty-five, Eric was about to shake hands with Dr. Allen George, who was making his way from the hotel's entrance flush with excitement.

"Oh, my, Dr. Knudson, I trust I'm on time. Lydia had some concerns, so I've spent most of the morning with her. Poor thing, she's so worried about the outcome. But rest assured, I told her everything's going to be just dandy, although I needed to step out for a bite to eat and voila, here I am, hungry of course, and you?"

Eric clasped his hand in Allen's, saying, "Absolutely and I'm looking forward to lunch, but please call me Richard."

"And me, Allen. So good to have another American to correspond with. All this translating gives me a headache. Shall we?" He led with his right hand extended toward the large Mercedes that waited.

Once they were deep in the sanatorium's compound, Allen asked, "Have you ever seen the castle before?"

"No, only in pictures" Eric told him.

"Then shall we have a little drive by before lunch?"

"Absolutely."

"You'll be interested in knowing that it was built in

1935 for the Meyendorff family. Some people still refer to it as such even though Lenin took full occupancy of it once the Great War began. Later, maybe sometime in the twenty-first century, I think, it became the official country residence of every Russian president that followed."

"I hear Turkov rather enjoys it," Eric said as they stopped at its gate to peer down a long drive.

"Oh, yes, as do other important guests."

Allen idled the car for a few minutes longer to admire the building's spires and then without preamble, said, "But we're hungry, so let's put an end to the tourist portion of our visit for the more austere sanatorium. I assure you, however, that what it lacks in décor, it makes up for in views and food."

As Allen promised, the building was plain but gave Eric his first glimpse of the apartment building that he and Fanny had failed to see the day before that in no way hinted at its purported opulence. Also as promised, the view from sanatorium's dining area was spectacular and opened onto the expansive lawn all the way down to the lake far beyond.

They ordered a lunch of broiled salmon and then launched into their respective practices. Eric related very little because from the start it was obvious that Allen's ego as a Los Angeles veterinarian wouldn't let him. All Eric had to do was pepper him with questions about actors and their pets to keep him going. Before long it was half past one and Allen was becoming noticeably anxious.

"Lydia will just kill me if I'm not in her room when she wakes," he told Eric. "Perhaps we should go."

Eric resisted. "I understand, Allen, but please if you must go, go. I can get myself back to the hotel."

"You wouldn't mind? Because I don't know when I could possibly return, especially since I still have to pick up a little gift for her. Goodness, my whole day has been nothing but deadlines."

"Not a problem, really. It was nice lunching with

you."

"Yes, and for me as well," he replied. "Thank you again. I so dreaded spending this entire trip without a good American mind to talk with."

"Yes, I can see how you'd miss the stimulation."

"Exactly. Perhaps we'll meet again during your stay. How long are you here?"

"Not long," Eric answered. "If all goes according to plan, I should be leaving tonight. It's been a long haul and I'm ready to go home to the wife."

"Oh, yes, I understand," Allen laughed. "Long journeys do that to a man, don't they? It makes us restless. Sorry, although if one gives it even the slightest bit of attention as I have, it's not hard to find similar comforts here in Russia."

Eric laughed in return before shaking his hand goodbye and sitting back down at the table to order another coffee. He needed to linger, he needed to wander, and he needed to get lost on the property if he was ever going to locate the person he'd come to find.

Eric sat another twenty minutes and then pushed back his chair to leave. As he did, he caught sight of Glory walking between the buildings. She was wearing a gold scarf around her neck that was tucked into the collar of a knee-length, camel hair coat. On her head she wore a blonde fur hat. She looked dipped in the very honey Fanny had mentioned earlier when he suggested they use her to find DuBethonee. Perhaps he was right. He threw his napkin on the table to find out if he could.

His search led him to a pillared back stoop at the apartment building where a janitor could be seen hefting two large bags into the dumpster. As the man swung the second one over its rim, Eric stepped forward and knocked him out cold. He then removed the janitor's belt and the keys, draped him over the dumpster's edge, and tipped him inside. He used the belt to secure the lid.

281

Racing back to the stoop, he opened the door and made his way to the front foyer. It was large and marbled like the kind you might find inside Meyendorff Castle. Damask drapes of silk brocade hung floor-to-ceiling in its stately windows. The area was eerily silent, except for the sound of the faint drag of someone wearing softer, leather slippers down the hall. Out of curiosity, he peeked around the corner as an elderly man shuffled away to the left. He waited until he heard the ding of an elevator rather then the closing of an apartment door and followed in the man's footsteps. One elevator was stopped at the seventh floor; the second was in motion.

After reaching the seventh floor himself, Eric stepped out into a foyer that served a single apartment and put his ear to the set of highly polished, double wooden doors. At first he heard nothing and then shortly, a set of footsteps approached and a woman's voice said, "Good day, madam, please call if you need anything else."

Eric slipped behind an identical set of damask drapes to those in the lobby. The apartment door opened and out stepped the woman. It wasn't Glory but maybe she was a housekeeper or an assistant. Either that, or he had the wrong floor.

As she waited for the elevator doors to reopen, she appeared to grow angry over some issue and was taking it out on her collection of keys that clattered loudly. Eric used the distraction to step out and wrap his arm around her neck. She collapsed immediately. He laid her on a divan near one set of drapes and used the drapery ties to bind and gag her. He grabbed her keys and opened the door.

Glory could be heard speaking sternly on the phone, first in Russian, then French, and then again in Russian. He wondered if the person listening could understand both languages at the pace she was spewing them. He spotted a broom closet and decided it was as good a place as any to hide. For now.

He continued to listen as she hung up the phone and began moving noisily about to make a drink and then to flip on the stereo. She was upset but he could tell that she was trying very hard to let the music soothe her. The phone rang again and she answered. This time her voice was sweet.

"Yes, grandmother, I'd be delighted," she said in French. "Now? Oui, of course, immediately."

He heard her place a glass on the counter and tap her nails against the granite counter top, saying, "God help us."

After she left the kitchen, Eric cracked open the closet door. Glory was moving quickly through a lavishly appointed living room and into another area. He followed but only as far as he could without being seen. She then entered another room off the hallway and opened and closed a few drawers. She next walked to the back of her apartment where he assumed she was entering the master suite. Eric tiptoed down the hall. When he reached his destination and peeked in, she wasn't there.

Eric was stumped and looked all around.

Where did she go?

He looked in her palatial bathroom.

Wow!

It seemed plucked from the Palace of Versailles with gilded, mirrored walls and an alabaster-soaking tub trimmed in highly polished silver. White silk curtains floated around it. To its left was a spacious walk-in closet filled with designer clothes and where the gold scarf and hat she'd worn earlier lay thrown on a mink-covered ottoman.

Everything mesmerized him. He imagined them here…together.

He reentered the master bedroom and felt around the walls for hidden panels or doors. He looked under her heavy four-poster bed, threw back drapes and sheers, and opened and closed trunks and cabinet cases. Glory was nowhere to be found.

He then ran his fingers over the heavy frames of her

bedroom paintings, tilting them and checking behind them, coming first to one bearing a small bronze plate with the title "Feodor Bruni--Maenad giving drink to Cupid" and then another by Taras Shevchenko titled "Odalisque." He found nothing but dared not question their authenticity.

Next he stepped up to a wall-mounted baroque mirror and felt around its edges. Nothing again. He turned and leaned against it, wondering what to do next.

Where the hell did she go? You can't just disappear. She had to go somewhere.

As he moved away from the mirror, it clicked. He turned back and pulled it wide.

Inside was a staircase. He followed it down, tiptoeing his way with every step. At the next floor, there was an illuminated panel with several buttons next to a windowless door. He pressed his ear to it. Nothing again. He descended to the next floor and the next, with each floor having the same illuminated panel and windowless door.

Which one? Eric wondered. *Which one?*

He reached the ground floor and still didn't know which door Glory had gone through, so he turned to climb back up the stairs. Just as he did, he heard the muffled voice of a woman shouting at someone. He turned back to listen again. He pushed against the door. It moved. He could now hear other people talking further inside the apartment.

How many were there?

He figured there must be at least three. First there was an older, more commanding female voice shouting orders that he assumed was DuBethonee, if he indeed had the right apartment. That was one. Glory would be two, even though he hadn't heard her speak. And the man defending himself was three.

Anyone else? Yes. There was a fourth.

And it was the fourth that kept begging softly, "Madam, Madam, please."

284

36
Fannie's Fire Fight
Barvikha Sanatorium

Fanny spent the forty-five minute drive from the Domodedovo Airport with his mind focused on connecting with Eric at exactly three in the afternoon. By now Eric's lunch with Dr. George should have been over and because of that, the closer he got to the hotel, the greater his anticipation became. Everything was in reach…DuBethonee, Glory, America…and never had his country or home seemed more dear. Of course, he knew everything could be wiped away if it became a disaster, but for the most part, he wanted only to have this mission behind him.

He pulled into the Radisson in time to witness Dr. George wrestling with a large duffle in the trunk of his Mercedes and could hear him shouting to the bellman over the Harley's popping, "I've got it. Really. No, it's not necessary. I don't need any help."

His face was sweaty from exertion. Fanny feared he wouldn't make it into the hotel with such a heavy load, so he shut down the bike and stepped from it. He then walked over to a luggage trolley and dragged it with him to the Mercedes.

"Perhaps this'll help," Fanny offered the doctor who looked up in surprise.

"Oh! You're Richard's friend, of course. I hardly recognized you on that Harley. Nice bike. Do you enjoy it?"

"Name's Francis, and to answer your question, there's nothin' like a Harley. But what ya got here?"

"Oh, nothing, really. A little something for Lydia."

"Not so little," Fanny replied.

"No," Allen said, "but then nothing ever is when it comes to women, is it?"

Fanny reached in and lifted from beneath the duffle. That something moved. The doctor looked him with eyes that pleaded, *please?*

Fanny played along and helped load the duffle onto the trolley. He gave it a good look, anticipating another movement. It remained still. Allen, however, was a tangle of nerves and grabbed the trolley to pull it toward the elevator. Fanny followed.

"It's a dog," Allen whispered. "A rather large dog that happens to be so heavily sedated that it's dead weight."

"A dog."

"That's right, for Lydia, a borzoi."

"How authentic."

"Well, she loves all things Russian and this wolfhound is the only thing she asked for when we decided to visit Barvikha."

"Then why isn't it in a cage or on a leash?"

"A cage? What, are you kidding me? This is how it was given to me. They said 'open the trunk' and dumped the bag in there. I simply had to rush back here just to see if it's alive. The market can be such a disgrace sometimes."

"I see," Fanny said as he checked his watch. It was three o'clock and Eric was nowhere in sight.

"Do you? I will, of course, have to make arrangements until Lydia is well enough to actually appreciate it, but for now I just want to get this heap of bones up to my room and out of this bag. Can you help me?"

"Sure."

Allen pressed the button to his floor.

Once inside the room, the doctor threw his valet ticket on the dresser and unzipped the bag. A white, silky borzoi bitch of about eight months old stirred.

"My goodness she's beautiful," he exclaimed as he caressed the sleeping dog before hefting her out of the bag and placing her on the bed. "Lydia will just love her," he said to Fanny over his shoulder while he examined the dog more fully.

Fanny said, "I've no doubt, but, ah, you had lunch with my friend Richard today. How'd it go?"

"Richard? Oh, yes, well, we had a delightful lunch with much discussion. He's an interesting man, Francis. But I'm afraid it took longer than anticipated and unfortunately, I had to leave to go tend to Lydia and, of course, this animal. Richard stayed behind. Said he'd find his own way back here."

"So he's still there?"

"I can't say because it's been a while now. All I can really tell you is that he stayed behind."

Fanny checked his watch. It was now ten minutes after three. Not good. Eric should have been in the lobby waiting. Something was up. He cleared his throat while reaching across the dresser for Allen's valet ticket.

"You won't mind if I borrow your car then, would you?"

"My car? Whatever for?"

"To retrieve my friend."

"Certainly not! He said he'd find his own way back and I need to get to Lydia."

"Do you see him anywhere?" Fanny snapped as he opened the hotel room's door.

"I'll call the police," Allen yelled.

Fanny pointed to the dog, and said, "Go ahead."

Allen retreated.

"Don't worry, Doc, you'll get it back."

"I'd better!"

Fanny hurried to Eric's room but there was no response to his knock. So he inserted his own magnetic card, grasped the handle and with added pressure, he pulled, pushed, and then pulled and pushed up simultaneously. The door popped open. The room had been recently serviced. Fanny sprinted to Eric's satchel, grabbed it, and went next to his own room hoping Eric might be there or at least had left him a message. But on arrival he found nothing and no one.

"Not good," Fanny kept repeating as he grabbed his own luggage.

He returned to the valet area where the Mercedes still waited and jumped in with their bags. The bellman ran to him.

"Sir!"

"Yes," Fanny said as he handed the stub over. "Dr. George's, I know. I'm borrowing it to run an errand. You can call him if you like."

The bellman reluctantly waved him off as Fanny drove from the resort.

He reached the sanatorium's grounds within twenty minutes, and with Allen's special pass still on the dashboard, was given immediate entrance. He steered the Mercedes down the lane until he reached the building. As he looked for a parking place, he saw a man step out of the adjacent apartment building with his gun drawn on another man fleeing.

The man shouted for the other to halt.

But the other man, however, ran faster until he jumped into a car, threw it into gear, and gunned it, only to slam into and topple over a concrete planter that brought him to the halt the first man had wanted. He raised his gun in self defense.

Fanny jumped into the action.

First he tipped over the second planter with the Mercedes to block the circular driveway and then he backed it to the side of the building, popped the trunk, and jumped out. From behind, a motorcycle roared. Fanny grabbed the Mercedes' tire iron and turned in time to whack the driver in the throat, throwing him from his bike. It was a guard. The bike powered forward until it fell to the ground. It's tires spinning.

Meanwhile, two new guards came running. So, Fanny threw the tire iron to the ground, climbed back into the driver's seat, and charged them.

"You're asking for nothing but trouble," he said as he reached into his pocket to remove the Harley's fob.

With his right thumb, he slid its panel half open to expose what explosives were there and tossed them out the window. The guards catapulted into the air. Fanny gripped the wheel of the Mercedes and doubled back by cutting across the lush lawn to face the gunfight. Eric, he knew, was in this foray somehow and by God he was going to find him or die trying.

37
The Gordian Knot
Barvikha Luxury Apartments

At the same time that Fanny had taken Allen's Mercedes, Eric was standing in the hidden stairwell with the mirrored-paneled door partially opened to better listen to the conversation inside the apartment. After a few minutes, he slipped through and again heard a soft click. He froze, wondering if he'd triggered a silent alarm, so as a precaution, he pulled his Glock from his waistband.

He moved forward, stepping into a small powder room elegantly over embellished in red roses. He then tiptoed down the hall toward the main salon and into a richly filled library. When he was finally able to get closer, he saw Glory's reflection in the glass of a tall china cabinet. She was pacing the room, smoking a cigarette while DuBethonee, whom he now knew was her grandmother, was fanning herself while seated in an embossed Louis XVI chair. DuBethonee's lips were drawn tight in anger. The two men, one of whom was clearly Niembriev, stood facing her. Both had their hands on their hips and were pressing their arguments.

"Please, madam. I beg of you," the man next to Niembriev implored.

"Nonsense!" DuBethonee rattled, tapping her cane hard against the floor.

Eric's eye caught the sparkle of a chandelier. It was immense, and if Eric was to place a bet, he'd wager that the crystals hanging from it were diamonds, some the size of twelve-inch spikes. It was stunning. And once the chandelier had presented itself, other diamond crystals came sharply into focus. Eric took in the more elaborate details of the room. Diamonds were everywhere. They were on cabinet knobs and lamp pulls, hanging as trim on drapes, and embedded in the floor between some of the marble tiles. It was amazing. Everywhere he looked, he spotted diamonds in blue, yellow, pink, chocolate, and white. Their translucence glinted whenever a beam of light passed through them. The apartment was a testament to Popigai's untold fortune. He closed his eyes to clear the image and focused again on the men in the room.

DuBethonee now stood and, using the cane that was also encased in diamonds, walked toward them. She stopped in front of the other man and in Russian said with a slow growl, "Do not disappoint me or I will have you killed, Usai."

"Madam!" he said, raising a closed fist to his mouth as she beat him with her stick. Niembriev stepped back.

"Now get out! Get out!" she screamed.

Usai left the apartment as Niembriev turned to her. "Madam, what is it you'd like me to do with him?"

"I do not have to tell you, Major General, that he has outlived his usefulness!"

Niembriev nodded and picked up his hat. He tapped his fingers on its brim and as he put his hand on the door to leave, he said, "Leave it to me, Madam. He will be punished."

She hissed at his back.

"Grandmere," Glory whispered as she approached her grandmother and led her back to her chair. "It'll be all right."

Eric waited a few minutes while Glory calmed her grandmother before stepping into the room. He wasn't sure why he felt so emboldened at that moment, except that the opportunity seemed preordained. He was meant to face DuBethonee alone…without Fanny at his side, which was why he'd told him to leave without him if it came to pass. And here it was.

Glory screamed. DuBethonee did not. Instead she glared at him without moving a muscle. He moved further into the room as DuBethonee watched like a preying cat, first at Glory, then at Eric, then back again at Glory.

"What? How? I…I mean, why? Why are you here?" Glory stammered as she moved to wrap her arms protectively around her grandmother.

DuBethonee shrugged herself loose and demanded in Russian to know who he was.

Glory stood, facing Eric, and answered. "This is Eric Dane, Grandmother. The man in Washington."

"Washington?"

"Yes, the one uncle asked me to…to…"

"Ah, yes, Washington. The lover. But why is he here? In my apartment, no less? Have you seduced him so successfully?"

"No…I don't know why he's here, Grandmother," Glory answered apologetically.

"Please," DuBethonee said slowly and with some glee. "Let us speak only English then, my dear, for the sake of your paramour."

Eric stepped closer as Glory held up her hands to plead with him.

"Eric, please, please, just….just stop," she said with a tremble in her voice. "Tell me why you're here and why you're pointing that gun at my grandmother." She could say no more.

Eric kept his sight trained on DuBethonee whose steely eyes penetrated Eric's own. In his peripheral vision, he watched Glory panic, and knowing what he now knew of her participation in the entire affair, steeled his heart as well.

"Eric," she begged again, walking toward him with her hands in prayer. "Please, do not do this. I…I…I beg of you. Don't hurt us, especially my grandmere. Take me. Kill me if you must kill someone but do not kill her. She's old, Eric. She's going to die anyway. I'm who you want."

Eric braced himself against Glory's approach that now partially blocked his view of DuBethonee.

Glory changed tack. "I'm on your side, Eric, you know that. Look how I helped your friend in Paris. Surely he told you how I helped him find my uncle? If I wasn't on your side by doing that then whose side am I on? He killed him. He killed my uncle, Eric. You know that, right? I gave your organization my uncle."

"My organization, Glory? Really? Because Fanny tells quite a different story," Eric replied.

"What?" she asked while folding her hands over her heart.

"You know what I'm talking about. Your goon. The one that took him away. We ended up together at the Popigai, Fanny and I, where we were nearly killed by your pals, Rabokov and Niembriev. But guess what, Glory? Popigai is no more. We escaped and I'm betting with the information we relayed to our *organization*, there are no survivors."

"Not true!"

"Technically, you're correct, because that was Niembriev who just left here, wasn't it? With Usai?"

Glory's eyes widen. Eric watched as certain realities gained a foothold inside her pretty head, forcing her mouth to open but emit no sound. Finally she blinked and said, "Eric, you don't know what you've done here."

"Oh, but I think I do, Glory. I've entered your hermit kingdom and am standing in front of the Queen Bee herself. Something no one else has been able to do."

"Not true."

"No?"

DuBethonee chuckled coarsely with, "I assure you it

was well before your time."

"Grandmother's correct. Since her reign, no one has ever gotten this close. She's protected our survival by performing in perfect sync with the gods. Our ties are as strong as the impenetrable knot of cornel."

"What knot is that, Glory?"

"The knot Midas used to tie his father's cart to a post at the palace of Phrygia," Glory said. "The Gordian knot, Eric. The one no one could untie."

Eric shook his head slowly in disbelief. "It's only a legend."

"No, it was real and so are we'" Glory said in defense of her people. "We rule as strongly today as they did then."

"You're dreaming. Because if what you say is true, then you also know that Alexander the Great used logic and sliced right through the rope below that knot, Glory."

DuBethonee sneered, "As you have used here."

Eric saw that DuBethonee had now raised a small pistol at him. Glory, however, had not because she was still staring at him and too stunned by his presence. Instead she let out a screech and lunged to grab Eric's wrist. He blocked her, wrapped an arm around her waist, and twisted her away to his right. As he did, she yelled, "I will kill you for this! I will not give you my grandmere! Never! It's too much to ask! Too much I tell you!"

Eric wrestled with Glory as DuBethonee took aim. He heard the ring of a gunshot but didn't believe he'd pulled the trigger. No, that sound came from DuBethonee's direction.

Glory screamed again as from over her shoulder he popped off two shots of his own, one striking DuBethonee in the head, the other in DuBethonee's chest. Glory slumped in his arms.

Eric lowered her to the floor and took a pillow off the nearby couch to press into her wound. He then looked at DuBethonee who was wide-eyed and holding the gun in a limp hand that now drooped from the chair's armrest. Blood oozed from her forehead into the wells of her eyes and down the sides of her nose. Eric stepped quickly over to the immortal Queen Bee to take the pistol from her and then returned to Glory to lift her head.

She looked at him through half-closed lids and said softly, "I'm sorry. We said no games but I played you because I had to. It's because…I have my loyalties."

Eric watched her for a moment without speaking.

"You understand, don't you? My family's empire? Its legacy is tied to the heavens. There's no way out for us, Eric. Our ties can never be cut."

"There are no more ties, Glory. Not even at Popigai. Everything's been destroyed."

Glory blinked.

Eric heard a slight, final exhale escape from her perfectly formed mouth. He picked her up and placed her on the elegant couch. He studied her face. Even in death she looked beautiful. But beauty fades, Eric knew, and more importantly, beauty conceals. Glory wasn't who he thought she was and it had been Fanny who'd tried to tell him all along. It had been his own conceit, though, that had kept him believing that Glory was innocent and wouldn't hurt him or their mission. But again, it was Fanny, Fanny, Fanny…who was where? His most loyal friend was out there somewhere.

38
The Final Ride
Moscow, Russia

Eric raced to the door to leave DuBethonee's ground floor apartment by way of the main entrance. It was the same exit that Niembriev had used not ten minutes prior.

As he stepped outside, he saw Usai and Niembriev standing in the circular driveway behind the opened doors of their two cars. Their pistols were raised in an exchange of silent gunfire. Fanny was seen making a wide loop across the lawn in Allen's Mercedes. Fresh tracks in the gravel road and a cloud of dust indicated this wasn't his first pass.

Eric assessed the situation and raised his gun to fire first at Usai, who was on the driver's side of his car and closest to him. At the sound, Niembriev turned in surprise. The sudden move caused him to fall backwards, but he somehow managed to catch his car's doorframe and right himself. Eric ran toward him, firing three more shots at close range. Two of his shots went into Niembriev and the last again into Usai.

Fanny, meanwhile, now raced up the drive and with a fishtail stop, shouted for Eric to jump in.

Eric grabbed the car's door handle and had barely seated himself before Fanny gunned it. They flew past the now dead Usai and Niembriev as well as the fallen concrete planters to speed away from sanatorium. Along the way, Eric saw Fanny's handiwork. A guard's motorcycle laid in a clump in the middle of the lane where a metal pipe had been cast aside. Two other guards were sprawled on the torn up lawn.

"You do all that?" he asked Fanny with a nod at what lay behind them.

"Maybe," Fanny answered. "But you know damn good and well that when you're in trouble, there's nothin' I wouldn't do."

"Apparently, and the same here, believe me."

"What happened inside?" Fanny asked

"I was in her apartment. DuBethonee's, that is. I handled it."

"As in?"

"I shot her."

"And Glory?"

"Glory was shot by her grandmother."

"So the hermit kingdom's done? We've shut it down?"

"Don't know, I, mean, Arnoult did tell me that if I killed the Queen Bee, I'd kill the entire operation.'"

"Good, then let's get outta here because I wanna go home bad, real bad."

"Me too, but how are we supposed to get there?"

"Oscher."

"Really? By what method?"

"He's got a plane waitin' for us at the Domodedovo Airport and once we're there, we're outta here."

Since the gate was no longer attended, Eric jumped out of the car and swung it open to allow the Mercedes to pass through. After it passed, he closed it and jumped back in.

They entered the highway with haste and without anyone aware as yet of what had transpired behind the sanatorium's high walls. They drove for several minutes before Eric turned in the seat to face Fanny.

297

"I owe you an apology, man," he said.

"Forget it," Fanny replied.

"I won't because that wouldn't be right. You knew from the start that Glory was on the other side."

"No, I didn't. I just knew she was on the outside and needed to stay out there if we were gonna have any chance at all at focusin' on the job."

"You were right just the same is all I can say. I appreciate it."

"Well, you've kept me straight millions of times, so we'll call it even. Besides, I probably owe you an apology too."

"What for?"

"For not thinking you'd be man enough to step up."

Eric nodded in concession. "You always were a parishioner of little faith but answer me this, how is it that you're driving Allen's Mercedes?"

"I borrowed his valet ticket."

"You mean you stole it?"

"No, I negotiated for it," he said with a grin.

"How and to which part of M.I.C.E. did you appeal to? His massive ego?"

Fanny's grin turned into a smile. "You've got the right letter but I appealed to something a little more effective. Something he'd understand."

"Like what?"

"Extortion."

At that Fanny released a riotous laugh that rose precipitously between the two men as they drove further into Moscow. Everything that they'd held pent up came out in happy tears and bangs on the dash with their hands. Eric rocked in his seat, as Fanny held tight onto the steering wheel. They arrived fully spent at Domodedovo Airport but eager to depart. A private jet area beyond the main terminal was where they were headed. Fanny had scoped it out earlier in the day, so the route was familiar. Waiting there was the promised Lear jet.

Eric slapped him on the back and asked, "You mean we're going home in *that*?"

"Looks like it," Fanny said with the smile that had yet to leave his face.

A set of stairs led up to the closed hatch that popped open as they stepped from the car. A flight attendant appeared once they began to climb.

"Welcome aboard, gentlemen," she said, and then to Eric she added, "Mon cher."

Eric stopped.

"Annette," he said in surprise.

"I knew it," Fanny whispered.

"Oscher thought you'd appreciate a familiar face to bring you in from the cold."

"And not a better face to do it," Eric said as he greeted her. "But it does kind of blow your cover, doesn't it?"

"That it would," she responded by leading them gently into the body of the plane, "But I don't mind. Truth ta tell, it was music to mine ear."

About the Author

Elaine Gallant holds a BA in Journalism and a concentration in Creative Writing from the University of Central Florida. As a freelance writer, recreational golfer, and certified tennis instructor, she has written travel articles related to both sports for magazines, newspapers, and Internet web sites. Her work has appeared in numerous publications, including: *Golf Orlando, Golf for Women, Golf Life, Orange Spiel, Women's Courterly, ADDvantage Magazine, Florida Tennis,* and *TravelGolf.com.* She has also contributed research to *The Payne Stewart Story* by Larry Guest. She additionally contributes to *Neighbors of West Maui* through her West Maui Book Club, established in 2005. (www.WestMauiBookClub.com)

Elaine is, and has always been, a passionate world traveler. She and her husband now reside in Hawaii where she focuses on short story and fiction writing.

Made in the USA
San Bernardino, CA
24 March 2020